Playing With Fire

"No matter what you might believe, Tucker, I am determined to become a famous photographer. I plan to start a business here. In fact"—Emily walked over to her trunk, furiously flicked the locks open and flung out the clothing she intended to wear on the journe___ ___ck to town—"I have some wonderful ideas ___ ___ it to set into motion."

She straightened, ___ ___ ___ gasped when she found h___ ___.

"While you're ___ ___ ___ in motion, this'll give ___ ___ ___ k about." He grasped he___ ___ ___ her into a rough embrace. Wh___ ___ ___ain, Sam smothered the sound with ___ ___ is mouth covered hers. This time there w___ ___ gentle exchange of curiosity, but a white-hot flame leaped to life in each of them the minute he touched her. . . .

—from "Picture Perfect"
by JILL MARIE LANDIS

SWEET HEARTS

BY
JILL MARIE LANDIS
JODI THOMAS
COLLEEN QUINN
KATHLEEN KANE

JOVE BOOKS, NEW YORK

This is a work of fiction. Names, characters, places, and incidents are either the product of the authors' imaginations or are used fictitiously, and any resemblance to actual persons, living or dead, business establishments, events or locales is entirely coincidental.

SWEET HEARTS

A Jove Book / published by arrangement with the authors

PRINTING HISTORY
Diamond edition / February 1993
Jove edition / January 2000

The Penguin Putnam Inc. World Wide Web site address is http://www.penguinputnam.com

ISBN: 0-515-12710-8

A Jove Book®
Jove Books are published by The Berkley Publishing Group, a division of Penguin Putnam Inc., 375 Hudson Street, New York, New York 10014. JOVE and the "J" design are trademarks belonging to Penguin Putnam Inc.

PRINTED IN THE UNITED STATES OF AMERICA

10 9 8 7 6 5 4

SWEET HEARTS

PICTURE PERFECT

by

Jill Marie Landis

Dear Reader,

It's hard to believe that Valentine's Day is here again. I hope you were all blessed with a year of laughter and love.

When I sat down to choose a setting for the characters in "Picture Perfect," a special place immediately came to mind. A favorite retreat for myself and two of my fellow writers is nestled deep in California's Tehachapi Mountains .in an area called Walker's Basin. Once or twice a year we sneak away from husbands, phones and city life and spend a few days at Rankin Ranch, where all we have to do is read, write, and horseback ride through some of the most beautiful country in California. Of course, the incredible meals are high on our list of priorities.

In the name of research, we three take notebooks and pens in hand and seek out anyone we can find who is willing to give us any shred of information we might incorporate into our novels. It isn't always easy to track down the elusive ranch owner, Bill Rankin, one of his right-hand men, Juan, or any of the wranglers, especially when we're certain they can see us coming and find plenty of things to do on the "other side" of the range.

One day, to my dismay, I found myself part of a group cutting a longhorn bull out of the herd so that one of my companions could "get a closer look for descriptive purposes." I was already as close to Arturo-the-Bull as I wanted to get, and the horse I was riding was of like mind. Thankfully, my friend got her close-up-and-personal look at a bull, and I was still able to make it to dinner.

Nothing, not even "Wait for the Wrangler" signs, can dampen our determination to track down authenticity. It was during one scouting session, when we were afraid that we might have accidentally over-watered a pen full of thirsty pigs, that I came up with the storyline for "Picture Perfect." What if a heroine, intent on her career, crossed paths with a rancher who was certain that he needed nothing less than an interfering photographer poking about the place? The heroine, Emily Richardson, is not only determined, but capable, talented and beautiful. The hero, Sam Tucker, is stubborn, cranky, and determined to protect his broken heart. But love is in the air, Valentine's Day is on the calendar, and of course, every romance must have a happy ending.

This Valentine is dedicated to Bill Rankin, his family and staff, and the Picture Perfect Rankin Ranch in Caliente, California. Also to Dorsey Kelley and Chelley Kitzmiller, partners in crime. I owe thanks to the staff of Rancho Los Cerritos in Long Beach, California, for taking the time to help me research early photographic methods and materials.

My wish to all of you is a Happy Valentine's Day, joy and peace.

—JILL MARIE LANDIS

California
Early January 1886

The back wheel of the wagon jolted over a rock and landed with a thud that sent Emily Richardson bouncing across the high buckboard seat. She sprawled against the bearded, unkempt driver, Ezra Jacobs, who held the horses' reins threaded through his fingers, his gaze everywhere but on the steep, sharply curved road.

Emily managed to push herself to a sitting position again and gripped the edge of the wooden seat. ''Are we almost there?''

The old man spat a stream of whiskey-colored tobacco over his shoulder, then turned to her and smiled, his mouth checkerboarded with holes where teeth were missing. ''Jest about.''

It was the same answer he'd been giving her for an hour now. As he worked the tobacco plug in his cheek his bearded jaw twitched up, down, then around like a cow working cud.

Emily tried to swallow her fear, but the bile in her throat from a none-too-settled stomach prevented any real success. Two hours ago they had started up the steep, rutted road carved precariously through the hills. Since then the team had steadily pulled upward. She decided it would be best to give up wondering when the torturous journey to Tucker Basin would end and tried to concentrate on the view.

The land that fell away from the side of the road was peppered with clumps of sage, rabbit brush, and thicker, twisted red branches of manzanita. Here and there the more substantial trees Ezra called black oak stood tall above the rest. The yellow-brown California foothills were like nothing she had ever seen around Chicago. At home such "hills" would certainly be called mountains, but the misnomer didn't surprise her. There had been little she'd seen in the west that reminded her of home.

She closed her eyes and turned her face skyward to drink in the heat of the sunshine, only a tad guilty at savoring such wonderful weather when she knew everyone back in Chicago was no doubt suffering the wind and snow so common in January.

After a noisy throat clearing and a long stream of expectoration, Ezra Jacobs asked, "'Zactly how'd you say you came to be stayin' out at the Tucker place?"

"I don't recall saying," Emily told him bluntly, knowing full well after three long hours in his company that Ezra Jacobs's skin was as thick as the fleece-lined buckskin jacket he wore. She gave him a quick sidelong glance—quick because the instant she took her eyes off the winding road, her stomach lurched. He was watching a cloud float lazily across an otherwise clear blue sky as his hands seesawed the reins.

Perhaps engaging him in conversation might somehow draw his attention back to the road. "I met William Tucker a few weeks ago when he was a guest of my father's. Papa is always entertaining stockmen at home." She thought of her large, boisterous family—Mama, Papa, three sisters, and two little brothers—she'd left in Chicago and smiled to herself. She doubted she'd even been missed yet in the constant confusion.

"So." Ezra chuckled beside her. "You met little Willie, did ya? How's he doin'? Seems he's always off someplace puttin' on airs."

For the life of her she couldn't imagine how anyone could think of the striking, dark-haired, well-tailored man who stood over six feet as "little Willie." "He is doing just fine. In fact, Mr. Tucker was quite the gentleman when I met him," she informed Jacobs coldly.

"Oh, Willie's that, all right. That's why he takes to runnin' all over the country 'stead of puttin' in his time at the ranch."

"My father claims William Tucker is quite the successful businessman." Quite a catch as a husband, too, is what her father had told her, but Emily wasn't at all interested in that. She snuck another glance at Jacobs and regretted it as soon as the horses began to negotiate a particularly treacherous turn.

Emily held her breath until she heard her companion remark, "That's the last of the bad 'uns."

"Thank God," she mumbled under her breath. "As I was saying, Mr. Tucker seemed quite intent on his mission. My father thinks rather highly of his idea of setting up a cooperative of ranchers to avoid paying a broker to sell their beef to the stockyards." She hoped Jacobs didn't ask her for any more details, since what she had just told him was virtually all she knew about exactly what William Tucker had been doing in Chicago, and those few facts she'd gleaned from her father.

"Don't get a bee in your bonnet, missy. I was jest thinkin' out loud."

"I'm very grateful to Mr. Tucker for being kind enough to invite me to his ranch when he heard about my project."

Ezra arched a brow and looked over at her. "Which is?"

She tried to ignore the tobacco stain on his shoulder. Obviously his shots weren't always well placed. "I am a photographer—"

He cut her off again. "Knew that already from loadin' all that gear in the back of the wagon."

"As I was saying . . ." Forgetting for a moment where she was, Emily crossed her arms defiantly. The wagon rumbled over the top of the last hill, throwing her backward. The low seat back gave little support and she nearly toppled into the wagon bed before grabbing hold of the seat again.

She sighed and tried again. "As I was saying, I am interested in preserving the western way of life in pictures, photographs to be exact, much the way the artists Karl Bodmer and Alfred Jacob Miller did when they traveled the west and captured the landscape and inhabitants in sketches and oils."

"Don't think I ever met 'em."

"Well, of course not. They reached their prime in the 1830s." Emily rolled her eyes in disgust.

"We're at the top," he informed her.

She paused to look around and found that they were, indeed, at the top of the broad range of hills. Mist jacketed the valleys between row after row of ridges. What looked like low balls of shrubs on the distant hillsides were in reality the same gnarled scrub oak, dark green and untamed, that grew around them.

She turned around fully and looked back the way they had come. There was no sign of another human for miles. Only the rutted tracks in the pebble-strewn road that wound its way back toward Tehachapi gave any indication that anyone else had ever passed this way.

"Now all we gotta do is cross this ridge and we'll be on the way down t' Tucker Basin." He snapped the reins across the horses' rumps and smiled over at Emily. "They know you comin' in?"

She sat up straighter and pulled the hem of her fitted jacket down over the neat waistline of her velvet-trimmed, flaired woolen skirt. "Of course they know. William Tucker assured me he would make all the arrangements personally."

Ezra spat.

Emily tried to ignore him, which was easy to do now that the worst of the road was behind them and the breathtaking view all around. As she studied the dramatic landscape an idea came to her. "Stop."

"What?" He leaned toward her.

"Please, stop. I'd like to take a photograph before we go any farther. It would make a good opening, to take a picture of the basin from this altitude. That is Tucker Basin and the Rocking T Ranch, isn't it?"

"That's right. This is Tucker Ranch, too. We been on it for the last hour."

She looked around, awed by the extent of land and the thought that so much could belong to one family.

It took Emily the better part of an hour to set up her camera and bring the basin into focus.

Ankle-deep in mud and manure, Sam Tucker drew off his hat, wiped his forehead with his arm, and shoved his hat back on. He wished he could shrug off his boredom as easily as he could wipe off sweat; there was nothing exciting about loading hay on the flatbed wagon and there never would be—still, it was a job that had to be done.

When he paused long enough to look across the wide basin and up at the surrounding hills, he knew why he stayed and why his grandfather before him had claimed this land. The Rocking T Ranch was in his blood. He wasn't about to leave it or let it go, even when times were hard, not for anything in the world. Not even for the woman who'd left him because of it.

Beside him his foreman, Ramon Valdez, worked in companionable silence just as he had done since Sam had taken over as head of the Tucker clan.

When Ramon straightened and nodded toward the hills, Sam stopped what he was doing and stared. Coming down the road at breakneck speed was Ezra Jacobs's familiar delivery wagon, swaying and bouncing over the ruts in the road.

Sam was content to stand and watch with a shake of his head as Ezra cursed his team of horses and rode the brake the last few yards to the bottom of the hill. True to form, the grizzled old driver finally brought the careening wagon to a halt on the drive behind the two-story, wood-frame ranch house. Deciding to let Aunt Vida take care of greeting Jacobs, Sam was about to turn back to work when he noticed a flash of deep green and watched in awe as a slight, feminine figure straightened up from the floor of the wagon and pulled herself back onto the wagon seat.

"*La señorita*," Ramon said softly.

Sam sighed. *Willie again.* He stripped off his gloves and shoved them into his back pocket. "Finish up here, Ramon, and then you can turn half of those line horses out to pasture."

The muddy ground, churned to thick loam by a multitude

of hoofprints, muted the sound of his spurs as Sam crossed the corral toward the house. The drab brown wagon stood in sharp contrast before the bright yellow paint and forest-green millwork trim that adorned the house. Involuntarily he clenched his teeth and swore. It hadn't even been two weeks since the last "guest" Willie sent them had departed, and now here was another.

A young one, too, from the looks of her, and a lot more fit than some of the others had been. Sam watched her from beneath the brim of his hat, slowing his pace in order to study the newcomer before he was forced to meet her. She was slight, shorter than average. A brunette, he saw by the curly strands that trailed from the little hat sitting askew on her head.

Despite her trail-weary expression she was a real good-looker. No doubt Willie expected him and Vida to entertain and lodge her until he got home to pay court. The girl was standing beside the wagon now, fiddling with her skirt before she jerked down the hem of her fitted jacket; Sam couldn't help noticing how it fit her form perfectly. She just continued to glare coldly at Ezra Jacobs. Her voice, which held a stern, forbidding note, rode to him on the late-afternoon breeze.

"If you think I intend to pay you for nearly breaking my neck, not to mention all my equipment, you have another thing coming," she warned.

Sam was nearly upon them when he heard Ezra argue, "Gotcha here, didn' I? That was the bargain as I see it, so ya owe me my two dollars."

"I'll give you one dollar and you should be glad to get it." She fumbled with a dainty bag hanging from draw-strings around her wrist.

Sam stepped up to the two of them and watched her

register surprise as she noticed him for the first time. Her eyes were a dark, deep bottomless black. Beautiful eyes. Eyes that might pull a man in deep if he wasn't careful. All too much like Lillith's eyes. He ignored the girl and looked at Ezra as he dug a pair of coins out of his pocket. "Here's your two bucks, Ezra. I take it this is one of Willie's deliveries?"

"You got it. This and some mail's all I'm carrin' today." The old man spat into the mud.

Like a pesky fly, she was at Sam's elbow in a minute. "Listen here, sir, I am perfectly capable of paying my own way, it's just that I don't see that this man deserves—"

Sam walked in the opposite direction, rounded the wagon, and looked over the tailgate. "All this *hers*?" he asked Ezra.

"Yep."

"Hell of a lot more than they usually bring." Sam avoided looking at her. She was standing beside him now, nearly on tiptoe, staring into the wagon bed.

"That, sir, is my equipment. My photographic equipment, a darkroom tent, backdrops, chemicals, and slides. I would appreciate it if you would handle it gently. After all, it has not had a very easy time of it, nor have I."

Finally, slowly, Sam turned his gaze on the girl. She was definitely too pretty and all too close for comfort. A hint of light, powdery perfume tickled his nose, reminding him of how long it had been since he'd been around a desirable woman. Sam's hands tightened on the edge of the tailgate.

The top of her head came to his chin. Her eyes were wide, round and dark. Her lips were full, almost pouty. The rich green of her traveling clothes highlighted the deep rose of her cheeks.

Sam swallowed hard and turned away, concentrating on

the load under the tarp in the back of the wagon. "You want *all* this unloaded?"

"I would certainly appreciate it," she said, her tone somewhat less starched.

Sam turned toward the corral area and whistled loud and long. Ramon looked up, answered Sam's wave with one of his own, and started across the lot.

The woman beside Sam fidgeted. He could feel her growing unease and chanced another look at her. A worried expression marred her finely drawn features.

"Is there someone here who's in charge?" She looked absolutely unnerved now.

Sam let her stew. He watched as she studied him and then Ramon, who was halfway across the drive. She looked up at the house behind them, at the deserted porch, the trees, and back up the road she had survived. "William Tucker assured me there would be adequate female companionship here. . . ." Her positive statement belied the skeptical expression in her eyes.

Sam eyed her carefully from beneath his lowered hat brim. "Willie tends to make promises he can't hold to." When he saw her complexion deepen to a bright rose, he backed off a bit. "Aunt Vida's here. She looks out for everyone like a mother hen. You have no cause to worry." He turned to Ramon and said, "Let's get this stuff up to the porch."

The man nodded and waited while Sam stepped aside and Ezra began to unfasten the tarp he'd thrown over the woman's belongings.

Her relief was instantaneous. "You can't believe how relieved I am to hear that," she said. "I was not looking forward to going back up that hill and down the other side—at least not anytime soon."

Sam made no comment as he watched Ezra grumble his way to the back porch with a load of wooden boxes. Ramon followed with a small trunk on his shoulder.

The girl cleared her throat. "I'm Emily Richardson," she said softly. "Of Chicago."

He looked down to find her waiting expectantly, watching him again with her serious, dark eyes. Sam shifted his weight and sighed, planting his hands in his back pockets. "I'm Sam Tucker, ma'am. Willie's my younger brother."

Her face brightened instantly at the mention of Willie's name. Sam looked away. The enthusiasm in her voice gave him cause to envy his little brother for the first time in his life.

"William is *such* a gentleman. And so thoughtful. He was instantly sympathetic to my cause. When I told him about my plan to capture life in the west in a series of photographs, he invited me here *immediately*." She was practically beaming now.

Sam couldn't hold back a comment. "I'll bet."

Emily Richardson paused long enough to look around, so long in fact that Sam found himself taking the opportunity to take a little survey. Willie had good taste. He'd grant him that. Sam was almost convinced, looking down at the girl, who, at close inspection appeared to be no older than eighteen, that Willie was probably hightailing it back home this very minute to be with her.

She turned around and caught him staring. "William didn't tell me he had a brother."

"Sometimes he forgets the minute, unimportant details of life." *Like how to duck when a mule starts kicking.*

The screen door slammed and Vida Tucker appeared on the back porch. Sam smiled up at the sight of his aunt's robust figure. The wide white apron around her middle was like a welcome banner against the backdrop of the big house. Beside Vida, Carmen Valdez, Ramon's wife, hovered with a curious expression as she watched the men return to the wagon for another load of goods.

"Bring that little filly on up here, Sam," Vida called out with a good-natured shout. "If I know Ezra, she'll need a good dose of tea to settle her stomach."

"That's my aunt Vida," Sam told her as he stepped up beside Emily Richardson and waved toward the porch. "Her aim in life is either to cure a body or stuff it full of food."

"I definitely feel the need of a little healing right now." Emily Richardson turned toward the house, but before she started off, she turned back and smiled at Sam.

Sam felt his insides drop to his spurs.

Damn it to hell, Willie. I don't have the time or the nerve for this sort of thing anymore.

All the way to the house Emily wondered why the big man behind her appeared so put out and why William Tucker had failed to mention his brother, Sam. Maybe his older brother's sour disposition was the reason why. She chanced a glance back in the man's direction and found him staring hard at the ground as they walked toward the comfortable house nestled in a grove of trees.

Emily decided then and there that she wasn't going to let one sour temperament drive her off until she had reached her goal. After all, she was a guest at William Tucker's invitation, and he had seemed genuine when he extended it.

They reached the steps to the porch and Sam Tucker politely waited for her to mount them before he did. His aunt Vida, a full-figured woman who towered over Emily, smiled and took her elbow to lead her into the kitchen of the house. A quiet, raven-haired little woman with bright snapping eyes hurried through the door before Vida Tucker and pulled a chair out at the kitchen table. Emily sat. All the while Vida smiled down at her and nodded.

"What a nice surprise," Vida told her. "Welcome to the Rocking T, Miss—"

"Emily," she volunteered as she took off her hat and gloves. "Emily Richardson. Of Chicago."

"Nice to meet you," Vida assured her. "This is Carmen Valdez, she helps me with the housekeeping. That was her man, Ramon, who brought in your things. And you already met my nephew, I assume?" Vida, with her salt-and-pepper braids wound around her head like a crown, looked to Sam. "You minding your manners, Tucker?"

Sam Tucker had stopped to wipe off his boots on the cast-iron scraper outside the backdoor. Now, hat in hand, he stood, obviously uncomfortable in his own kitchen. He was far more handsome than his younger brother, a fact Emily found amazing, because until she met Sam Tucker, she had thought William the best-looking man she'd ever laid eyes on. Her own mother and sisters had agreed.

Jet-black hair and suntanned skin perfectly complemented his green eyes—eyes, she noted, that continually avoided her gaze. Dressed in work clothes, he was ruggedly built, broad-shouldered, but narrow at the hips and waist. There wasn't an ounce of spare flesh on this man Sam Tucker.

"Well?" his aunt demanded. "You mind your manners or not?"

Emily watched the tall man arch a brow and smile wryly at his aunt.

"I tried," he muttered.

"Don't mind Tucker," Vida warned. "He hasn't been one to socialize much lately."

Not sure of how to respond to such a blunt statement, Emily concentrated instead on the luscious aroma in the kitchen. "Something smells delicious."

"Pot roast and potatoes," Vida told her. "We'll be havin' supper at six-thirty sharp every night."

Emily's stomach rumbled and she wondered if she could hold out until then. She was more than surprised when Sam Tucker said, "How about you giving her a slab of bread and butter, Vida. She looks about to blow away."

"Why, thank you, Mr. Tucker. I am famished." Emily smiled up at him and his expression immediately darkened. Without knowing how, she had obviously angered him again in some way. Glancing across the room, she noticed Vida was watching Sam closely, too. Carmen Valdez slipped out the door and disappeared into the room beyond the kitchen.

Feeling decidedly uncomfortable during their exchange, Emily tried to clear the air. "I can't help but notice that I seem to have descended upon you without warning. William assured me he would let you know that I was coming and that everything would be fine. If I'm in the way, or if I have arrived at an inconvenient time, I can leave and make other arrangements."

"Why don't you."

"Nonsense!"

Sam and Vida spoke at once. It was clear to Emily that Sam Tucker would be happy to see the last of her but that his aunt was delighted to have her company. Emily stood up uncertainly. "I think I'd better catch that driver before he goes. . . ."

Vida turned on Sam immediately. "Tucker, you apologize right this minute. She's Willie's guest and I don't want this girl making the trip back to town tonight. Besides, we're gettin' famous for our hospitality and I won't have it said Vida Tucker ever turned anyone away from her table." She flushed and smiled. "Well, from *your* table, anyway."

Emily watched the man struggle with his conscience for half a second before he grudgingly apologized. "Don't mind me." He pinned her with a meaningful stare. "Just stick to the house and try to stay out of the way. That's all I ask."

With that, he stormed out the backdoor, shoving his hat on over his ink-black hair as he went.

While Emily watched him stalk across the yard Vida puttered at the tall cupboard, pulling together a pot of tea, bread, butter, and jam. She set them down in front of Emily and then lowered her bulk into the opposite seat.

"Don't mind Tucker. His bark is worse than his bite."

Emily lifted the teacup to her lips, blew on the steaming liquid, and attempted a sip. She winced and set the heavy cup on the saucer again. "He didn't seem very thrilled at the thought of having an unexpected guest."

Vida settled back and brushed crumbs off of the front of her otherwise spotless apron. "We've had a slew of them since Willie's been traveling the country gathering the support of the ranchers."

Emily swallowed a bite of the best bread she had ever tasted. "I didn't realize. I promise to be on my way just as soon as I have the photographs I want."

"Now, as I said, don't pay Tucker any mind." With a glance toward the backdoor, Vida shook her head. "There's not much that's gonna take that man out of his black mood. Sometimes I think he's been that way so long he doesn't want to change."

Curious enough to ask why, Emily took another bite of bread instead. It was no business of hers why Sam Tucker was perpetually angry. Besides, she suspected that if she waited long enough, Aunt Vida would volunteer the information. "So, William is in the habit of sending guests your way?"

"Land sakes, yes! None as pretty as you, though. That boy has sent us some real characters. The last one to leave was a woman in her fifties, peaked little thing. Built like a sparrow. Had a bad case of lung trouble that her doctor was sure a few weeks in the sunshine would cure."

"Did it?"

"No. But she went home looking rested, at least. Then there was the time Willie invited three writers to come out and see the 'real west.' They 'bout drove poor Tucker crazy, followin' him around the corrals and pastures, writing down everything he said fast as they could catch it, trippin' in the cow paddies and overfeedin' the stock because they couldn't stand to hear the newly weaned calves bawlin'."

Emily hid a smile and said half-aloud, "No wonder he told me to keep out of the way." Then, to Vida she added, "I am determined to document a day on a ranch in photographs. That will mean taking pictures of the workings of a ranch from dawn to dusk. I certainly hope Mr. Tucker and I don't butt heads too often."

"Well"—Vida laughed and slapped her hands on her thighs—"like I said, his bark is worse than his bite. Besides, I think it'll do him good to have to put up with a pretty gal for a while. Maybe you'll have a bit of luck thawin' out that heart of his."

Emily seriously doubted she could do any such thing, as if she even wanted to. Polishing off the last of her bread and jam, she licked her lips and told Vida, "As long as I let him get his work done and he lets me do mine, I think we'll get along just fine.''

After a nap, a sponge bath, and a change of clothes Emily was ready for dinner promptly at six-thirty. She walked down the narrow stairway that led from the upper floor of bedrooms to the entryway at the front of the house, admiring the dainty floral pattern of the wallpaper along the way. The house was neatly appointed, the furniture highly polished, the linens crisp and white. Vida Tucker took obvious pride in the way she kept her nephews' home.

Led by the heavy aroma of pot roast and onions, Emily found the dining room, but it was deserted, so she went into the kitchen to see if she could be of any help. The place was a beehive of activity as Carmen Valdez carried plates heaped with food to a side room filled with the boisterous sound of men's voices.

''Let me get these men fed and then we'll all sit down to eat,'' Vida said as she dished up a man-sized mound of mashed potatoes onto a plate already filled with pot roast and vegetables. ''You'd best stand back so you don't get a spot on your dress.''

Emily glanced down at her elegant pink woolen gown with its deep flounce around the skirt then looked back at Vida, who had not changed for dinner. Feeling overdressed but determined to fit in, she asked, ''Can I be of any help?''

Carmen bustled past and picked up two more full plates.

''That was the last of 'em,'' Vida told her. ''You can go on into the family dining room. Tucker will be down in a minute.''

Pausing to catch a glimpse of the men in the side dining room, Emily peered curiously around the door frame. A long table with short benches that seated two each nearly filled the narrow room. Four cowhands bent over their meals, all talk having ceased while they devoured the savory dinner.

Emily realized Vida was at her elbow, her face flushed from the heat of the oven as she wiped her hands on the apron she had just untied. "Let's go in and sit down. Carmen will serve our dinner, then she's going to go on home. She and Ramon live in one of the small cabins near the pond."

"I hope you'll let me help you with the dishes," Emily said as they moved into the dining room.

"No need for that," Vida said as she indicated the chair Emily was to use. "The men grumble about it, but they all take turns with kitchen duty."

Emily wondered if Sam Tucker ever put his hands into a pan of dishwater. Movement in the doorway drew her attention and she caught the object of her thoughts standing there watching her intently. He had taken obvious pains to clean up for dinner. His hair was still damp and glistening in the lamplight. Black pin-striped wool pants, a fresh white shirt, leather vest, and shining black boots completed his outfit.

She smiled in greeting.

He merely nodded and took a seat without speaking.

The three of them seemed lost at the long, formally set dining table. Crisp white linen cloths and napkins, shining china, and crystal were not exactly what Emily had expected to find at the Rocking T.

She smiled at Vida and attempted to make polite conversation while Carmen set their filled dinner plates in front of them. "Everything looks lovely, Mrs. Tucker."

"Land sakes, call me Vida. And then pass the butter, please."

Despite the fact that she was all too aware of the big man silently pretending not to watch her from the end of the table, Emily said, "This all looks so elegant, I'm glad I dressed for dinner, after all." She snuck a peek at Sam Tucker and found him studiously spreading butter on a thick slice of bread.

"We don't do things up like this every night, but I like to have a new guest sit down to a fancy meal the first night they get here. You're just lucky I had a urge to fix pot roast this morning. Most of the time you'll get chili verde and bread." Then Vida looked across at Sam Tucker and said, "I left Willie's letter out on the desk for you. He said he'll be home before Valentine's Day with a big announcement." She looked at Emily and smiled as if waiting for Emily to comment on what Willie's "big announcement" might be.

Emily merely smiled back at her and shrugged. She had no idea what William would announce, but when she glanced down the length of the table at Sam Tucker, she was met by another of his dark looks.

They ate in silence for a time and then Emily said, "Mr. Tucker, I suppose I should warn you, I am here to do a photographic study of life on a ranch. What I had planned was to take pictures step-by-step throughout your day beginning with the very first thing you—"

Sam Tucker carefully laid his knife and fork down beside his plate. Too carefully. "No."

Vida frowned. "Now, Tucker—"

Emily merely accepted the challenge. She hadn't battled three sisters and two little brothers all her life for nothing. "What do you mean, no? I don't mean to inconvenience you. It will be quite painless."

"Listen, little lady, we have work to do here. My men

and I can't be posing for any pictures. Besides, I've been told life here on the ranch is nothing but a bore. There isn't anything we do during the day you need to waste time on.''

Pushing her plate away, Emily refused to back down. "I disagree with you there, Mr. Tucker. This is a unique way of life, one that very few easterners know about, but most of them are curious. Just look at the interest in the novels about life in the west—''

"All exaggerations," he interjected.

"All hold a grain of truth. I want to present an accurate record through my photographs. Willie was more than gracious when he extended his invitation.''

"I'll bet.'' Sam Tucker studied his plate.

"I assumed someone here would be willing to help," she added.

He leaned against the back of his chair and continued to pin her with his steady gaze. "You assumed wrong.''

Vida was hard-pressed to remain silent any longer. "Now, Tucker, I don't see what it's going to hurt to let her take a few photographs of your men working.''

Emily felt herself blush with embarrassment. She wasn't about to beg Sam Tucker for anything. There were plenty of other ranches around, and if need be, she'd just try to get herself invited to one of them. She brushed back her skirt to stand, careful not to catch the soft pink wool against the chair legs.

"I'm sorry to have inconvenienced you in any way, Mr. Tucker. If you can have a man take me back over the mountain, I'll leave tomorrow morning and find a place to stay in Tehachapi." She turned to Vida. "Dinner was delicious. Thank you.'' Emily remembered to smile, sincerely sorry to have to leave the pleasant, motherly woman behind with such an overbearing, contemptuous—"

"Good," Tucker said, all too smugly. "I'll have a wagon waiting out front for you at daybreak."

Humiliated, Emily left the room and headed for the steep staircase in the entry hall. One foot on the bottom stair, she could hear the continued conversation in the dining room without strain.

Vida's voice came to her clear and sharp. "Tucker, there wasn't any call for you to be so rude to that child. Especially not when Willie wants her here. He'll be home shortly, so I think the least we can do—"

"I told her the truth, that's all. There's nothing worth seeing around here. She'd only be in the way."

"All women aren't like Lillith."

Lillith? Emily moved up two steps, hating to eavesdrop, but willing to hear Vida Tucker put her stubborn nephew in his place. The sound of china being cleared from the table was a familiar one. Emily often shared the chore with her sisters at home.

The strained silence lengthened until she heard Tucker say in a low, controlled tone, "I told you never to mention that woman's name in this house again."

"Some things are best brought out into the open and gotten over with, Tucker. It's time you put her behind you."

The scrape of chair legs against the highly polished floor alerted Emily that someone was leaving the table. She picked up her skirt and silently hurried up the remaining stairs to the second floor, wondering all the while who the woman named Lillith might be and what she had done to deserve Sam Tucker's undying hatred.

* * *

It was almost pitch-dark in the room when the four-poster bed started shaking and Emily, startled out of a deep sleep, bolted to a sitting position. Everything around her seemed to be creaking and rattling. The windowpanes and the crystal prisms on the lampshades chimed. The house itself was rumbling and groaning in protest. She wanted to shout to whomever was making the ruckus to stop, but her voice was lodged firmly in her throat.

When the shaking worked itself into a roll, and wave after wave shook the bed, she managed to scramble out from beneath the covers and head for the door. Merely crossing the room was like walking over the heaving deck of a sea-tossed ship. Frantically she tried to open the door and finally managed to twist the knob. By the time she was out in the hallway, the motion had subsided to a faint shuddering and the incessant noise coming from all quarters faded. Then, within an instant or two, the house stopped moving and the noises sighed to silence.

Relieved, Emily leaned against the door frame. Down the hall, another door opened and Sam Tucker emerged holding a lighted lamp aloft. His shirt was unbuttoned down the front. He was barefoot, and his pants had been hastily donned, as evidenced by the way they hung from his hips. They were barely buttoned.

Properly averting her gaze, Emily stared up at the shadowy figure towering over her in the semidarkness.

"That was a good one," he commented coolly. Extraordinarily cool given the situation.

"What *was* that?" she gasped, hoping she could hear his answer over the roar of blood pounding through her veins.

"Earthquake. Haven't had a shake like that for some time."

Emily mumbled to herself. "*Earthquake?* Earthquake! No one told me anything about earthquakes." She looked back up at Sam Tucker and thought she saw him smile.

"Could be another one close on its heels."

Yes, she decided. The perverse creature definitely *was* smiling. He looked downright ghoulish standing there in the darkened hall with the halo of light illuminating his features.

"Is Vida all right?" she managed to ask.

Tucker turned around and glanced at his aunt's closed door. "Probably back to sleep already. Quakes only upset her when the dishes get broken."

Emily tried to push away from the doorjamb and stand under her own power. Her legs were trembling, but they worked. "I probably won't get another minute's sleep all night long."

Tucker tried to ignore the frightened, wide-eyed look of the girl standing just beyond the glow of the lamp but found his usually cold heart begin to thaw. She looked like a waif standing there in a proper, wide-yolked flannel gown that covered her from neck, to wrist, to the tip of her toes. And cute little toes they were at that.

He ran a hand through his tousled hair and held the lamp higher, casting her in more light. She was trembling like a newborn calf and he reckoned if he hadn't grown up used to the fact that the earth could jolt around beneath him anytime it wanted, he'd look just as scared.

"How about some hot milk?" he asked of a sudden.

"What?"

She looked as if he'd lost his mind and he figured he just had. Why else would he offer to play nursemaid in the middle of the night? *When are you going to learn, Tucker?*

He cleared his throat. "I said, would you like some hot milk? It'll help you get back to sleep."

He watched her tilt her head and eye him suspiciously. "I *thought* that's what you said. Why are you suddenly so concerned, Mr. Tucker?"

Wondering whether it was an unconscious movement on her part or not, he watched as her hand went to the throat of her gown and then fell away after she was certain it was buttoned to the neck.

"Most folks call me just plain Tucker," he said. "As for why I offered the milk . . . well I guess 'cause I gave you an awful hard time at dinner." Now that she was leaving, he figured he could afford to be magnanimous.

She smiled. It was slow in coming and held a hint of suspicion, but it was a smile nonetheless. For some reason it made him smile in return.

"I'll just get my wrapper," she told him, and turned to step inside her room.

Sam waited at the top of the stairs so that he could guide her down with the lamp. He found an anticipation building inside that he hadn't experienced for three years and knew that any man who could feel excited simply because a woman agreed to share a glass of milk at midnight was a man whose life had become hideously routine.

Emily hurriedly rifled through her trunk until she found her heavy plaid wrapper, slipped it on, and drew the sash tight. Her slippers were beside the bed. She found it remarkable that they hadn't moved during the earthquake. Following the soft lamplight in the hallway, she joined Sam Tucker at the top of the stairs and let him lead the way. Thankful for his good mood and a few brief moments alone with him, Emily hoped to convince him that she should stay and begin her series of photographs here on the Rocking T.

He was amazingly at home in the kitchen as he motioned her out of the way and took a crock of milk from the icebox then poured some into a pan. He had to stir the fire in the stove to life and throw in a piece of wood from the wood bin, but Emily was more than content to wait for the fire to heat up enough to warm the milk.

The room was so chilly her breath almost fogged the air. She shivered where she sat on the cane-bottom chair and finally stood, crossing to the stove to soak in some of the building heat.

"California is a very surprising place," she said, hoping beyond hope he would pick up the thread of conversation.

It was a minute or two before he committed to join in, but join in he did. "How so?"

She watched, speechless, as he began to button his shirt over the broad expanse of his chest. He seemed to be quite suntanned for the dead of winter, quite a bit more suntanned than anyone she knew. His chest was covered with a thick mat of dark, wiry hair, his pectoral muscles highly developed. As far as a photographic subject of the details of the human body—

"I said, how so?" he repeated.

Emily tore her eyes away from his fingers as he worked the last button closed and swallowed. "Well . . ." She found it hard to concentrate for a moment, so she met his gaze and caught him staring down at her curiously. She cleared her throat. "By that I meant . . . what was I saying?"

She was certain he was trying to hide a smile again. "You were about to tell me why California is such a surprising place."

Relieved, she laughed. "Oh, yes. Well, it's just that here

it is January already, and the sun was shining to beat the band today.''

"To beat the band," he repeated.

"Exactly. But I have noticed that the temperature drops quite startlingly at night and it stays very chilly indoors. In the shade outside as well. It makes it quite a challenge to choose the right attire.''

He was watching her closely, but didn't comment, so Emily felt the need to fill the void. "Then, of all things, an earthquake! I can't wait to write my family all about it.''

Still barefoot, he walked over to the table, took the chair she had vacated, and sat down. He reached out to turn up the lamp he had set in the center of the kitchen table. "Do you have a big family?''

Finding it easier to talk now that he wasn't standing practically on top of her, Emily smiled. "Oh my, yes. I have three older sisters and two younger brothers, so I truly am a middle child. Which I like, actually. I've always gone quite unnoticed.''

"Fishing for compliments?''

She didn't like the chill she heard in his tone. "What exactly do you mean by that?''

Sam leaned back and rested his foot on the opposite knee, seemingly quite content to rile her. "What I mean is, since there's no way someone with your looks could go unnoticed, I figure you dropped that little statement to get me to comment on them.''

"My looks?''

"Yes.''

Emily was taken aback. Barbara, her oldest sister, had always been the pretty one. Catherine, the next in line with natural blond curls and long lashes, had been proclaimed the classic beauty. Cynthia, the sister closest to Emily in age, had been spoken for at sixteen. By the time her sisters were her age, they were already legendary for their personalities, charm, and good looks, while she, at twenty-two, was known for nothing more than her radical ideas regarding women pursuing professions.

"Why, Mr. Tucker, I'm nothing out of the ordinary, and you know it."

Tucker watched her with a wary eye. She might be nothing out of the ordinary in Chicago, but she was by far one of the most stunning women he'd seen in a coon's age. When he had first seen her arrive, dressed in her fancy duds, trail weary and dusty, he thought her pretty. Tonight, with her rich brown hair falling softly about her shoulders, the hint of lace teasing her chin, and a gown that encouraged his imagination to ponder what might be hidden beneath it, he found her downright captivating.

He knew enough from his own experience with a con-niving woman to let the subject of just how captivating she might be drop, for it led nowhere but straight to trouble. Besides, she was here at Willie's invitation; that made her Willie's claim and his brother would be home by Valen-tine's Day, which was a little over a month away. He'd no doubt expect his valentine to be around.

Sam stood up and went back to the stove. The milk was simmering in the pan, so he moved to the cupboard and took down two mugs. He set them on the sideboard and then, after wrapping a dish towel around the pan handle, he poured the steaming liquid into each cup and set the empty pan on the dry sink.

Emily took one of the mugs from him, and for an instant, when their fingertips met, she thought she saw him frown. This someone named Lillith, she decided, had hurt him very, very badly. Sipping the warm milk carefully, she waited to see if he would linger over his cup or drink it and be done with her.

He lingered.

She sipped in silence.

Finally she mustered the courage to try to extend her stay. "What do you have planned for tomorrow, Mr. Tucker?" She watched one of his dark brows arch as he sized her up over the rim of his cup.

"You mean after you are gone, Miss Richardson?"

She managed to hide her answer to that as she took another sip.

He sat back and set the mug on the table for a moment. "Tomorrow, first light, we're going to ride out and round up a few of the mamas that are out too far from the barns. I want 'em brought close in before they drop their calves."

"Mamas?"

"That's right."

"With babies?"

"Calves, not babies. But they aren't here yet."

"That's why you have to go get them? Because the mamas aren't here?"

He sighed. "No, Miss Richardson. The babies"—he cleared his throat, obviously frustrated—"I mean the calves aren't here yet. The mamas are still . . ." He paused, as if trying to come up with an appropriate word.

"Pregnant?"

"Exactly."

She was surprised to see him color with embarrassment. "Does that word offend you, Mr. Tucker?"

"No, Miss Richardson, but it's just not something I'm in the habit of talking about around a lady."

"Pregnant cows embarrass you?"

He shifted. "Could we talk about something else?"

His sensitivity surprised her. He looked far too rugged to care what subject he talked about with her or anyone. But she was not about to let him off that easily. "Why are you bringing them closer to the house?"

"To the barn. Because we've had one good snow and just because it's already thawed doesn't mean we won't get another. In fact, Ramon said he can foresee a storm coming."

"And this Ramon is some sort of psychic?"

"No, he's my foreman."

Pleased with the way they were chatting somewhat amiably now, she smiled. "Oh, that's right. He's married to Carmen and they live close by."

"The hands with wives and families live in the cabins down by the pond. The single men bunk in the bunk-house behind this one. They take their meals in the dining room."

Feeling more self-assured in his presence, she set her empty mug on the table and leaned forward. "This is exactly the type of thing I want to photograph. The cabins by the pond, the bunkhouse inside and out. There are the vignettes of life that must be captured before they're gone."

"Where they going?"

Emily stood up, carried away by her enthusiasm for her dream. "Who knows where a way of life goes? No one sees it passing until it's too late and it's gone. What if Matthew Brady had not recorded the war in photographs?"

"This isn't a war, it's a cattle ranch. Besides, we aren't going anyplace. This is my home."

He was frowning again. She knew she had to do some fast

talking and quick thinking in order to get him to agree. "Of course it is. But think of future generations. What will you tell your grandchildren when they ask what this place was like? Think of how wonderful it would be to show them a photograph."

At the mention of children his scowl deepened and she knew she was once again treading on thin ice. "Or . . . or think of those folks back east who will never have the chance to experience firsthand—"

"The answer is no, Miss Richardson."

"But if I could just—"

"*No.*"

"I wouldn't be in the way."

"Still no."

"Just a few photographs. Landscape shots. No people if that's what bothers you."

"I don't think—"

"*One* day. Just give me one day."

He sighed. His shoulders sagged in resignation.

Emily smiled. She had him now. "Well?"

He stood up and collected the mugs and carried them over to the dry sink. She watched him stand with his back to her, leaning forward on his hands as he wrestled with his decision. She held her breath.

He turned around and leaned casually against the dry sink. In a barely audible mumble he said, "I guess it wouldn't hurt if you stayed one more day and took some pictures of the buildings."

"Oh, thank you, Mr. Tucker!" She was so elated she almost hugged him. A foot in the door was better than nothing at all.

"Call me Tucker."

"Only if you'll call me Emily."

He turned, prepared to leave the room, but first he collected the lamp from the table. "We ride at dawn, so I think I'll turn in."

Already making mental plans for the morrow, Emily followed him to the kitchen door. He paused to let her precede him up the stairs. "I can't tell you what this means to me, Tucker," she whispered, afraid of waking Vida. The hushed sound filled the empty stairwell.

Sam Tucker stared at her plaid flannel wrapper and followed her swishing little bottom up the stairs with an intense frown marring his features. Somehow or other she had wormed her way into staying another day and he would have to face her again across the dinner table. Tomorrow, he vowed, he'd be on guard against her devious ways. Tomorrow he wasn't about to let her talk him into one more day. And after that? Day *after* tomorrow he would see the last of Miss Emily Richardson. Of Chicago.

When they were halfway up the staircase, the earth shifted again, not with a long, rolling wave, but with a severe jolt that knocked Emily off her feet. Sam, two steps beneath her, held tight to the oil lamp with one hand, braced himself against the wall, and grabbed for Emily with his free arm as she tumbled into him.

He blew out the lamp, afraid if the tremors continued, he might drop it and set them and the house on fire. He could feel Emily trembling against him and drew her closer.

"Is it over?" she whispered.

"Rose petals," he mumbled.

"What?"

Without meaning to speak out loud, he had named the fragrance that surrounded her. Unwilling to let go of her just yet, he warned, "There might be one more tremor." There certainly were a few affecting his hand as he slightly. tightened his grip on her arm.

Maybe he would spend the remainder of a sleepless night in his bed, wondering why for the life of him he had held her so tight, and why, when she lifted her eyes to his in the shadowed hallway, he had covered her lips with his own. But as they stood there on the stairs he did just that. It wasn't a kiss of passion, not by any means. The exchange was more of a curious tasting, a test, a delightful sampling of something so unexpected they were both caught unaware.

"Oh, my—" Emily said when he released her. She stepped back to take firm hold of the banister.

"Oh, no." Tucker's reaction was definitely one of chagrin.

They stood there enshrouded in silence so thick it became utterly deafening. He could hear her soft, rapid breathing. She could sense his total frustration.

"I think we should—"

"Let's just forget—"

Emily laughed nervously when they both spoke at once. He waited for her to say something, anything, to help him over the awkward moment.

"I was about to suggest we both forget what just happened, Mr. Tucker."

"Words out of my own mouth," he agreed.

"Well, then. I'll see you tomorrow." Emily kept a firm hold on the banister as she climbed the stairs and then headed straight for her room.

She heard him moving behind her, felt him holding back so as to avoid running into her in the dark hallway. Once inside her room she closed the door and leaned back against it, one hand pressed to her lips.

Whatever possessed her to let Sam Tucker kiss her like that was beyond her reasoning. She had all but melted against him, clung to him there in the dark stairwell long after the fright from the second earthquake had subsided.

It wasn't as if she'd never been kissed before, either. After all, she thought with a tilt of her chin, she was twenty-two years old. Just because she was almost an old maid didn't mean there hadn't been stolen kisses or whispers exchanged during a soiree or garden party. Just because she had never met a man who appreciated her need to fulfill her dream of becoming a photographer of note didn't mean she had given up all thought of marrying someday.

But this? This unexpected, overheated, toe-curling reaction to a sudden kiss from a man who didn't even seem to like her very much—she didn't know what to think.

Shivering from the cold, she finally gathered her wits enough to cross the room and slip back into bed. The soothing effect of the warm milk had been shattered by the second quake. Refusing to lie awake for hours staring into the dark, Emily mentally went over what she planned to photograph come morning and how she could convince Sam Tucker she needed to extend her stay at the Rocking T. And when she was plagued by unbidden thoughts of the way his kiss had warmed her to her toes, she closed her eyes, shook her head, and waited for the memory to pass.

It was cloudy the next morning, the overcast sky the color of dull slate that hung heavy above the surrounding hills. Sleep had finally come to Emily somewhere in the wee hours of the morning. Deep in slumber, she had missed the dawn. It was nearly eight o'clock when she got up and moved about the room, hastily donned her green traveling suit because it was the warmest outfit she had with her, and hurried down to the kitchen, where she hoped it would be warmer.

"Good mornin', Emily. Tucker told me you'd be stayin' another night and that you were going to be taking some photographs today after all."

Emily smiled and helped herself to a mug and coffee as Vida pulled some warm cinnamon buns from the oven. "Yes, I am. I was able to convince him to let me stay one more day and take a few photographs of the buildings." Suddenly she was struck with an idea that might convince Tucker to extend her stay even longer. "I'd like to take one of you here in the kitchen, too, if I may."

Vida's hand flew to her neat braids, her fingers quickly feeling to be sure every strand was in place. "Why, I look a sight. I don't know what you want to do that for."

Emily could tell the older woman was not only pleased, but flattered, even as she protested. "I was counting on capturing all the facets of ranch life. The kitchen is a very integral part, and so is the cook."

"Well, if you put it that way, then I'd be happy to oblige." Vida set the plate of warm buns on the table and poured a cup of coffee for herself. "Now, you want me to fix you some eggs?"

Emily sat down and chose a bun. She set it on the plate in front of her and licked the sticky frosting and cinnamon from her fingertips. "This will be plenty."

Vida took a bun for herself and shook her head with a smile as she eyed Emily. "I'd like to have been a fly on the wall when you talked Tucker into letting you stay. Folks don't usually get around him so easy."

It was almost impossible to keep the color from staining

her cheeks as she recalled her exchange with Sam Tucker last night. Wriggling in the chair, she avoided looking at Vida and began to tear the cinnamon bun into bite-sized pieces. "After the earthquake, which, by the way, I can't believe anyone could sleep through—"

"Oh, I woke up, but I'm one to ride 'em out, and if the house doesn't fall down around my ears, I go right back to sleep."

"Anyway," Emily continued, "Tucker and I ran into each other in the hallway and he offered to fix me some warm milk so I could get back to sleep."

Vida looked sincerely astounded. "You don't say?"

"It's true. I was fairly amazed myself. Then we started talking about this and that and he finally agreed to let me stay and take pictures of the outbuildings, the house, the men's dining room."

"The hands' dining room?" Clearly Vida looked puzzled.

Instead of explaining her objective again, Emily changed the subject. There was something she had to know and she hoped that Vida would not be offended when she asked. "I couldn't help but overhear you refer to someone named Lillith twice last evening. Can you tell me who she is?"

When Vida pushed away from the table, Emily was afraid she had overstepped her bounds, but Tucker's aunt merely crossed the room to the stove and picked up the coffeepot to refill their cups. "Tucker's wife."

Emily almost choked on a mouthful of cinnamon roll. When she could manage it, she swallowed and asked, "His *wife*?"

"His former wife. She divorced him three years ago."

"Really?"

"Sure did." Vida sat back down, glanced at the backdoor

to be certain there was no one on the porch, and continued, "Tucker was a different man then. He laughed, he smiled. He enjoyed life. Met her in San Francisco. Lillith was an actress. Told me one day she wanted some respect, so she thought marrying a man like Tucker, a rancher with roots and a good name, would bring her that.

"They got married and she moved in here. Found out there was no place to wear all her fancy gowns, nowhere to show off, none of the attention she was used to."

Emily folded her hands in her lap. She tried to imagine Sam Tucker laughing. "Tucker didn't pay any attention to her?"

Vida shook her head and sighed. "He was head over heels in love with Lillith. But he's a rancher. That's all he's ever been, all he ever wanted. He couldn't make up for all the crowds and he couldn't take the time to travel the way she wanted. They argued from the get-go, loud enough for everyone to hear. Finally she told him this place was going to drive her crazy, that she was 'too bored to breathe,' and that if she didn't get out, it was likely going to kill her."

"So she left," Emily concluded.

"That she did. Broke his heart. He thought it didn't show, but he won't go anyplace at all anymore and he's ornery as a bear. That's how Willie ended up being the one to do all the travelin' to arrange the co-op between the other stockmen and the stockyards."

Vida's story explained Tucker's reluctance to open up to her, his claim that there was nothing about ranch life worth documenting. But the kiss? When she realized he probably hadn't been as close to a woman in three years as he had been to her last night, Emily understood.

Sam Tucker was a man in need of caring in the worst way.

She smiled at Vida. "Thanks for telling me all this. It explains a lot."

"Glad I did. Sam's got a reason to be bitter, but I think it's high time he gave it up," Vida admitted.

"Well, since he's agreed to let me stay today, I'd better get to work, hadn't I?" Emily stood up and put her napkin on the table. "Can I help you clear up?"

"No, you just run along and get those photographs you wanted."

Emily looked around the warm kitchen with its butter-yellow curtains and well-scoured floor. "I still plan to start right here, if you don't mind."

The weathered outbuildings—the barn, stables, and feed shed—were solid, familiar shapes in the thickening fog that had gathered in the basin and hidden the rounded peaks surrounding the ranch proper. Sam dismounted, thankful he was wearing his heaviest fleece-lined coat before he rode out that morning. He glanced toward the house and wondered briefly how Miss Emily Richardson of Chicago was spending her time, because the fog had obviously ruined any chance of taking photographs.

He handed his big-rumped bay over to Tim, the young wrangler, and headed for the house. Smoke from the chimney hung low over the outbuildings and mingled with the fog. The leafless oaks that surrounded the house marked the bleakness of winter. He cupped his gloved hands and blew on them to ease the cold from his fingers.

Sam ducked as he cleared the threshold of the back porch and let the screen door bang behind him. As he closed the interior door he heard laughter in the kitchen and ducked to take a peek in the back window. Aunt Vida and Emily

Richardson were talking, heads together, as they studied something on the kitchen table.

Sam sighed. He pulled off his gloves and shoved the ends in his back pocket, then took off his hat and raked his fingers through his hair. He took a deep breath before he stepped gratefully into the warmth of the kitchen.

Vida hurried to get him hot water so he could wash up. Emily Richardson looked up with a smug smile on her face.

Sam knew he was in for trouble.

"Good day, Mr. Tucker. I have a few surprises for you," she said all too cheerfully.

As he looked down into her dark eyes, let his eyes roam over her flushed cheeks and the full pout of her lower lip, he couldn't help but remember every detail of the kiss they had shared in the stairwell last night. It had been sweet. Tempting. Blood stirring—

"Mr. Tucker?"

He wrestled with his concentration. Shrugging out of his heavy jacket, he handed it to Vida, who stood waiting to take it from him, straightened the leather vest he wore over a thick plaid shirt, and said, "What, Miss Richardson?"

She blinked rapidly. Her expression sobered at once. "I asked you to call me Emily."

"And you were supposed to call me Tucker."

Emily smiled once more. "I guess you're right. Well then, *Tucker,* have a look at these. What do you think?" She indicated a group of photographs spread across the kitchen table.

"You've been a busy lady," he said after a quick glance at the half-dozen pictures. He took a step forward to get a better look.

"That I have. I've been pleasantly occupied since breakfast. When Vida told me it was nearly time for supper, I was amazed the afternoon had flown so quickly.''

She stepped up beside him, too close for comfort, he thought as he stared down at her work.

Emily chatted on. ''This was nothing like taking photographs of subjects I'm familiar with. With each shot I had to pause and think about composition, lighting, and the effect I wanted to achieve. There's a story to tell through the work and I aim to get it right.''

He picked up a picture of Vida standing beside the stove. The image captured the laughter that always shone in his aunt's eyes. Pots and pans covered the stovetop, the details so clear he could almost see steam coming from the teakettle. The photograph was unlike any of the stiff, formal portraits he'd seen. This was the real Vida in her element, in command, alive, enthusiastic about everyday life. He set the photograph back down on the table, forced to grudgingly admit something to himself.

Miss Emily Richardson of Chicago was a very talented photographer.

''Well?''

She waited for his response. Sam picked up another image on paper, this one of the interior of the bunkhouse. It reminded him of life suspended—a pair of boots lay discarded under a bunk, a pair of chaps hung lifeless from a hook on the wall. Horseshoes and calendars were tacked to the mud-daubed walls. Textures stood out in the still life: the wadded chinks of mud between the long walls, the rough striped blankets on the beds, the cold, slick metal of the rifles that hung on the walls. It told a silent story of the hard lives of the men who inhabited the elemental environment.

''*Well?*'' she asked again.

He let her stew.

Sam picked up a third photograph, a study of the great stone fireplace in the parlor. Each memento set on the hearth and mantel stood out in deep relief—the longhorn horns over the fireplace, his grandfather's Hawkin rifle, his mother's precious china vase with a peacock-feather fan propped behind it, a tall, silver candelabra spattered with candle wax. Beneath the mantel, the rough stone fireplace opening was stained black with soot. Andirons stood at attention, poker at the ready.

The objects hinted at the composition of life in the west, where elegant remnants of eastern pasts were lovingly displayed alongside the rough-hewn necessities of everyday life.

He set the photograph down carefully.

Emily Richardson was tapping her foot, her dainty leather shoe revealing her irritation as it hit the floorboards.

He glanced over at her, pinned by her dark-eyed stare.

Sam shrugged. "I like 'em."

Her foot stopped tapping. "Why?"

Sam pulled a chair out from the table and sat down. His aunt, carefully avoiding the photographs, immediately set a cup of coffee in front of him. "What do you mean, why?" he asked Emily.

She sighed in frustration. "*Why* do you like them? *What* do you like about them?"

Vida laughed. "She's been at me for half an hour, Tucker. Might as well think of something to tell her."

Emily shook her head and told them both. "It's not enough for you two to tell me you *like* them. I need to know why you like them, what you see in them. I want to know if I've expressed the essence of the message I'm trying to get across."

Sam took a sip of coffee and crossed his booted foot over

his knee as he leaned back and let the hot, black liquid warm him. He pointed to the bunkhouse picture. "This one shows the bleakness of the men's lives." His finger touched the edge of the fireplace photograph. "This one, I think, is about east meets west, leftover refinement on the range, you might say. And this one"—he picked up the photograph of Vida at the stove—"this one is a kitchen come to life. A scene we live with every day and take for granted."

He glanced up at Emily Richardson and found her gaping at him.

He took another sip of coffee and swallowed a smile. "Didn't know I had it in me, huh?"

Excitement radiated from her. She pulled out a chair and dragged it up beside his, plopped down, and leaned toward him. "You are exactly correct, Tucker. It's astounding."

He shrugged off her amazement. "Nothing astounding about it. You have quite a talent. You make it easy to see a story in every picture—which, the more I look at these, is the way it should be." He thought of the stiff formality displayed in the only photograph he possessed of his parents and wished someone could have captured them as they really were, not as two lifeless, wooden cutouts.

Sam passed her the photograph of Vida. "I'd like to buy one of these."

Once more he caught her off guard. "You would?"

Tucker nodded. "Yep."

Vida leaned over their shoulders and studied the picture of herself. "It's just me doin' what I do every day."

Sam smiled sideways at her. "That's why I like it. It's real." He turned back to Emily, who looked as contented as a fox in a henhouse with a bellyful of chicken. "It's alive."

She blushed. He liked catching her off guard. Sam took a deep breath and hoped he wouldn't regret his next pronouncement. "If you promise to keep out of the way, you can stay for the rest of the week," he told her.

Unprepared for her reaction, he almost sloshed the remains of his coffee on her precious photographs when she reached out and hugged him around the neck. Then, immediately, she let go and turned beet red. But Emily Richardson didn't flee the scene.

"*Thank* you, Tucker! Thank you so much," she said.

Shifting, uncomfortable under her intense regard, he glanced over at his aunt and caught her smiling from ear to ear.

Emily slogged through the mud and manure in the corral. She had given up trying to save her ankle-high shoes an hour ago. The sun was up, barely. It illuminated the sky above the humped peaks of the Tehachapi Mountains. A scarf around her head did little to fight off the biting cold as she carried the last of her supplies, a box of spare film covers loaded with chemical papers inside their glass plates. Her camera stood like a three-legged stork in unfamiliar waters. Emily ducked beneath the black hood that shrouded the back of the camera to check the focus. Since there was no time for the long exposure with both men and animals involved, she decided to use the flash powder, which would be ignited just before she hit the shutter spring.

"How you doin', miss?"

Nearly upsetting herself and the camera, Emily whipped the cloth off and found the man assigned to readying the horses for the day standing directly behind her.

"Just fine, Tim. You startled me."

The young man tipped the brim of his hat. "Yor pardon, ma'am. I didn't mean to."

Emily forced a smile and turned back to her work. As she

ducked under the cloth again she explained: "I want to have this all set up so that I can get at least one shot off before you men leave." She knew she had to work quickly. Although she had agreed to stay out of the way, she had not exactly promised Tucker she would not try to capture some photographs of the men at work.

She had avoided him this morning, skipped breakfast in order to let him think she was sleeping late as she had the previous day. Last evening had passed without event; supper was less strained than the first night, if not downright pleasant. On one occasion Sam Tucker had even smiled over something she had said. When he announced he would be up and out by dawn, rounding up the last of the remnant "mamas," she became determined to get a picture of the men in the corral as they were about to ride off.

After one last check Emily knew she was ready. Three of the men sauntered out of the kitchen and crossed the yard to the stables. They laughed and joked with Tim, teasing him about being out in the dark with a pretty lady all by himself. One asked if he knew what to do in the dark with a "gal." Tim dipped his head, obviously embarrassed. Emily pretended to ignore their boisterous exchange and called out to them. "Gentlemen, I am a photographer, Emily Richardson. Of Chicago. After you collect your mounts, I'd like you to bring them over here in front of the barn and gather 'round."

Tim opened the heavy gate to the back corral, where the horses stood saddled and ready. The others began leading them over as Emily directed, admonishing them against lining up formally. "Just stand around and talk as you might usually do. Relax." She was afraid they were all too aware of the camera to do much more than line up and stand at attention. It was the type of photographic composition they were used to.

Ramon, the foreman, rode up from the group of small houses down the creek. He tipped his hat to her and then, in Spanish, asked one of the others what was going on. After a cowhand explained, Ramon joined the group, but didn't dismount. Instead he leaned against the saddle horn and watched her as she filled the flash pan with flash powder.

The sound of conversation and laughter filtered over her shoulder. She glanced back toward the house to see the last four cowhands, along with Sam Tucker, come walking toward the corral.

Emily swallowed hard, trying to overcome embarrassment. The sound of voices died away. The men waiting in the corral watched their boss approach. The sly glances from beneath their brims were hard for Emily to miss. She was afraid sparks were about to fly between her and the volatile Sam Tucker and she knew they all knew it.

None of them had to wait long.

"What's going on here?" Tucker stomped up to her, pointed at the camera, and then crossed his arms over his chest.

Emily looked up at him, forced to tip her head back to look him in the eye. She balled her gloved hands into fists, then slowly opened them. "I'm taking a picture of all of you before you ride off."

"Impossible."

"Why?"

"We don't have time to pose." He turned away. "Mount up, boys."

When he started to move away, she went after him. "Just a minute, Tucker. The men don't mind."

"I do."

"Why?" she demanded.

He turned on her. "Why? Is that the only word in your vocabulary? Because I mind. I don't want to take the time, that's all."

"You just want to be an ornery old coot," she mumbled.

His hands went to his hips and he glared down at her. "What did you say?"

"Nothing your aunt Vida wouldn't agree to." Emily tried to smooth his ruffled feathers. "I'm ready now. This will only take a second."

"I said you could take pictures of the buildings."

"You said nothing of the kind when you extended my stay to a week. There were no stipulations then."

"Because I thought the old ones still stood."

"I thought the opposite."

"Well, you're wrong," he snapped.

They stood in the ghost-gray light of dawn glaring at each other as their breath fogged and fused between them.

"You are the one wasting time, Mr. Tucker."

He jerked off his hat and slammed it against his thigh and glared over at the camera. "Get the damned thing ready," he grouched before he strode off to mount up.

Afraid he'd change his mind, Emily hurried back to the camera. Before she ducked beneath the cloth again to check the focus one last time and cock the shutter spring, she made certain most of the men were in view. If the photograph was not exactly what she wanted, there was little she could do about it now. Sam Tucker was in no mood to wait for everything to be perfect.

Three of the men stood beside their horses talking softly, paying her no mind. Ramon was still leaning forward, his arms crossed on the saddle horn. Sam Tucker led his own horse out of the corral and two others were mounted and ready to ride.

She quickly struck a match, held the shutter ball ready, and lit the flash pan, intending to catch the men casually unaware.

The flash exploded and all hell broke loose.

Horses reared and whinnied before they fled. Men cursed and shouted, trying to bring the frightened animals under control. Emily slipped from beneath the cover cloth just in time to scream at the sight of a frightened mare bearing down on her from across the corral. Instinctively she grabbed for the camera and wrapped her arms about it as the galloping horse bolted out of the open gate, but not before sending Emily down on her back into the mire—camera and all.

She caught her breath, and then slowly and carefully she sat up, her arms still hugging the camera tightly. Emily winced, not only at the pain, but at the sight of Sam Tucker, flat on his rear end in the mud, swearing a blue streak. There wasn't a horse left in sight.

Sam pushed himself up, sat in the mud and manure, and glared across the corral at Miss Emily Richardson, of Chicago, who for the moment was ass-deep in the same muck, staring stubbornly back at him with her godforsaken camera clutched to her breasts. The skirt of her green wool traveling suit was hiked up, revealing the lace on a frilly pair of knee-length bloomers and the eyelet edge of her petticoats. Her matching emerald hat was riding low over one eye, its decorative feather broken and dangling sadly beyond repair.

Sam sat there fighting the urge to erupt in a fit of temper, wanting to shake her until her teeth rattled. He knew if he laid a hand on her, there was no telling what he might do.

As if she had read his mind, he saw her quickly hand her camera up to Ramon, who had offered assistance. He fumed as he watched his foreman pull Miss Emily Richardson up to a standing position, and then actually smiled a satisfied smile when he saw her twist and turn to get a look at the damage to her backside. The entire length of her was mud-coated. Standing, she reminded him of a playing card, one side brown, the other green.

He heaved himself up, knowing full well that he was in the same condition. As he moved across the corral, finally in control enough not to cause her bodily harm, Sam watched her eye him quickly, snatch her camera from Ramon, and turn toward the house.

"Hold it right there, Miss Richardson," he called out.

She froze in midstride, but didn't turn to face him. In half a dozen steps he was beside her. He reached out, put a muddy gloved hand on her shoulder, and spun her around so that she was forced to look up at him.

Ignoring the humbled expression in her big brown eyes, overlooking the slight trembling of her lower lip, he took a deep breath. In a low, ominously controlled voice he said, "I don't care how much it upsets you—or my brother, for that matter. I want you to pack up your gear and be ready to leave as soon as I can get a man to hitch up a team to take you back to Tehachapi. Do you understand?"

He expected an argument. At the very least he expected her to make excuses for what happened. But she did neither. Emily Richardson merely hugged her camera closer and stalked off toward the house.

Sam took off his hat and almost ran his muddy glove through his hair, but stopped in the nick of time. He shook his head and shoved his hat back on. "Damn it, Willie," he mumbled to himself as he watched Emily on the march with a defeated slump in her shoulders. Having his brother's romantic interest in residence was as bad as having Willie around.

This morning's fiasco was not all that out of the ordinary. Ever since they'd been children, Willie had been possessed of the uncanny ability to create disasters around the ranch. When Willie rode out to get a wayward cow out of a sinkhole, he usually wound up in it with her. When his little brother sought out strays, he often ended up miles away, lost himself. Branding cattle, Willie ended up burned. Shoeing horses, Willie got kicked.

Sam thought the luckiest day of his life had come when Willie decided to get involved in the cattlemen's association and volunteered to make frequent trips back and forth to the stockyards to handle the business end of things. Lucky, that is, until all the "guests" started to arrive. But not until Miss Emily Richardson had anyone been as much trouble, or at least as disturbing. And not until Emily did he feel his heart in danger of a thaw.

As he followed her across the yard, dogging her steps but keeping a distance so that he wouldn't have to exchange another word with her, he wished he'd never laid eyes on her.

Sam pulled on the seat of his pants, the uncomfortable dampness having soaked through to the skin. Well, he thought, there was no going back now. Willie would be in for a big surprise when he got back and found his valentine gone.

* * *

"I've never been so humiliated in my life," Emily groaned as Vida Tucker took the muddy skirt she handed her from behind a fabric-covered dressing screen.

"Don't take on so, honey. It could have happened to anybody."

Emily sighed. "No, it most likely wouldn't have happened to anyone but me. I should have known better than to use flash powder around horses." She handed over the shirtwaist blouse that had been muddied in back through her jacket. Emily sneezed as she untied the waistband of her bloomers, shoved them down, and bent to pull them off. Reaching to give them to Vida over the screen, she sneezed again.

"You hurry up and get into that hot tub and soak the cold out of your bones and don't worry about these things. We'll have 'em washed up in no time."

"Thank you, Vida." Emily put on her plaid wrapper and, tugging the belt closed, emerged from behind the screen. "I'll take a soak and then start packing."

Vida Tucker halted before the door and frowned, her lips pursed. Then she said, "You're Willie's guest, not Sam's. You don't have to leave if you don't want to, you know."

Emily shook her head. "There's no way I can stay now. Not after what I've done. Tucker will never forgive me and I can't say as I blame him." She drew the wrapper tight and shivered as a sudden chill shook her.

Vida scowled. "We'll see. You just get in the tub."

Emily waited until the older woman closed the door and then moved the folding screen around the high-backed copper tub. Slipping her wrapper off again, she tossed it across the top of the screen and then tentatively stuck her toe in the steaming water. Grateful for the soothing warmth, she slowly stepped into the tub and sank into the water with a sigh.

In a room down the hall Sam shoved open the bedroom window and flung dirty water out of a washbasin. "Damn woman's using the only tub," he mumbled to himself as he closed the window and crossed the room to refill the porcelain washbowl with hot water from a bucket on the floor beside the washstand.

His muddied clothing lay in a heap in the middle of the floor. A fire crackled in the corner fireplace, effectively cutting the chill. Grumbling under his breath as he worked, he quickly dipped a washcloth into the basin, finished his sponge bath, and dropped the cloth into the bowl. Within minutes he had dressed for the second time that day. Striding over to the mirror hanging above his oak dresser, Tucker stared at the frustrated image of the man reflected there. His scowl was so fierce he almost frightened himself.

With a quick flick of his comb he slicked his damp black hair back into place and then met his own gaze in the mirror. Guilt assailed him when he thought of the forlorn look he'd seen in Emily's eyes before she'd turned her back on him and disappeared into the house. Then he remembered the way her lower lip had actually trembled when he told her to get packing.

"She's not Lillith," Vida had reminded him that first night. Her words came back to him now.

No. Miss Emily was definitely not Lillith. His former wife would have ranted, raved, and refused to budge, but he couldn't recall ever seeing her cry, not even to get her way.

Emily Richardson didn't seem the type to try that either. But she had been on the verge of tears out in the corral, no doubt about that. The longer Sam thought about it, the more sure he became that her show of emotion had been brought about by the embarrassment and humiliation of the moment rather than to manipulate him into letting her stay.

The thought didn't do much to make him feel any better

A soft knock outside the door brought him around. Expecting to find Emily on the threshold, he put down his comb and crossed the room, slowing his steps when he reached the door, ready to stand firm in the face of her badgering him to let her stay and finish her work.

He almost smiled.

When he opened the door and found it was only a scowling Aunt Vida with her arms full of muddied emerald wool and lacy white underclothing, all thought of smiling slipped away.

He turned around and, as he bent over to retrieve his dirty clothing from the floor his aunt stepped into the room and closed the door behind her.

Sam knew what was coming. He sighed.

"I want you to apologize to that girl as soon as she's through with her bath."

As quickly as he could, he blocked the disturbing thought of Emily Richardson sitting nude in *his* copper bathtub. "Me apologize?"

"Exactly. And tell her she can stay."

"Not when somebody might have been killed out there this morning. This whole fiasco was her fault." None too gently he dumped the clothing on top of the arm load she already carried.

Vida retaliated by shoving the combined loads back at him. Sam found himself peering down at her over the pile, a piece of eyelet lace teasing his nose. Despite the mud her clothing smelled suspiciously of rose petals. He frowned.

"I don't see what the big fuss is," Vida went on. "So the

gal put a few of you on your behinds. The men have the horses all rounded up and are having a good laugh over a cup of coffee. If you had any shred of a sense of humor left, you'd be laughing instead of sulking around here like a old bear.''

''Now don't try to talk me out of this, Aunt Vida. She's got to go.'' He started for the door, prepared to carry the laundry down to the kitchen for her. He stood beside the door, waiting for Vida to open it for him.

She didn't offer. Instead, lowering her voice, she stepped up beside him. ''I think there's only one reason you want that girl out of here so bad, Tucker. I think for the first time in years you have a hankerin' for a woman and it's scaring the hell out of you.''

The memory of a stolen kiss in the stairwell haunted him. He gave her his most quelling stare. ''You're barkin' up the wrong tree.''

Vida eyed him right back. ''I don't think so.''

''She's Willie's,'' he said, afraid to admit, even to himself, that his aunt might be right.

''Willie's not here,'' she reminded him. ''Besides, I think she's taken a cotton to you.''

''You're crazy.'' He fumbled the clothing around until he could reach out for the door handle himself. Before she could say anything else—not that anything she could say would disturb him as much as what she'd already said—he headed out the door and down the stairs.

Forty minutes later Sam stood outside the door to the bedroom Lillith had moved into when their relationship was ending. Balancing a tea tray in his hands, he took a deep breath and tapped on the door with his toe. The heady scent of lemon mingled with the aroma of chocolate cookies on a dainty plate on the tray.

When he heard Emily's footsteps on the other side of the door, Tucker regretted letting Vida bully him into bringing up the offering. *Nothing like self-torture, Tucker. You're getting to be an expert at it.*

The door swung inward to reveal Emily Richardson eyeing him suspiciously as she held her plaid flannel wrapper closed with one hand at her throat. Obviously still disheveled, her hair had been scooped up off her neck and pinned atop her head, but a few damp tendrils had managed to escape. Her cheeks were still flushed from the steamy bath, her ebony eyes still suspiciously bright. She didn't say a word, just stared up at him contritely.

He lifted the tray an inch and shrugged. "Aunt Vida sent this up for you."

Emily glanced down at the offering. There were two cups and saucers on the tray. She didn't know whether to take it and close the door in his face or see if Sam Tucker's temper had settled down some. She knew one thing for certain. She was through begging. In fact, as she watched him stand there awkwardly with the tea tray in his hands, she almost felt sorry for him. Almost.

"Come in," she said finally, moving aside to let him enter.

He paused inside the threshold and surveyed the room. Unlike Lillith, who had always strewn her clothing from one end to the other, everything that belonged to Emily Richardson was neatly folded or tucked out of sight. Her crates of photographic equipment were arranged in one corner; her jars and bottles of chemicals and solutions were arranged on the washstand. The closet door was open, revealing the temporary darkroom she had set up. The camera on the tripod lurked in the corner.

Emily watched him as he looked around and then chose the small escritoire near the window as a resting place for the tea tray. Once again it struck her that he was one of the biggest men she'd ever met. Everything in the room—the washstand, the small desk, the bedside tables—seemed dwarfed as he lingered there by the escritoire staring out the window with his hands shoved deep into his pockets. As always, he had dressed carefully, his shirt topped by a vest—this one of striped wool. A gold watch chain was looped across the front.

As she waited for him to say something she wondered if perhaps the tea was a peace offering.

Sam stared out at the rounded mountaintops. Low clouds rode the ridges and valleys, clouds he suspected were full of snow. He braced his hand on the window frame and noticed the lavender-striped wallpaper his mother had chosen years ago, back when his heart was still intact and he was possessed of the sense of humor Aunt Vida so thoughtfully kept pointing out was lost.

Behind him Emily sneezed. He turned around and found her pulling her wrapper still closer around her throat.

"Sit down," he ordered as he pulled out the diminutive chair that matched the escritoire.

Surprisingly she did as he asked without argument. Sam looked down at her bare pink toes and her feet, one atop the other. He crossed the room, reached for the afghan draped over the foot of the bed, and promptly carried it back to Emily. He spread it over her lap, knelt down, and gently tucked it around her feet.

Emily watched in silence, blinking away tears for the

second time that morning. What in the world had come over Sam Tucker?

She reached out and felt the teapot. It was hot to the touch. "Would you care for a cup of tea?"

Sam looked down at the tray and for the first time noticed that there were two cups on it and understood the sly smile Vida had given him when she handed him the tray.

He started to decline, then realized if he did so, he'd have no further excuse to linger, and for some reason he felt compelled to stay. "Sure. Why not?"

Emily picked up the teapot and poured them each a cup of tea. "Lemon and sugar?"

"Whatever."

She gave his cup a liberal dose of the sweetener and avoided giving him any lemon. *He's usually sour enough,* she thought. Handing him the cup, she waited to see if he would continue to stand, obviously so ill at ease being in the same room with her.

Tucker chose to put some distance between them. He sat down on the edge of the bed, glanced toward the door, which he had left wide open as propriety dictated, and took a sip of tea. Vida might have gotten him this far, but he'd be damned if he apologized for his anger of the morning.

After two more sips he realized Emily was stubborn enough not to say a word either. He looked at her over the rim of his cup and found her dark eyes studying him intently. Somehow the thought of her in Willie's arms caused a dull ache somewhere in his chest, but he could certainly see why his kid brother wanted her.

Emily was determined to wait until Tucker said something to her. She watched him sip his tea, shift his weight, glance toward the window. He looked up once, met her gaze, his expression darkening. She wondered what he was thinking, what about her put him in such a dark mood. The only conclusion she could come up with was that he was still besotted with his ex-wife, that the woman had broken his heart beyond repair.

Wondering if it was indeed too late for any woman to put his broken heart back together, Emily was startled out of her thoughts when he finally spoke.

"Snow's comin' in."

She set her cup down carefully on its saucer and tucked her hands on her lap beneath the folds of the multicolored afghan. "I'll get packed right away so it won't keep me from getting over the mountain to town."

Tucker knew this was his last chance to change his mind and tell her she could stay. Ignoring the half cup of tea that was left, he walked over to her, set the cup down on the tray, and then leaned an elbow on the back of the small writing desk. He imagined himself putting his fingers beneath her chin and gently tilting her face up until her dark eyes looked deep into his own. He knew what it would be like to savor the taste of her mouth, to tease her plump bottom lip with his teeth, to nuzzle her neck and inhale the soft, rose-petal scent that clung to her.

He knew it would be exquisite torture, so he didn't do any of those things, but merely let the opportunity slip away.

"It won't snow till late tonight or tomorrow. There's plenty of time for you to get back to town."

Emily's heart plummeted to her toes. She wasn't fool enough to kid herself that her disappointment was limited to her photography. She hated to think she would never see Sam Tucker again, and did not wish to let him think he'd won the battle of wills they'd waged since she'd climbed down off Ezra Jacobs's wagon two days ago.

"You may be able to throw me off the Rocking T,

Samuel Tucker, but I intend to stay in Tehachapi until I've accomplished my goal.''

"The name's not Samuel. And what goal is that, Miss Richardson? Landing a rich rancher for a husband? Landing Willie in particular?''

She looked stunned. "What an incredibly cruel thing to say.''

Sam knew the comment had been uncalled for the moment the words were out, but he'd been unable to stop himself. He knew, too, he had no right to drive her away from Tehachapi just because he couldn't stand the thought of his brother having her.

Emily had recovered enough to stand and pull the afghan into her arms. She shook it out, folded it, and padded over to the bed on her bare feet. "No matter what you might believe, Tucker, I am determined to become a famous photographer.''

"What's wrong with Chicago?''

"Too many photographers already in business in the city. Tehachapi, if you will recall, has none.''

"Tehachapi, if you'll recall, is a flyspeck on the map.''

"A growing town. Everyone wants a likeness of themselves now and then. I plan to start a business here. In fact''—she walked over to her trunk, furiously flicked the locks open and flung out the clothing she intended to wear on the journey back to town—"I have some wonderful ideas I can't wait to set into motion.''

He watched her bend over her trunk, her round little bottom in the air as she dug for some hidden article. He couldn't keep himself from moving silently across the room to stand behind her, where he could better appreciate the view. She straightened, turned around, and gasped when she found herself flung against him.

"While you're setting all those ideas in motion this'll give you something to think about." He grasped her forearms and pulled her into a rough embrace. When she gasped again, Sam smothered the sound with his lips as his mouth covered hers. This time there was no gentle exchange of curiosity, but a white-hot flame leaped to life in each of them the minute he touched her.

Emily started to resist until she realized that in his arms was exactly where she had wanted to be since he'd walked in. While he continued to press his kiss upon her, a kiss that only increased in demand, she savored the moment, hanging on to a glimmer of hope that perhaps his heart was salvageable, that she could bring laughter back into his life.

Sam felt her relax under his onslaught and in the back of his mind he cursed himself. Not only had he betrayed his brother, but he had crossed the line he'd vowed never to step over again. Not when the price was too high—the hurt too deep.

As if scorched, he let go of Emily and stepped back. Without a word he turned to leave. The soft sound of her voice stopped him at the door. "You have given me something to think about, Tucker, if that was your intent."

Sam stopped with his hand on the door frame, but didn't turn around to face her. "Forget it." Willie was going to want to kill him for this.

"You told me to forget it the first time. It's getting harder, you know."

It's getting harder, all right. He knew she was too naive to understand her innuendo. He started out the door.

She issued her next statement like a challenge. "I'll be ready to leave in thirty minutes."

Sam turned around and found her awaiting his reaction. He kept his face void of emotion as he said, "Fine."

He disappeared down the hall. When she heard his footsteps on the stairs, Emily sank to the edge of the bed and reached out to grab the footpost. Pressing her forehead against it, she closed her eyes. In the process of trying to repair Sam Tucker's broken heart, her own had become badly bruised.

"I think that'll do it, Mr. Blum," Emily told the editor of the *Tehachapi Mountain News*. She handed him the advertisement she had penned and smiled as she paid him a deposit on the fliers she planned to distribute to the stores along Railroad Avenue.

"I'll have those done for you by midweek," the gnome-faced man assured her as he wiped his ink-stained hands on his leather apron. "Your idea of running a Valentine's Day special might just encourage some of the other shopkeepers along the avenue to do the same thing."

Happy to hear her idea praised, she smiled as she gathered up her reticule and threaded the drawstring ties over her wrist. "They just might at that. For your sake I hope so. See you later, Mr. Blum."

Cold air struck her in the face as she opened the door and stepped out onto the wooden walk that fronted the newspaper office. Thankful that the shop she had taken a three-month lease on was only a few steps away, Emily pulled her heavy woolen coat about her and then, head down, hurried on.

Her shop. The reality of having a business of her own was still as bright as a shiny new penny. Although not grand, the space she had rented had an entire wall of windows that allowed in enough light for her photographs. There was a closet with space for a darkroom, and even a reception area where customers could sit and wait until she was ready for them.

After pausing to look up at the sign over the door, one that had cost her an entire three dollars to have lettered in gold leaf, Emily turned the key. Just inside the window, balanced on a windowsill behind the tapestry café curtains, sat another carefully lettered sign that read OPEN on one side and CLOSED on the other. Emily flipped the sign so that OPEN faced outward and took off her coat as she hurried through the reception area to the back room.

As she hung her coat on a rack near the door, she caught a glimpse of the photograph of Vida Tucker standing beside her oven. A sudden sinking feeling struck her, and even though she tried, Emily couldn't shake it off. Nor could she ignore the memory of the night she and Sam had shared warm milk in that very kitchen, then a kiss on the stairs. Such thoughts inevitably led her to recall their exchange the day she left the ranch, to relive the memory of the kiss he'd pressed upon her and her own heated reaction to it. One that had been too heated, it seemed, for it had been two weeks since Sam had his foreman, Ramon, unceremoniously drive her into Tehachapi and leave her at the local boardinghouse. Two weeks, during which time Emily had convinced herself that as much as she was attracted to him, as much as she wondered what would have happened if he had allowed their relationship to flourish, she would never see or hear from Sam Tucker again.

Shaking off the sadness that threatened to engulf her, Emily straightened her shoulders, determined to complete the work waiting for her in the darkroom. Sam Tucker be damned. She was here, she was doing what she had dreamed of doing most of her life, and if the business she had acquired in the last few days was any indication of the potential she could tap here in Tehachapi, then she was one lucky girl, with or without Sam Tucker.

Still, no matter how hard she tried to convince herself otherwise, she knew deep in her heart she'd rather be with him than without him.

He was cold, wet, hungry, and his temper was as short as a cow with no legs. Tucker rode into the corral and turned his big bay over to Tim, sudden anxiety churning in his gut when he spied the spring buggy drawn up at the front of the house.

Emily. For two weeks she'd been his first thought in the morning, his last thought at night. So it wasn't surprising that he wondered if perhaps she'd come back to visit Vida.

He wasn't fool enough to think she'd come back to visit him. Not after the way he'd treated her that last day. He looked over at the house and hesitated, took off his gloves, shoved them in his pocket, and then decided it wouldn't do any good to stand out in the snow and torture himself.

Sam started toward the house.

When he reached the back porch, he slowed up, listening for the sound of voices inside, but the windows were shut tight against the cold. He stepped up just below one of the east windows and, on tiptoe, peered over the sill. The kitchen was empty. Feeling somewhat relieved, he scraped his boots on the scraper by the step, entered through the backdoor, crossed the porch, and went on into the house. The faint sound of laughter filtered through the rooms.

He washed his hands in a pan of soapy, lukewarm water in the sink, splashed some on his face, and toweled himself dry. Moving through the dining room toward the parlor, he paused in front of the mirror over the dining-room fireplace and finger-combed his hair, all the time telling himself what a fool he was for making something out of nothing.

Sam moved to the door that led to the parlor. The sound of deep-throated laughter rang out. A man's laugh. More to the point, Willie's laughter.

His brother was home.

Sam pushed open the door and stopped dead in his tracks. Willie sat on the low settee, his back to the door, and beside him sat a woman—ramrod straight, her hair tucked into a saucy royal-blue hat, slim-waisted and round-hipped.

Sam wanted to back out the door before Emily turned and saw him there. He didn't think he could bear her look of triumph. She was back, but so was Willie.

"Come on in, Tucker," Vida called out when she noticed him lingering uncertainly in the doorway.

Willie stood at the sound of his brother's name and rounded the corner of the settee, arms extended in a flamboyant greeting that was so like him. "Tucker! Damn but it's good to see you, brother. Come on in and meet my new bride."

The word *bride* stopped Tucker in his tracks. His gaze shot to the woman on the couch. He watched her slowly, dramatically set her teacup and saucer on the butler's table pulled up before the settee. He held his breath, waiting for her to turn and face him, steeled himself as she stood and straightened her skirt.

"Come here, Annette. Come meet my big brother."
Annette.

"Annette?" Sam coughed on the word as a doll-faced blue-eyed girl with honey-blond hair tucked up beneath her hat crossed the room to slip into the welcoming curve of Willie's arm.

Willie smiled like a Cheshire cat and tweaked one of the

bobbing curls that teased his new wife's cheek. "Annette Benedict Tucker, may I present my brother, Sam?"

"How do you do, Mr. Tucker?" The girl, who couldn't be any more than eighteen, smiled up at him.

Sam had a hard time finding words. From across the room he heard Vida prod, "Say somethin', Tucker. You look like a ton of bricks just fell on you."

"What about Emily?"

"Emily who?"

"Who's Emily?" Willie Tucker and his new bride both spoke at once, although where his tone held nothing more than curiosity, hers was laced with suspicion. Across the room Vida Tucker laughed and poured herself another cup of tea.

Sam rocked forward and then back on his heels, trying to find the words, trying to avoid the jealous frown that now marred the new Mrs. William Tucker's brow.

"Emily Richardson. Of Chicago."

Willie looked blank.

Sam added, "The photographer?"

"Oh, her." Willie straightened an already perfectly placed cuff link and then smiled a reassuring smile at his wife. "She's nobody. Well, I mean, she's the daughter of a business acquaintance. I met her one night at a dinner her father held at his home. Odd sort. She spent the evening talking about photography, which seemed a queer passion for a woman, if you ask me—"

"I didn't," Sam interrupted. "She was here, you know. Said you sent her." He eyed his brother suspiciously. "I thought—"

"Well, you thought wrong, big brother," Willie said, successfully deflecting any inference Sam might make about his possible romantic interest in Emily Richardson. "Something wrong, Tucker?"

"Something's wrong, all right," Vida commented from across the room. "You're brother just realized he's a bigger fool than I thought."

Sam stood outside the small corner storefront on Railroad Avenue smiling up at the neatly lettered script on a sign that read, PHOTOGRAPH PARLOR AND GALLERY, E. RICHARDSON, OF CHICAGO, PHOTOGRAPHER. He had to hand it to Miss Richardson, it hadn't taken her long to start up the business she'd confessed to having dreamed of all her life. He looked down at the smudged piece of newsprint in his hand and gave the advertisement another read.

VALENTINE SPECIAL
One time only offer will not be repeated.
Come in now and have your portrait taken as a gift for your Sweetheart
at Tehachapi's new portrait studio on Railroad Avenue.
Miss Emily Richardson, of Chicago, Photographer.

Vida had seen the advertisement in the paper and left it on his bureau. He ignored it for two days. Refused even to pick it up. Yesterday he'd folded it and shoved it into his pocket. Last night at supper he announced to Willie, Vida, and Annette that he was riding into town to pick up barbed wire. Vida had given him a long, knowing stare. Willie and Annette were too busy gazing into each other's eyes to question his motives for going on an errand any one of the men could have accomplished.

Now here he stood outside Emily's photographic studio wondering what to do next. He pocketed the advertisement again and noticed the Open sign propped inside the window. If he didn't act fast, she might just walk out and find him standing here trying to stoke his courage like a lovesick schoolboy.

Sam turned the knob and stepped into the waiting room. It was deserted. He closed the door without a sound. An appointment book lay open on the desk; Emily's next customer was due in an hour. Sam took a quick look around and then reached behind the café curtains to turn the sign in the window around. Then he locked the door.

He took off his hat and, without knocking, opened the door to the inner studio. At first it appeared deserted, but then he heard muffled sounds coming from behind another door against the far wall. Unbuttoning his heavy coat, Sam walked across the room to inspect the wall-sized canvas backdrop painted to resemble a well-appointed parlor down to the likeness of a fireplace in the corner. A padded, velvet upholstered chair with red satin tassels dangling from the arms stood front and center before the backdrop. A wall of high windows brought the sunlight indoors.

The sound of the door opening behind him caused Sam to turn around in time to see Emily emerge from her darkroom wearing one of her fashionable, very elegant gowns. The royal-blue fabric highlighted her creamy complexion. A long, silent minute passed while she merely stared back at him.

Finally she spoke, her voice as melodic and lilting as he remembered.

"Tucker." Her face mirrored her surprise.

He nodded. "Emily."

She stepped farther into the room and closed the darkroom door behind her. "How are you?"

He cleared his throat. "Fine. I'm fine."

Another pause and then, "And Vida?"

"She's fine." *You sound like a simpleton, Tucker.* A sudden thought came to him; he wanted a spontaneous reaction to the news and so blurted out, "Willie's home. He's brought a wife."

Her response was hardly what he expected. "How exciting! Please extend my congratulations and tell him I'll gift them with a wedding portrait.♥

Tucker frowned. Her smile and congratulations seemed genuine. "So you don't care then?"

"Care? About what?"

"About Willie being married."

She moved closer, a thoughtful expression clouding her dark eyes. "Sam, why do you think I would be upset about William's marriage?"

He rubbed the back of his neck with his hand and shrugged. "I just thought . . ."

Emily closed the space between them and looked deep into his eyes. "You mean you thought that William and I . . ."

He shrugged again. "Yeah. Yeah, I guess that's what I thought."

She crossed her arms. "Then you thought wrong."

He smiled for the first time since she walked into the room. "I guess I did."

Emily watched him carefully, trying hard not to set him off, trying just as hard to figure out why Sam Tucker had really come. He stood, hat in hand, as uncomfortable as could be in the middle of the studio. Taking pity on his obvious discomfort, she smiled and decided to start over.

"So, are you in town for the day?"

He seemed to be making up his mind about something as he glanced toward the door to the reception room. He set his hat down on the posing chair and, relaxing a bit, shoved his hands into his pockets.

"Yeah. I came to pick up some barbed wire. And—" he pulled the advertisement out of his pocket—"I thought I'd take advantage of your Valentine Special."

"You want me to take your picture?" *Why?* Was this just an excuse of his to be here, she wondered, or was it something else? Had he found someone? Had William brought along another one of his guests, perhaps? Someone that Sam Tucker didn't find as irritating as he had her? Had his Lillith come to her senses and realized just what a fine man she had thrown away?

"Can you do it on such short notice?" He turned around and picked up his hat before he sat in the posing chair. "Is this right?" He set his hat on his knee and threw his arm over the back of the chair.

Emily shook her head and walked over to adjust his position. "That's all wrong. If you insist on being seated, you should put one hand on the arm of the chair, the other you can rest on your knee." Hesitating a moment, she finally took his wrist and positioned his hand on his knee for him. Merely touching him set her pulse racing. Curiosity goaded her into asking, "Will the photo be a gift?"

When she glanced down, she found him watching her intently. His eyes shone as he smiled up at her all too jovially. "Of course. Your advertisement says the Valentine Special should be given to a sweetheart."

He purposely shifted in the chair, again forcing her to lean over him and readjust his position. Familiar, sensuous, the heady scent of rose petals assailed him. Sam Tucker smiled.

Emily pulled back. She hurried over to her camera, ducked beneath the hood, and focused, all the while trying to compose herself as easily as she composed the elements of a portrait. It wasn't at all that simple, not when her mind kept repeating, *a photograph for his sweetheart.*

Sam watched as Emily reappeared from beneath the black cloth and hurried over to the darkroom. She looked about to ask him another question when she paused with her hand on the knob. "I'm going to load the chemical paper into the frames and then I'll be right back."

She closed the darkroom door behind her and leaned against it. "Pull yourself together," she whispered into the darkness. After taking a deep breath, she began to move about with familiarity in the shadowy interior of the room, all the while wondering who the woman was that had finally been able to put the pieces of Sam Tucker's heart back together. If she'd stayed at the ranch awhile longer, she might have been the one to eventually win his love and trust.

True to her word, she was back in a moment. Sam waited while Emily shoved the frame into the camera and then pulled out the slide covers. She adjusted the lens again, cocked the shutter spring, and then went to stand in front of him again.

"This isn't quite the pose I would choose for you. It's rather stiff."

He smiled. "What would you suggest?"

"Somewhere outdoors. A photograph of you on the ranch. In your element. But of course, there's no time for that with Valentine's Day in a week."

"I guess not," he agreed.

"And since you said this is to be a gift for . . . for your sweetheart—"

"That's right."

Damn the man. She hated his smug, secretive smile. No doubt he thought this worthy payment for the day she'd set

him on his ass in the mud. And to think she'd tried to make
something of the way he'd kissed her.

"Is something wrong, Emily?"

"What? No. What makes you ask?"

"You looked perplexed. Maybe I should stand."

She shook her head. "No. This will be fine. Just fine."
Let's just get it over with. He was slouching forward in the
chair, his forearms on his knees. Emily sighed. "Tucker, if
you want this done right, you have to sit up." She put her
hands on his shoulders to push him back against the chair.

Before she could budge him, Sam threw his hat to the
ground and pulled Emily down onto his lap in a swift move
that left her stunned.

Finally she began to struggle in his arms. "Samuel
Tucker! Let me go." Emily tried to stand but found him
immovable. "What are you doing?"

"I'm doing what I came to do. And my name's not
Samuel. I told you that once before." He bent his head to
kiss her, but she braced her hands on his shoulders, locked
her elbows, and held him back.

"You came here intending to steal another kiss and *then*
have your photo taken for your sweetheart?"

He smiled, his lips inches from hers. "I came here for
more than a kiss. The photograph was an afterthought."

She watched his mouth lower dangerously close to her
own. "What about your sweetheart?" she managed to
mumble.

"I don't have one, but I was hoping you'd agree to oblige
me." His lips grazed hers as he spoke.

"To do what?" she whispered, fighting a very disturbing
but not uncomfortable feeling mounting inside.

He stared down into the depths of her dark eyes and said,
"To be my valentine. Will you, Em? Since you're not

beholden to Willie, do you think you could love me just a little?''

Emily's eyes flooded with tears at his earnest request. "Oh, Sam.'' She lifted her lips and welcomed his, marveling in the fact that such a strong man could be so very gentle.

He gathered her close.

She let him kiss her deeper.

When his tongue slid between her lips, she welcomed it and the heated response it stirred deep within her. Her arousal came swiftly, but not so overwhelmingly that she didn't wonder somewhere in the back of her mind if he was experiencing the same overpowering sensations. When the kiss ended, she reached up to run her fingers through his hair.

"Tucker?''

"Emily?'' he teased.

"If it's not Samuel, what *is* your name?''

He tried to kiss her again, but she pulled back. He could have easily overwhelmed her with his greater strength, but he complied with her wishes. "Promise not to laugh?''

She nodded.

"Samson.''

When a giggle threatened to escape, she pressed her lips to his again and was soon lost in another kiss.

Sam held her close, the discomfort of the rigid posing chair forgotten now that Emily was in his arms. She was all too warm and willing, all too tempting for him to do what he knew to be the gentlemanly thing and end the mounting intimacy. Instead he continued to kiss her, to explore the sweet recesses of her mouth with his tongue and allow her to do the same to him. He caressed her tenderly, his fingers tightening around her slim waist and then sliding up to brush the underside of her breast with his knuckles. The rich fabric of her gown was silky. He longed to slip it off her and expose her luscious curves to his sight.

Emily's eyes flew open when she felt his hand cup her breast. "Someone could walk in," she murmured. "I have another appointment—"

"Not for an hour. Besides, the sign in the window reads 'Closed.' And I locked the door."

Emily smiled up at him. "Very sure of yourself, weren't you?"

"I've never been more uncertain of anything in my life. After the way I treated you at the ranch, I didn't expect you to ever speak to me again."

"If I had followed my heart, I wouldn't have let you run me off. I think I've wanted this since the night you first kissed me."

"Are you sure?"

"I'm not a child, Sam. I know what I want."

His heartbeat matched hers in celebration. "No"—he gently cupped her breast—"you're certainly not a child. And neither am I. I don't intend to go through a long courting period when I know what I want. Marry me, Emily."

Emily took a deep breath. She knew she wanted this man with all her heart, but what of her lifelong hopes and dreams? As much as she loved him, she wouldn't have him at the expense of all else she'd wanted. "What about my work?"

He reached out to brush a stray wisp of a curl off her cheek and studied her closely. "Would you at least think about moving your business out to the ranch?"

She smiled, knowing how easy it would be to comply with his request. "I'll think about it."

"That's all I ask." He ran his hand down the side of her cheek. "Now, do we have to keep talking?"

Emily shook her head. "Not at all."

"How about that Valentine Special?"

She reached up and whispered against his lips, "It's yours. Just love me, Sam."

Sam Tucker smiled down into her eyes and pulled her close. "I do, Em. I do."

IN A HEARTBEAT

by

Jodi Thomas

Dear Reader,

I would like to wish you a Valentine's Day full of love and laughter.

February fourteenth always reminds me of the first time I fell in love. I was seventeen and had one goal in life: to get a date before I got out of high school. The teacher lectured that Valentine's Day in senior English about love and marriage. She asked a tall, thin boy in the row next to me when he planned to marry.

"I don't," Tommy told her. "I think it would interfere with my career. I want to go to college."

I'd been trying to talk to Tommy all semester and saw this as my chance. I leaned over and said, "Bet you ten bucks you're married by the ten-year reunion."

We made the bet with everyone in class as witness.

Ten years later, he paid up. I'd married Tom when we were seniors in college. He was my first love and we've been happily married for twenty-two years. When I started writing about love, there could be no other pen name than Thomas.

Which leads me to my story.

Texas was a lonely place for the soldiers who fought along the frontier line, and Fort Griffin was no exception.

My family and I stopped by the remains of the old fort one winter day in 1990. Longhorns now graze on the parade grounds and only a few bricks from each building still remain.

A park ranger was kind enough to show us every detail of the fort.

When he seemed reluctant for us to leave, I asked, "Are we your first visitors today?"

"Lady," he answered, "you're the first folks I've seen in almost two weeks."

I decided that maybe the fort hadn't changed so much after all. When I was thinking of the perfect place to set my Valentine story, this old fort came to mind. It would take a special kind of man to settle there and a special kind of woman to stay with him.

I hope you enjoy "In a Heartbeat."

—Jodi Thomas

Chapter One

Colt Barnett stormed onto the loading dock of the train station, amazed at the position he'd found himself in. If there was one thing he'd learned in the years he'd been assigned to Texas, it was that he'd rather wrestle a locoweed-eatin' longhorn than have any part of bringing a woman onto an army fort. But there'd been no time to wire Miss Joanna Whiddon to tell her not to come. He'd only gotten her letter the day she planned to arrive. He'd failed to mention in his ad that only male tutors need apply.

He could just picture the kind of woman who'd answer an ad to teach other people's children. She was bound to be homelier than a polecat caught in a hailstorm and about as even-tempered. Why else would she be teaching and not raising children of her own?

"She must have had a terrible life to sign on out here where she'll be lucky to keep her scalp through the winter," Colt said to himself as he stomped his way along the platform.

After a few minutes of confusion from arriving and departing passengers, the throng cleared and Colt looked around at the few remaining people. Three women waited while a porter unloaded luggage. One was obviously a lady, tall, well dressed, and clutching a Bible in her hand like a missionary suddenly dropped off in the wilderness. Another woman, dressed in black, was probably someone's recently widowed grandmother. The third fit Colt's self-made description of what a tutor should be. Short, plain, thick wire glasses, hair in a bun and "never married" written all over her.

"Miss Whiddon?" He towered over the little woman who looked like she might run if he spoke too loud.

All three women turned to face him. Colt removed his hat and looked at the old maid before him. "Miss Whiddon, I'm Colt Barnett."

The little woman lifted her eyebrows in confusion and shook her head slightly. She glanced from side to side as if debating darting around him.

"I'm Joanna Whiddon," the tall lady said softly, stepping between Colt and the unlucky candidate he'd guessed as the tutor. She shifted her Bible to her left hand and extended her right. "It is a pleasure to meet you, Captain Barnett."

She was the first woman Colt could remember who almost looked him straight in the eye without having to look up. She had a handsome face, but there was no smile on her lips or in her crystal-blue eyes.

Colt caught himself wiping his hand on the pant leg of his uniform before accepting the lady's handshake. He knew he was supposed to say something, but words seemed to roll around at random in his mind without forming one line of thought. This woman wasn't at all what he needed to help with his three half-wild children. She looked like she'd been pampered all her life, and if she wasn't toting a gun in that Bible, she'd be wise not to move any farther west.

The lady turned slightly toward the older woman. "I'd like you to meet my aunt Etta." Her voice softened as she said the older woman's name.

Colt managed to raise one eyebrow, communicating volumes.

"She always travels with me, Captain Barnett," the tutor continued as she made no secret of sizing him up. He had the feeling she saw every flaw in his Union uniform, from the slightly wrinkled yellow scarf marking him as an officer in the frontier campaign to his pants legs in need of a good pressing.

"You didn't mention an aunt traveling with you." Colt wished he could see a little fear or at least respect in her expression. He could deal with that more easily than with the challenge that seemed to be banked just behind the indigo depths of her eyes.

"I know I forgot to tell you about Aunt Etta in my letter." She smiled as if her secret would somehow delight him. "I hope there'll be no problem with room?"

Colt thought, Hell yes, there's a problem with room. I don't know what I'm going to do with the likes of you much less an aunt! Instead he shook his head as if brushing away a slight obstacle. "I don't think it will be a problem," he lied as he turned to the aunt and raised his finger to touch the brim of his hat. "Ma'am."

The older woman smiled as if she'd just walked into the middle of a play and suddenly discovered she was one of the actors. "Call me Aunt Etta. Everyone does." She lifted a small box that looked as disheveled from the trip as she was. "I brought the children some valentine candy. I hope you don't mind."

"I don't mind, ma'am." Colt couldn't imagine himself ever calling her aunt anything, but he managed to nod respectfully. "In my ad for a tutor I assumed it would be a male, or a female who'd board my children at her home somewhere out of Indian country. Not a female coming here to Texas. The fort is not an easy place for a woman to live.''

"I understand." Again he saw the challenge in her gaze. "Do you wish to terminate my employment?" Joanna asked.

Colt hesitated. He both admired and resented her directness. In a man he'd have expected it, but in a woman it was a little unsettling. "I suppose we could try it for a month."

Joanna nodded once in agreement. "Today is January fifteenth. If either you or I are not satisfied, my aunt and I will be on a return train one month from today."

"The day after Valentine's Day," Aunt Etta said more to herself than anyone around.

"February fifteenth," Colt agreed. He could ask for no fairer proposal. Though unsure of how to deal with these women under his command, he figured he'd manage. "If you'll show me your luggage, I'll load for the fort right away. You'll be riding with Sergeant Abe Buckles." Colt would have liked to load them back on the train, but somehow the idea of having them stay didn't seem as bad as having to face his three children alone. It had taken him three months to get one reply for help and he didn't plan on waiting another three months for some other tutor to answer his ad.

"We have our luggage," Joanna answered as she pointed at the two small carpetbags beside her.

Colt lifted the bags, suddenly very intrigued by these two women. He'd never known a lady to travel anywhere without a trunk. "This way." He moved toward the line of wagons getting supplies for the fort from the train.

As they waited for the wagons to be loaded he studied this new tutor carefully. Joanna Whiddon wasn't the most beautiful woman he'd ever seen, but she fascinated him. She had hair the color of spring sunshine and eyes the cold blue of an ice storm in winter, which softened with laughter when she looked at her aunt. She was the kind of woman a man wanted to step out with on Sunday morning, not like most of the women he'd seen in the west, who looked like they'd been cozied up to once too often on Saturday night.

Before he knew what was happening, they were heading toward Fort Griffin. He tried not to think of her as he rode in front of his men, but he couldn't get her out of his mind. He wondered if he'd ever see laughter in her gaze when she looked at him. When she saw the fort, he was much more likely to see fire.

The January wind was dry, blowing cold against Joanna's face as the wagons crawled slowly west. Rolling brown land, broken only occasionally by a scattering of trees, spread across what seemed to be an endless horizon. For the first time since she'd left home, she wondered if she'd done the right thing. When her father had declared that she was to be married, she hadn't had much time to contemplate her decision. But now, as she rode quietly on the wagon bench with her aunt and the stocky driver named Sergeant Buckles, Joanna admitted she may have been a bit hasty. This was not her safe hometown in Ohio, this was Texas, the legends and stories of which had always frightened her.

"I'm not a pioneer," she whispered. "I'm only a coward."

She wondered if the handsome Captain Barnett would understand. He looked at home in this country. Even though he was slightly unkempt, he was by far the most exciting man she'd ever seen. Not that she had much of a selection for comparison in her small town. She'd been looking over the heads of most of the boys by the time she'd half-finished school. In all her twenty-five years she could never remember seeing such a man.

Captain Barnett seemed as strong as this frontier. Wild and a little untamed. He was just the kind of man she'd imagined could thrive in this land. Just the kind who'd never understand someone running instead of fighting.

He'd send me back on the next train if he knew what I really am, she thought. Such a man could never understand that all she wanted to do was teach. Not settle a frontier. Not fight. Just teach.

"There's the fort," Sergeant Buckles shouted as though his passengers were hard of hearing. "Ain't much, but it's home."

Joanna looked across the open country to a slight hill and tried to believe what she saw. This was less a fort than a scattering of shacks and tents. There were no parade grounds or high walls for protection.

"That's Fort Griffin?"

"Ain't much to look at yet"—Buckles smiled with the pride of a parent—"but she'll be one of the finest along the frontier soon. Few months' more work and she'll start to take shape."

Aunt Etta giggled. "Looks more like a target right now."

Joanna put her hand over her aunt's. "I'm sorry I dragged you into this."

Etta pushed her away with a gentle pat. "No one dragged me into anything. I came because I wanted to. You think I'd stay another moment in your daddy's house after what he tried to do to you." She lifted her head. "I've got my pride, too."

Joanna smiled. Pride was about all Aunt Etta had, but she wore it closer than kid gloves on a sunny day. The only unmarried child among twelve children, Etta had moved from home to home without ever having one of her own. Her sisters always pampered her as if she were slow-witted. Her brothers usually attributed Etta's behavior to a loose grip on reality. But Etta had come through when Joanna needed her. "Thanks for coming with me."

"I wouldn't be anywhere else, child. Not anywhere else."

"You might change your mind when the weather warms and the Indians start causing trouble." Buckles laughed. "The fort ain't no place for women, though we already got a few. We have enough to worry about trying to keep the settlers' wives from gettin' too scared."

"I can handle myself, Sergeant Buckles." Etta straightened proudly. "No one has to worry about me."

Buckles's laugh sounded more like a hiccup. "Sure thing, ma'am." He pulled the wagon up to the row of small cabins. "This here's the captain's place." He made no offer to help the women down. "Might want to handle yourself out of the wagon, Miss Etta."

"I'll do that, Mr. Buckles, and don't be getting familiar using my Christian name until I give my permission."

"Yes, ma'am," Buckles answered as he removed his hat. He'd learned a long time ago always to give a woman respect when she demanded it. "I'll be more careful in the future."

Joanna laughed and backed off the bench. It wouldn't take the sergeant long to learn that Etta had all bark and no bite to her ordering. Just as her foot touched ground, fingers closed around her waist.

"Welcome to Fort Griffin." Colt's voice was formal, but his hands were warm even through her wool traveling coat.

"Thank you," she whispered as he held a hand up for Aunt Etta.

Before Joanna could ask any questions, the door to the cabin flew open and three children dove toward the Captain. They were barefoot and dressed in overalls much in need of mending. Their faces were a mixture of mud, freckles, and mischief.

Colt stumbled backward as he wrestled them in his arms. "Calm down!" he shouted, but there was no anger in his voice. "Settle down, I said. There's someone I want you three heathens to meet."

Joanna smiled as he tried to stop all three children from wiggling, but he only had two hands. As soon as he turned loose of one, another jumped into action. Finally, he had all three standing in front of him. None of them came up to his belt buckle, but they all had his dark hair and eyes.

"These," Captain Barnett said proudly, "are my children. The twins, Drew and Terri, are five and Johnnie here is a year older."

Joanna knelt down to their level. "Hello." She extended her hand. "I'm very happy to meet you boys."

"Boys!" Johnnie yelled. "We're girls."

Joanna looked up at the captain, who seemed to be made of stone. He was looking at her, but there was no expression in his eyes. He needed her much more than she'd thought. But until this moment she hadn't realized how much.

Chapter Two

Colt carried the luggage through the door of his house. "The girls sleep upstairs in the loft." He carefully maneuvered the bags so that they didn't accidentally hit the children circling at his feet. "I can move my office next door. You and your aunt can bunk in that room." He pointed to the first of two doors on the opposite side of the house.

"Bunk?" Etta's thin eyebrows raised all the way to her hairline. "Sounds like fun."

Joanna could see the gleam of adventure in her aunt's eyes, excitement that hadn't been there before. "That will be fine, Captain." She glanced around at the room so void of furnishings it looked as if the house were unoccupied. Through an opening to the left she could see a kitchen area, as sparsely furnished as the rest.

Sergeant Buckles shuffled into the room as he hitched up his breeches. "Need a detail to move the desk and books from your study, Cap'n?"

Colt nodded, wondering how Sergeant Buckles always managed to guess a command five seconds before he thought of it. Aloud he said to the ladies, "Besides being the best driver on the post, Sergeant Buckles also cooks for me and the girls as well as keeps these quarters in order."

Joanna wondered what could get out of order in a house

so bare. No woman's touch had ever brushed these rooms. Whatever happened to the captain's wife, happened before he moved here. As she stepped toward him the large man moved quickly out of the room as if nervous to be so close to a woman.

Within seconds he marched back through the room, his arms loaded down with supplies. He glanced at the captain. "Am I still the cook, Cap'n?" He didn't sound too enthusiastic about his job.

Before Colt could answer, Etta chimed in, "I can cook for you and the girls. There's not much I can't stir up. That way I'll feel like I'm earning my keep around here."

For the first time in all the years Colt had known Buckles, he saw a look of true admiration in the sergeant's eyes as he stared at her.

And Etta seemed so excited, Colt couldn't say no. He'd spent his life around men, but he guessed Etta wanted, like most people, to be valued. "I'd be mighty grateful, ma'am. I need the sergeant for duty."

Etta followed Buckles into the kitchen, pulling things from the supply box even before he set it down. "Come along, girls," she ordered kindly. "I'll tell you about the time I fought a grizzly bear single-handed while we put the supplies away."

Joanna giggled at her aunt and turned to face the captain. "Thank you," she said simply. He didn't pretend not to understand what she was talking about. "My aunt really is a good cook."

"My pleasure." Colt looked into her eyes and wondered if this woman had ever really cared for anyone except her aunt. "I'll be direct with you, Miss Whiddon. I don't know if this is going to work out or not, but I'm willing to give it a try for the month. You'll have the run of the house and I'll try to stay out of your way as much as possible. I've had no chance to give my daughters lessons and it's time they started.'' His three children ran through the room and thundered up the stairs to the loft. He sighed. ''I'm willing to give anything a try. Anything.''

Etta ran past them, growling like a bear, and followed the girls up the steps.

''Even taking on a tutor and her aunt?'' Joanna held a tight grip on her Bible.

Colt's grin made him look younger. ''She's something, isn't she?''

Joanna let out a breath she felt like she'd been holding since they'd stepped off the train. ''Yes, she is, but no one's ever realized it but me. I couldn't leave her behind.''

''I don't think I need to warn you, this is not the place for any woman, much less an older one. Life's not easy on the frontier.''

Joanna lay her Bible down on the room's one table. ''Life's not easy anywhere, Captain, when you face it alone.''

Colt wondered if she was talking about herself or her aunt, and he felt suddenly embarrassed that it mattered. ''Then, if you'll excuse me, I've got my duties. I may be gone a few days.'' He nodded slightly toward the loft. ''Will you be all right here?''

''Of course,'' Joanna said hoping her tone sounded more confident than she felt.

Almost a week passed before the captain walked back into his house. He'd been in the saddle for so many hours he wasn't sure his legs would ever be straight again. The cold winter moon looked frosty in the cloudy sky as he took one last glance at the camp before opening the door to his cabin.

For a moment he just stood looking around as if he'd accidentally stepped into someone else's house. A warm glow came from the fireplace and the air smelled of baked bread. Only Miss Whiddon's Bible on the table assured him he was in his own quarters.

"Hello," he whispered as he looked at the three home-made stools pulled close to the fire. The room seemed more like a home than it ever had. Dried flowers banked both sides of the mantel and pictures drawn in charcoal almost covered one wall.

"Hello?" He stepped inside and moved to the fire. Funny that he should think of this place as home. Nowhere had ever been that to him. He was born on a fort in south Texas and had grown up moving from post to post.

"Anybody here!" he yelled.

"Quiet," someone whispered from the opening to the loft. Colt looked up as Joanna descended the steps. She was wrapped in a midnight-blue robe that hugged her neck and brushed her bare feet. He looked away trying not to think of how intimate it felt to see her in her nightclothes.

"Oh!" Joanna stopped as she reached the end of the steps. "It's you. I thought it was the sergeant coming in with the firewood."

"Sorry." Colt wasn't sorry at all, but he didn't know what else to say. "Am I only welcome if I'm toting wood, Miss Whiddon?"

"Of course you're welcome." Joanna moved beside him, looking him straight in the eyes as though she'd never feared anyone in her life. "This is your house, Captain."

At her last word squeals broke out from the loft. Suddenly voices filled the room. "Daddy!"

The girls were down the stairs and in his arms before he could say another word. They yelled and danced around him like forest elves who'd found a treasure. He hugged each one and endured wet, smacky kisses on his whiskery cheeks. Then all three talked at once in a language he had trouble understanding on the best of days.

Joanna stood back and watched this strong man with his daughters. He brushed his large hand over each one's curls as if checking to make sure they were all well and happy. His dark eyes turned gentle as he tried to answer their endless questions. He kissed away the hurt from Johnnie's cut finger and told the twins how grand they looked wearing his old shirts as nightgowns.

A longing appeared in the pit of Joanna's stomach and spread all the way to her heart. She never remembered being held by her father. It seemed every day of her life, all he'd ever done was give orders or criticize her for her shortcomings. Finally he'd given one order too many.

Now she fought the urge to join the children and be hugged for no reason at all. As she watched, her heart aching, Colt looked up over the girls' heads. For an instant she felt her soul stand bare before him, then she looked away.

"Ladies!" she shouted over the children. "Say good night to your father and go back up to bed."

They protested until the loud slam of a door shook the room. Aunt Etta appeared in the doorway of her bedroom, her hair woven into rag curlers, her face pale with cream, and her eyes bright with fright. She looked around the room and relaxed. "Lord to goodness, girls, I thought the Indians had attacked from all the racket you were making."

Joanna placed her hands on her hips. "They were just saying good night to their father."

Before they could protest, Aunt Etta spoke up. "Well, get it done and up to bed." She headed toward the stairs. "I guess I'll have to settle you down with the story of how I was once captured by renegades and had to swim the Mississippi to escape.''

The girls kissed their father and were even with Aunt Etta by the time she was halfway up the stairs.

Colt unbuckled his gun belt and laid it across one of the stools. "I've never seen them go to bed so easily." He stretched. "You've done wonders. I don't think I've ever seen them so clean either."

Joanna wanted to add, *Wait until you see your uniforms,* but only asked, "Would you like some stew?" The room felt suddenly quiet and empty without the children. "Aunt Etta left some warming on the back of the stove."

"You don't have to get it." Colt wasn't sure how to act around her. She wasn't a house guest or a servant . . . or a wife.

"I don't mind." She disappeared into the kitchen. "I'll sit with you while you eat so we can talk."

Colt sank into the rocker and stretched his legs out. He leaned his head back against the cushion that had been added to the chair in his absence and closed his eyes. Stew sounded good, but he didn't want to talk. If he could figure out a way, he knew he'd never talk to a woman for as long as he lived.

The memory of his wife drifted amid the smell of baking and home. They'd been happy those first few years. He remembered how he'd looked forward to seeing her at the end of every day. She was always full of laughter and dancing, like a little dream fairy who accidentally waltzed into the real world. But when Johnnie was born, things changed. Each night all he heard was how she hated being tied to the house with a baby all day. A year later when the twins were born, she hadn't even waited until they were a month old before she'd left him.

A rattling drew him back to the present, but Colt didn't open his eyes. He heard the front door open and knew from the heavy shuffle of boots who approached.

"Captain?" Buckles's voice pulled Colt wide-awake. "Cap'n, are you asleep?"

"No." Colt forced his exhausted body to straighten. "Not any longer." He ran a hand through his black hair. "How were things here while I was gone?"

"Nothing happened that can't wait till morning. I've mostly been helping the ladies get settled."

"Did you order anything they might need from town?"

"Yes, sir." Buckles dropped the wood in the pile. "They had quite a list. It may take a month or more to get some of the things."

"It doesn't matter." Colt didn't have to see his house through Joanna's eyes to know there were things missing. Things a woman would need and probably things little girls should have. "As long as I can afford it."

"Oh, that ain't no problem, sir. Miss Whiddon picked up the freight bill."

All the fatigue left Colt's body as he stood. "She what?" He knew that freight often cost more than the original prices of the items sent. No tutor could afford to pay such a bill, especially a woman.

Sergeant Buckles backed toward the door. "Oh, don't worry, Captain, I made sure you paid for all the supplies for the house and for the little ones. She just bought the decorations."

Colt's voice lowered slightly. "Decorations!"

"Now, Cap'n, I've been around you since your wife left, and with respect, sir, you ain't the easiest person to tolerate at times. But that Miss Whiddon, there ain't no saying no to that lady.''

"I think you're exaggerating." Colt forced his muscles to relax. "What's this about decorations?"

Before Buckles could explain, Joanna entered the room carrying a steaming plate of stew. "I'll tell the captain about them, Sergeant Buckles."

Buckles was out the door, his good-byes blending with the latch falling into place.

Colt took the plate and folded back into the rocker. He watched this woman who'd invaded his house as she sat on one of the stools and stirred the fire. She seemed in no hurry to start the conversation, and for once in his life he was willing to allow time to crawl by.

Finally she looked up at him. "I can teach the girls, but they need clothes and shoes."

Colt stared at his boots. He didn't want to admit that he didn't know much about what little girls needed. He'd seen that they were fed and spent many a night walking the floor with one on each shoulder when they were sick, but now they were getting older and he was lost.

"Order whatever you need."

"I did," Joanna answered. She looked at him directly, again, a look that told him she didn't fear his reaction to anything.

"You've no need to pay the freight. I can take care of my family."

Joanna realized she might have accidentally wounded his pride. "I only paid for freight on things I'm sending for from home. I didn't know how much room I'd have here. I sent for my sewing machine and books."

"But . . ." Colt didn't know how to approach the

subject of money lightly with this woman. "We haven't even agreed on your salary."

"I'm sure it will be fair." Joanna stared into the fireplace. "When I left Ohio, I brought only my own money and my mother's Bible. She died when I was twelve and Aunt Etta raised me after that."

A hundred questions came to Colt's mind, but he could only watch her sitting so silent and proud before him. The firelight danced in her blond hair and he found himself wondering how long the strands were when she set them free. He believed a person's past was a book you saw one page of at a time, so he wasn't about to pry.

He finished his stew with only the crackling of the fire and Aunt Etta's soft voice drifting down from the loft breaking the silence. Colt couldn't take his eyes off the woman in front of him. She stood and crossed the room with such easy grace, only her eyes giving any hint that all was not right in her world.

"Best stew I ever had," he managed to say as he stood.

"I'll thank Aunt Etta for you." Joanna smiled. "She claims to have learned how to make it from a Gypsy woman."

He smiled at her words and she thought how handsome he looked when he wasn't acting like the fort commander.

Before she could leave, he spoke his thoughts. "I'm glad you're here."

Joanna looked surprised. "So am I," she answered as she opened the door to her bedroom. "Good night, Captain."

"Miss Whiddon?" He lifted his gun belt and walked toward her. "About the decorations."

Her back straightened slightly and her hand whitened around the doorknob, but she didn't lower her gaze. "The ladies have decided we're going to have a St. Valentine's dance a week from Saturday night, so I ordered paper to decorate.''

''Ladies?'' Colt hadn't noticed more than a few settlers' wives around. ''What ladies?''

Joanna lifted her chin slightly. ''Those beneath your roof, to name but five.''

Colt started to object, but she vanished through the door before he could speak. He stood staring at the wood with his hand in the air and his mouth open, wondering what on earth she was talking about. This was his house. He should be able to get an answer. But the door might as well have been made of molten lead because he wasn't about to touch it.

''Talking to the door, are you, Captain?'' Etta's voice sounded from behind him. ''Won't get much of a response.''

Colt turned to confront the plump little woman, but she merely walked by him and also closed the door in his face.

''Must be a family trait,'' he mumbled as he headed to his own door. ''Well, they'll be in for a surprise in the morning if they think I'll allow a Valentine's Day dance out here in the middle of the frontier.''

Chapter Three

Joanna rolled her head over on her pillow and felt something damp and soft pat against her cheek.

"Miss," Johnnie's little voice whispered. "Are you awake yet? We've been waiting."

Joanna opened her eyes. There, not three inches from her nose, stood the three girls, already dressed in their overalls. She jerked and looked toward the window. Had she overslept? No, the sky was still the gray of predawn.

Reluctantly she rose up to one elbow. "Good morning, girls. What's the problem?"

Johnnie glanced at her sisters. "The twins got two questions, miss, and we didn't want to wait until Daddy woke up to ask."

Joanna pushed her hair from her face and slowly pulled her robe from the foot of the bed. "Questions go best with coffee. Let's go to the kitchen."

The girls all nodded and backed away enough for her to get out of bed. They followed Joanna to the kitchen and sat silently as she lit the fire in the stove and put on a pot to boil.

"All right." Joanna suppressed a yawn. "Ask those questions that can't wait." In the two weeks she'd been with them she'd quickly learned that the twins came up with all the questions about life and Johnnie did all the asking.

Johnnie propped her elbows on the table and placed her

hands inside her palms. "Drew wants to know if the angel Cupid was an Indian?"

Joanna fought down a laugh. "I'm not sure. Why do you ask?" She looked at Drew, but it was Johnnie who answered.

"He carries a bow and arrow that shoots people and makes them fall in love."

Joanna moved to the stove to check the coffee. "I guess you're right about that. But it's not what really makes people fall in love."

All three girls leaned forward and waited for the real answer. Joanna poured herself a cup and sat down across from them. "Cupid only does his work in stories. In life, people fall in love differently."

The three girls asked in unison, "How?"

"Well." Joanna tried to put into words what she herself had never understood. "Love happens when a man and woman spend time alone together. They look at one another in a special way and realize they need each other."

"Like my daddy needed you to come take care of us?" Johnnie asked.

"Well, that's important, but it's more than just needing someone to help raise your children and run your house. It's needing someone to share your life with."

"Like you have your aunt Etta?" Johnnie's brow wrinkled, showing how hard she was trying to understand.

"Even more than that," Joanna answered. "Love is having someone to share your dreams with when you're young and memories with when you're old."

Johnnie climbed down and came around the table to Joanna. The little girl placed her arm around Joanna's waist as smoothly as any tent preacher cornered a sinner. "Miss, would you consider marrying our daddy even if he didn't look at you in a special way?"

Before Joanna could answer, Johnnie flew up into the air faster than a leaf on a windy day. All the girls turned to see Colt standing behind Joanna as he held Johnnie five feet off the ground by the back of her overalls.

Anger fired in his voice but laughter danced in his dark eyes. "I'll not have you asking Miss Whiddon such questions. Off with the three of you and wash up for breakfast."

Johnnie held out her arms as though planning to fly in order to execute his order, but he gently lowered her to the floor. When he heard their footsteps on the stairs, he looked at Joanna. Her hair was wild and free around her shoulders and Colt fought the urge to reach out and feel how soft it was. "I'm sorry about that." He scratched at the whiskers along his jaw. "I guess I never got around to teaching them to hold back their curiosity."

Joanna pulled her hair to one shoulder and began trying to braid the mass together.

"No. Don't." Colt touched her fingers to still them before he realized what he'd done.

For a moment their hands touched, his covering hers. He felt as if he were frozen at this time, in this place, forever. Yet the warmth of her fingers reminded him he was alive. The feel of her hand beneath his seemed to penetrate the icy wilderness where he'd stored his heart.

He opened his mouth, but no words formed. He saw her look of surprise . . . and more. Something that made him want to lose himself inside her blue depths and heal all the wounds from the past. But his heart had scarred over five years ago and the only dragons he could fight were his own memories.

With a quick jerk of one fighting himself, he pulled his hand away and took a step backward. "I mean . . ." The very air seemed thick with the wonderful fragrance of her. "I mean, don't braid your hair on my account."

Joanna moved to the stove and tried to keep her hands from shaking as she poured him a cup of coffee. It was only a touch of hands, she told herself. Nothing more. But her body knew she was lying. In all her years of dancing with men, shaking hands, even holding hands while being courted, never, never had a touch affected her so.

"My mother used to say"—Joanna tried to think of anything else but how warm his fingers had felt sheltering hers—"a lady binds her hair by dawn and never lets it down till dusk."

Colt accepted the coffee she offered. "We've a few more minutes until daylight. Will you sit and have a cup with me?"

Joanna nodded and they sat across from one another. For a while they remained silent, enjoying the stillness of dawn and the company.

Finally Colt said softly, "It's been a long time since I've had coffee with a woman." His words made the act seem like far more than it was.

His long tanned fingers moved slowly up and down the handle of his mug and Joanna could almost feel his touch once more on her hand.

"I meant to tell you last night that I like the changes in the place," he complimented.

"Thank you," Joanna whispered, unable to look away. "We've been just having fun until all the supplies arrive."

She glanced up at him and felt suddenly embarrassed, as though he'd read her mind and knew what she'd been thinking. Standing quickly, Joanna marched to the stove and added another log. He was just a man, nothing more, she reminded herself, and she wasn't some sixteen-year-old girl who'd never had her hand touched. It was about time she remembered that she was his employee.

"If you'll excuse me, Captain." She didn't look back at him as she moved toward her room. "I'll get dressed and start breakfast."

Colt watched her go, wishing she'd stayed just a moment longer. In her robe, with her hair down, she was sure easy on the eyes. He might just enjoy having Miss Joanna Whiddon under his roof. She wasn't as cold as he'd thought and it was pleasant talking with her. For the first time in years Colt smiled for no reason at all.

Chapter Four

Colt's mood was as dark as the stormy northern sky when he loaded the girls into the wagon. He'd done what he could to cancel this Valentine's Day party, but Buckles had been right, Miss Whiddon was one determined lady. She'd organized all the wives for ten miles around and decorated the mess hall in red and white.

"Valentine's Day isn't for another week," he mumbled as he climbed in beside her on the wagon bench. "Plus it always struck me as a worthless holiday."

"This is close enough to the date," Joanna mumbled back, mocking him. They'd been playing a game, avoiding speaking directly about the dance. He hadn't been able to resist getting up before dawn in hopes of sharing coffee with her. She was usually up, but between the girls and Aunt Etta they'd never been alone again.

Colt raised an eyebrow and looked at her as he debated saying anything else. "I don't see much point in this when there are a hundred other things to be done around the fort."

Joanna decided to change the subject. "Well, one good thing, you got your clothes pressed. You look very polished in your dress uniform, Captain Barnett."

The captain threaded the reins through his fingers as he smiled to himself. "I'm not easily taken in by flattery, Miss Whiddon."

Joanna spoke her mind before she thought. "Or women, I'd guess." She realized how hard her words sounded, so she softened them with a question. "You don't think much of the fairer sex, do you, Captain?"

Colt urged the horses into a walk. "To tell you the truth I've never been around them much. My mother died before I could walk and my wife left after two years of marriage. Maybe it's the other way around. Maybe women don't like me much."

Joanna looked back at the three girls talking to Aunt Etta. "You have three girls who love you a great deal. Maybe you should spend a little time trying to understand them. Women don't always respond to orders like your men do."

"You're telling me!" Colt couldn't keep from smiling as he glanced over his shoulder. "They're a lot of trouble, but I wouldn't trade them for anything." He looked forward. "And you're probably right. The girls do look more civilized in dresses than in overalls."

"They're the reason you let me plan this party." Joanna simply stated a fact. She'd known it from the beginning. When he'd started objecting, all one of the twins had done was take his huge hand in hers and ask him to teach her to dance. From then on he complained only to force her into a lively argument about the party, but Joanna guessed he'd do little to stop it from happening.

Colt didn't answer but acted as if he was only interested in the clouds. Finally he said, "I wanted to drive the wagon over tonight because it looks like it might rain."

"It might," Joanna added, knowing that he was thinking of more than the weather.

They reached the mess hall and Colt climbed down to help first Joanna and Etta down, then he lifted each of his little ladies out of the wagon. "You girls look like angels tonight, so try to act like it."

The twins looked at one another and giggled. At five, their every experience was filled with emotion, be it joy or fear. Joanna took their hands and led them into the converted hall.

The children squealed with excitement when they saw all the decorations. Paper hearts and flowers were everywhere. All the tables except one had been stacked along the walls. The one remaining held a large bucket of punch and Aunt Etta's now famous valentine cookies. She'd sworn to make them every day until all the men at the fort got tired of the sight of her passing them out from the captain's porch. The soldiers had promised that this date would be years in the future.

Etta now proudly placed another basket of cookies on the table. She'd never had anyone rave about her cooking like these men did and she'd told Joanna more than once that she'd gladly put up with the threat of Indian attacks to stay at this fort.

A three-piece orchestra, consisting of a guitar, a small accordion, and a fiddle, began to play a waltz.

"Would you like to dance?" Colt interrupted Joanna's thoughts.

Joanna nodded slightly and took his hand. Even though she'd spent several nights under the same roof with him, eating meals together and talking by the fire at night, she'd never felt his nearness as much as she did when he placed his hand politely around her waist and swung her onto the floor. The morning when he'd stopped her from braiding her hair floated back in waves of warmth against her cheeks. His steps were wide and bold, but she had no trouble keeping up with him. He didn't speak, only waltzed. To her surprise Colt Barnett danced the Black Hawk waltz better than any partner she'd ever danced with.

Almost sorry to hear the music end, Joanna looked away, suddenly shy around a man who'd seen her all week at her worst and best.

As the music stopped he bowed low. "Duty calls. I've other ladies to dance with," he whispered, "but may I claim another turn later?"

When she looked up at him, she saw laughter in his dark eyes. A laughter that seemed silently to say, "Thank you." Then he was gone, dancing first with Johnnie, then with the twins, and finally with Aunt Etta.

Joanna accepted each partner's offer, but was careful not to dance with anyone more than twice. As the evening wore on she began to relax and truly enjoyed herself. Back home there were always about the same number of men as women. Because of her height she'd often found herself sitting out a dance or two in a row. No such thing happened here. Even Aunt Etta was busy every round. Though Joanna knew it was only because of the unequal number of men and women, she enjoyed the attention and felt pretty for the first time in her life.

Finally the evening drew to an end. As the band announced the last waltz a strong hand closed over hers. "May I have the last dance, Miss Whiddon?"

Joanna looked up at Colt. She'd watched him all evening, turning around the dance floor with his daughters standing on his boots. After each dance was over, he'd lift the child up and hug her gently. The kind of hug Joanna had always longed for and never received from her father.

"Of course, Captain." She placed her hand on his shoulder and felt the hard strength beneath her fingers.

This time she didn't look away, but kept her eyes on his

face as they waltzed. She didn't even think about the steps as they slid around the floor.

When he halted, he couldn't have missed the disappointment in her eyes. "The music's stopped," he whispered as his arms pulled her slightly closer instead of away.

Joanna quickly dropped her hands and her gaze. "Oh." She felt foolish, as though she'd publicly announced how happy she'd been in his arms.

But he only stood in front of her, waiting for her to look up again. When her eyes met his, he whispered, "Thank you for the evening. I'm sure it's been good for the morale."

Joanna locked her arms behind her. "You're welcome. I think the girls had a grand time tonight."

"And their teacher? Did she have a grand time as well?" All the hardness eased from his face.

"Yes," Joanna answered, wishing she could tell him just how happy she was.

Etta's voice interrupted, "Captain, I think you'll have to carry Johnnie home. The poor child just high-stepped one too many times."

Colt laughed and lifted the half-asleep child into his arms. "I'll take the girls and your aunt home, then come back and help you get the mess hall back in order. I want the men to be able to eat here in the morning."

Joanna nodded and looked around. Men were already pulling the tables back into place. She kissed the little girls good night and began folding away the paper hearts.

By the time the captain returned, she was ready to leave. He lifted a wet cape over her shoulders and said, "Rain's starting, better put this over your head until we get in the wagon."

His arm rested over her shoulder as they ran. With one swift movement he swung her up into the seat and jumped in beside her. As they hurried to his cabin the rain continued, turning the ground to liquid with its pounding.

Joanna felt the damp soak into her bones and shivered beside Colt. Without a word he pulled her close, warming her with his arm as they rode the last few yards.

"Hold the reins!" he yelled as he climbed down from the driver's box and led the horses toward the barn. His body was only a shadowy outline in black, with his hat low.

Joanna's fingers turned to ice, but she held the reins. She pulled his cape close around her, realizing he'd given her his only protection from the weather.

With an eerie creaking she heard the barn door open. A moment later they were inside, where the air was damp and thick with the smell of hay.

Colt unhitched the horses, then raised his arms to help her down. "If you'll wait till I get the horses bedded down, I'll carry you across the yard to the house. Otherwise you'll ruin that dress of yours."

Joanna moved into his waiting arms, aware of the strength and power in this man as he held her suspended in the air. He lowered her to the ground slowly, as though in no hurry to move away from her.

"I can help with the horses," she volunteered. "I grew up on a farm."

"Really?" Colt moved back to the animals, pulling the harness as he went. "I had you figured for a city girl."

"That just proves it then, Captain. You were right."

Colt continued to work. "Right about what, Miss Whiddon?"

"You know nothing about women," she answered as she helped.

Colt's laughter was rich and full inside the quiet barn. For the first time since they'd met, she felt that he relaxed.

Maybe it was spending the evening away from his worries, or maybe it was the spirits mixed into the punch, but Colt Barnett finally looked relaxed.

"You have a nice laugh, Captain." Joanna bit her lip, suddenly wishing she could pull back her bold words.

"Thank you," he answered as he wiped the leather dry and hung it away.

Joanna crossed to the doorway and watched the rain pour in solid sheets. She could hear him moving behind her, putting everything in place. Finally he joined her at the door.

"Mind if I ask you a question, Miss Whiddon?"

"No," she answered, dreading what might come.

"Why'd you answer my ad?" He moved against the door frame so that he was only a few inches from her. If she'd shifted slightly, their shoulders would have touched.

Joanna continued to stare into the rain. "I needed a job," she lied. "Plus, I've always wanted to teach."

Colt was silent so long she wasn't sure he'd heard her. Slowly he ran his hand along the doorjamb and let out a long breath. "That's not what I mean. I'd guessed you needed a job, but why all the way out here in Texas? Why a tutor? A fine, good-looking woman like you surely had several offers of marriage."

"Is that a compliment, Captain?" She didn't want to tell him how few she'd had over the years.

Colt laughed. "Am I that rusty?"

"You're doing fine. That's probably the finest compliment I've ever had." Joanna looked out at a world that seemed all gray and lifeless. "You're right about one thing. I did have an offer for marriage. Several, in fact, over the years. The last was such a good offer that my father planned to make sure I accepted. So Aunt Etta and I packed and left before he could get back from town with the preacher.''

"He wanted you to marry some no-good, right?" Anger bubbled in Colt's words.

Joanna laughed. "No. In fact, the man he wanted me to marry was a successful farmer. Maybe someday he'll be the best in the state.''

Colt looked at her, raising one dark eyebrow. "But the man had a dark past?"

"No. I've known Milton all my life. His family are all fine folks.''

Colt leaned his head slightly sideways. "Did you think he'd beat you?"

"No!" Joanna couldn't even imagine such a thing from Milton.

Frustration showed in Colt's face. "Then what?" His whole body seemed to tense in frustration. "If I'm going to try and understand women, I might as well start with you. But I don't seem to be getting anywhere.''

She realized she had to be honest no matter how silly it might seem. "All I ever wanted was to be a woman one man would love in a heartbeat." Joanna tried to keep the tears from falling as she put words to her feelings for the first time. "But it never happened. As the years went by I realized it never would. All I'd ever be was second choice, the consolation prize, even to Milton. I was the one who was always asked after the girl a man loved had turned him down.''

She stared into the rain and knew her life had been nothing more than the same gray reality. "Every year my father offered more and more land along with my hand as though I was wilting merchandise that had to be sold quickly before all the value was gone.''

Colt crammed his fists deep into his pockets and fought the urge to pull her to him. If she could have seen his face, she would have known how her words touched him, but the darkness hid his eyes as the night covered her shame enough to allow her to continue.

"I heard Milton say once that he'd love another in a heartbeat, if she'd let him." Joanna was silent as if gathering courage from the storm. "I'd have given anything if he'd felt that way about me. But he didn't. He let me down by not loving me enough and my pride wouldn't allow me to accept less. Even though I've loved him since we were children, I couldn't accept him knowing he didn't truly love me. He loved another girl who wouldn't marry him."

"You left with nothing rather than take what he offered?"

"Yes."

"But he offered marriage. A home. Children. Everything."

"Everything except a heartbeat. I wanted to be the woman in his heart, not just the woman in his house. I wanted to be loved, not just needed. I wanted him to look at me when he talked of marriage and not at my land."

"And if he appears again?" Colt had a feeling any man worth his salt would follow Joanna wherever she went and take her back home.

"He can't change the way he feels any more than I can accept anything less from a man."

"Do you still love him?"

"I've grown weary of loving a man who thinks of someone else first. I like him, I've cared for him since we were little, but nothing more." She almost added that Milton had never made her temperature rise by just touching her hand. "If Milton and I married, I'd always wonder, was it me or her in his mind?"

Colt didn't know what to say, he could almost feel his muscles cry out to hold her. He knew what it was like to love someone who didn't bother to return that love. He'd also been the one who came in second and he'd sworn when his wife left that he'd never throw himself open to that pain again.

"So you packed your bag and ran," he whispered, remembering how he'd felt that night he'd come home and found Buckles trying to keep three babies from crying. He'd wanted to close himself off and cry also, but there had been no time. He had three children to care for.

"I didn't run; I just . . . left." Joanna wished she could look braver in his eyes. "If my father would have allowed me to teach, I never would have answered your ad."

Colt didn't move for a long while. He just stared into the rain. His handsome face closed to all feeling as if he were locking away a memory.

Finally he turned to her. "We'd better make a run for it."

Joanna nodded and lifted her arms. Colt's hands went around her formally as he lifted her up into his arms. "Ready?" he whispered, and carried her out of the barn and into the rain before she could answer.

Joanna pressed her face against the scarf at his neck and held on tightly as he ran through the rain. She could feel his heart pounding against her side and his arms iron tight around her as he moved through the downpour.

With long strides he bounded onto the back porch and lowered her to her feet. Joanna didn't move away, but turned to stare into his dark eyes that seemed to burn with an anger far older than their acquaintance.

"Thank you," she whispered, her breath frosty in the few inches between them.

Without thinking of the consequences, she lifted her hand and pushed the wet hair back from his forehead. He's really a very handsome man, she thought. Bravery was carved in his jawline as solidly as iron seemed to be molded into his strong arms. "You have an angry fire in your eyes, Captain."

He moved an inch closer. "And you have cold winter in yours," he answered. "Tell me, are you made of ice?"

Before he could move away, she closed the distance between them and whispered against his cheek. "I don't know. No one's ever come close enough to find out."

Something deep inside snapped in Colt and he couldn't resist any longer. He pulled her against him and covered her mouth with his own. He'd taste the winter or feel the fire of this woman before he died of longing to know.

Joanna had been kissed before but she'd never been kissed like this Texan kissed her. There was something wild and demanding in his touch. He held back nothing and he wanted all she would offer. There was no politeness in his hold, only a need so old and deep it resounded from the past and promised into the future.

His kiss deepened with a desire far greater than she'd thought a man like him would ever have. His arms were so tight around her she could hardly breathe.

All her life she'd dreamed of being kissed just once with all the passion in a man. Joanna moved her arms around his neck and ran her fingers into his wet hair. His kiss grew more demanding as he parted her lips.

The cold and rain disappeared around her and all she felt was the warmth of his arms. Her logical mind told her this was only a moment captured outside the reality of their lives, but her heart begged her to take all she could and store it up for the lonely years to come. She gave herself over to the passion of his kiss, willingly drowning in the pleasure.

He pulled away slightly, breaking the kiss but continuing to brush his lips against her cheek. "I . . ."

Joanna turned, her lips blocking his words. She would hear how he was sorry later. She would listen and forgive his rash act, later. Now all she wanted was to feel a man in her arms and believe for once that he was kissing her, only her, and not wishing she were another.

Something rattled, pulling them back to earth. In an instant he was away from her side, leaving only cold and silence between them. He bent to pick up his cape, which had slipped to the porch, as someone opened the backdoor.

"Oh." Aunt Etta shone a light into the night. "There you are, Joanna. I've been waiting up for you."

Joanna tried to make words form on her lips, but the memory of Colt's kiss was still fresh.

"We were just seeing to the horses," Colt mumbled as he straightened and threw the cape over one shoulder. "Quite a night, isn't it?"

Joanna glanced up at him. The lamplight reflected in his dark eyes, making them seem full of fire. He held her gaze silently, willing her not to look away.

"Well, you two better get in out of this weather." Aunt Etta stepped back into the house, taking the light with her.

As Joanna followed she felt Colt's light touch at her waist. A touch that lasted only a moment, but told of his nearness. She wanted to look back and see if the kiss had meant as much to him as it had to her, but she made herself march forward. She'd spent enough years being hurt when she took a second glance; for once in her life she wanted to remember only the beauty of a moment and not look too deep for a love that might not be there.

"You'll never guess what came while we were at the party." Aunt Etta moved to the table and lifted a telegram from atop the Bible.

"What is it?" Joanna had no doubt Aunt Etta had already read the contents.

"It's from Milton." Etta smiled, her eyes cutting to Colt. "It says he's coming."

"But how could he know where I am?"

"Your father must have told him when we sent for your things."

"It's impossible."

Joanna thought she heard a mumbled curse before Colt's bedroom door slammed.

Chapter Five

Joanna read the telegram for the tenth time then tossed it into the fire, wishing she could get rid of Milton so easily. She couldn't believe he was coming. She'd known him all his life, and he hated leaving his land. The thought that her father might have increased the acreage again if he married her crossed Joanna's mind. Her father had started worrying about her marital status when she'd been eighteen, but he hadn't decided to do anything about it until she turned twenty-two. From that summer on he'd made no secret of promising land to any young man who won her hand.

Looking out the window at the cold February morning, Joanna remembered what he'd said the day she'd left. "I won't have you wasting away like my sister, Etta. You're getting married today or there'll be hell to pay."

Tears welled up in her eyes as she remembered the look on Etta's face when her father had said those words. Aunt Etta had never been anything but kind and giving. She hadn't deserved the pain reflected in her eyes when she'd looked around praying for a place to hide.

Milton was the same kind of man as her father, God-fearing and hardworking. He loved the land more than he ever would a woman, no matter if she was his wife, daughter, or sister. Joanna would live alone before she'd marry such a man.

Only now Milton was coming. What did he hope to do? Drag her back home like a runaway child? Well, she was old enough to know her own mind and decide her own future.

"Want some apple pie?" Aunt Etta shouted from the kitchen.

"No, thanks," Joanna answered. She smiled toward the doorway to the kitchen. She'd never seen her aunt so happy. For once she wasn't helping in someone else's kitchen, she was the queen in her little world.

"Then I think I'll take it over to Abe, I mean Sergeant Buckles!" Etta shouted back. "He's working in the captain's office next door, and you know how he loves my pies."

Joanna smiled. "Everyone loves your pies. Ask him while you're there if he's seen the captain. It's been three days." She didn't want to think of the real reason Colt had been staying away from the fort. He'd left a note the morning after the dance that said he had to ride out to check on a report of trouble at an Indian camp to the north.

Aunt Etta opened the door with her free hand. "I'll be back before the girls wake up from their nap."

Joanna waved. This was getting to be a habit of Etta's . . . visiting Sergeant Buckles. To be honest the two had a lot in common. They were about the same age and both had spent their lives taking care of others.

Joanna made herself stay busy as the evening passed. She taught the girls to write the word *Texas* and cut out a paper shape of the state.

After they'd been tucked in for the night with one of Aunt Etta's stories about how she saved a family from a tornado in the middle of a snowstorm, Etta went to bed, and as always, Joanna poured herself the last cup of coffee.

She curled into the rocker and watched the fire. She'd

spent the past three days thinking of what she'd tell Milton.
But before he came, she had to talk with Colt and tell him
she was sorry about the kiss. Maybe if he believed that little
lie, he'd allow her to stay on as tutor.

Joanna was almost asleep when the door creaked open.
Colt looked exhausted as he moved in from the cold. For a
moment he didn't seem to see her as he crossed to the
fireplace. He stretched and removed his coat. His broad
shoulders rippled with muscles as he locked his fingers and
reached into the air.

When he turned his back to the fire, he saw Joanna. A
hundred emotions seemed to cross through him, kalei-
doscoping in his eyes. For a moment she thought he was
going to reach for her and pull her against him, but slowly
he forced the hardness into his face.

"I thought you'd be gone by the time I got back." His
words were as cold as the wind. "Your month will be up by
the end of the week."

"Am I fired?" Joanna stood.

"Of course not," he snapped. "I only figured your man
would have come by now."

"He's not my man." She forced herself to keep her voice
low. "I'm quite satisfied with my employment here, unless
you have some objection, Captain."

He watched her closely as though he didn't trust her
response. "No objection," he whispered, locking his hands
behind him. "Only, I half wish you were on the train back
to Ohio."

Joanna felt the pain of his words all the way to her soul.
"You do?"

"Yes," he answered as he moved away from the fire and
into the shadows. "There's trouble coming. Big trouble,
and I wish I knew you were somewhere safe."

Joanna closed her eyes and tried to stop the tears from falling. He hadn't wanted her gone, only safe.

He moved between her and the fire as he lifted his coat and rifle. "Well, we'd best get some rest. Tomorrow's likely to be a busy day."

As he straightened he looked into her blue eyes and saw the tears. Suddenly his formal manner was forgotten. He dropped his coat and moved closer to her. "Don't be afraid," he whispered. "You have to know I'd protect you and the girls with my life."

Joanna pushed the tear away from her cheek with her fingertips. How could she tell him that it wasn't the fear of an Indian attack that frightened her, but the thought that he would send her away if he could?

I'm playing silly games with myself, she thought. I let myself believe that one kiss could mean something between two people. He probably thought it was nothing, not even worth mentioning.

Colt took a step toward her, then backed away. "I'm sorry I mentioned the Indians. We won't know anything until tomorrow. I didn't mean to worry you."

Joanna pulled the ribbons of her pride together. "I wasn't worried about an attack." She moved to her bedroom, suddenly wanting to be alone.

The captain didn't follow. "Miss Whiddon," he whispered before she reached the door. "About the other night. I didn't plan what happened on the porch."

"I know," she whispered, wondering why he didn't just say he was sorry and that it would never happen again. The best kiss in her life and he felt he had to apologize for it. "Good night, Captain," she whispered as she hurried into her bedroom. She thought she heard him start to say something, but her heart couldn't bear an explanation of what had been magic to her.

She pulled off her robe and curled up beside her aunt as she fought back the sobs. What a mess she'd gotten herself into. She could list his shortcomings all night long, but Joanna had to face one fact. She'd fallen in love with Colt and all he wanted was a tutor for his children.

She closed her eyes and drifted into sleep. Far into the night she dreamed she heard him call her name. Then he touched her shoulder gently and she came fully awake, realizing she wasn't dreaming.

"Joanna," he whispered. "I need to talk with you."

She crawled from the bed and followed him to the main room. She knew her hair was wild around her shoulders, but his tone was too urgent to delay.

When they reached the fireplace, he stooped to add a log. When he stood, he was only inches from her. "I just got word that we may be attacked at dawn."

Joanna sucked in her breath.

"Don't worry," he quickly continued. "We're better armed and protected than you might think, but I need your help. Can you wake your aunt and the girls? Try not to excite them but get them dressed and over to the mess hall within the hour. There's a cellar under the building and I think it will be the safest place for you all."

Joanna nodded and turned to follow his orders, but his sudden grip on her hand pulled her back.

"One other thing. I couldn't sleep last night thinking about how I had lied to you." He pulled her gently toward him. "I'm not sorry about the kiss."

Joanna looked up into his black eyes that reflected the firelight. "Neither am I," she whispered.

Colt relaxed his grip. "I'll promise you it won't happen

again. It wouldn't be fair to you. You have to understand one thing about me, Joanna, I no longer believe in love.''

Suddenly the air seemed thick between them. She had trouble breathing with him so close. ''I'd better get the girls, Captain Barnett,'' she mumbled, and stepped away, wishing she was strong enough to hit him and make him believe in her.

Colt's face hardened into a mask. ''Thank you, Miss Whiddon.'' He was all officer now. None of the man she'd held that rainy night remained.

Half an hour later Aunt Etta was walking toward the mess hall with the girls following her like little ducks. She carried a huge basket of food in one hand and Joanna's Bible in the other. ''Come along, girls. We're going on a picnic just like I did the winter of the great dust storm that blew away half the livestock in Ohio. Just wait and see, it's going to be great fun.''

Joanna brought up the rear, her arms loaded with blankets. She'd never loved her aunt more than she did right now. She knew Etta had never been on any adventures except in her mind, but somehow it didn't matter in the least.

Sergeant Buckles met them at the door. ''Captain says to set up in a corner here on the ground floor. If any trouble starts, then you can move to the cellar.''

Joanna nodded. ''I'll go ahead and take the blankets down now and save you the trouble.''

Aunt Etta handed Buckles her basket. ''That's wonderful news. Now we can cook in the mess kitchen. Have you got the coffee on?''

The sergeant looked confused. ''Coffee?''

''Of course.'' Etta took the lantern from his hand and shooed the girls toward the kitchen. ''Everyone knows men have to have coffee to be wide-awake at dawn. Hurry up, we don't have more than an hour before sunup."

Joanna walked from sentry to sentry, carrying the pot of coffee in one hand and cups in the other. Each man told her she should be back inside but thanked her for the hot brew. When she finally reached the captain's post, she had only one cup left.

"What are you doing out here?" His voice was laced with anger . . . and concern.

"I had to bring coffee," Joanna said as if the words made some sense.

"But we may be attacked!" Colt was so angry he sloshed the hot liquid over his fingers.

Joanna wiped his hand. "Oh, I'm not afraid," she whispered. "I don't believe in Indians."

Colt pulled his hand away. "You've gone as crazy as your aunt Etta with all her tales."

"Not at all," Joanna countered. "If you can't believe in love, I can't believe in Indians."

Colt raised one dark eyebrow and stared at her. "Not believing in love doesn't get you killed."

"Maybe not on the outside, but on the inside a man's heart can dry up and blow away."

"Would you rather me believe in your Valentine's Day? In hearts and flowers and all that nonsense?"

"It's better than dying inside and refusing to feel anything."

Colt's voice was low, filled with anger and pain. "This advice is coming from a woman who ran away from marriage? Who gave up a man she thought she loved because she didn't think he loved her enough?"

Joanna's free hand balled into a fist. She'd never wanted to strike someone as much as she did him. She'd told him why she'd taken the job in trust and now he was throwing that trust in her face.

"Maybe, Miss Whiddon"—Colt's voice was only for her ears—"you don't know as much about men as you think you do. Whatever gave you the idea I'm dead inside?"

He tossed his coffee in the dirt and handed her the empty cup. "Take my advice and get back inside where it's safe."

"Is that an order, Captain?"

"You're damn right." Before she could say another word, he'd turned his back to her.

Joanna stormed back to the mess hall, wishing the Indians would attack. She was angry enough to whip the lot of them.

If Captain Colt Barnett didn't get killed today, she just might do the job herself tonight.

Chapter Six

The morning crept by with the sounds of the children playing in a corner of the mess hall and a few of the wives talking as if nothing were wrong. Joanna tried to think of anything but the argument she'd had with Colt. It made no sense. Why hadn't she just dropped the subject and walked away? Why had she allowed him to upset her so? He had a right to believe or not believe anything he wanted about love.

Buckles hurried into the mess hall just after lunch, his smile spread wide. "The captain said it's all right to go back to your homes. Seems the rumors were just that, nothing to worry about."

Aunt Etta jumped up and hugged Buckles. "Praise the Lord!" she shouted.

Joanna couldn't miss the smile widening across Sergeant Buckles's face.

He patted Etta's shoulder gently. "Now, don't you worry none. We'd fight to the last man to save a cook like you."

Giggling like a schoolgirl, Etta gathered her things to head back to her own kitchen. "Sounds like you're trying to wiggle an invitation to dinner out of me, Sergeant."

"And if I am?" Buckles patted his stomach.

"Then consider yourself invited."

Joanna smiled at the older couple but didn't want to be

part of their lightheartedness. "I'll stay behind and clean up," she yelled after Etta. "You go on without me."

Johnnie waved good-bye as she and the twins followed Aunt Etta. "Don't forget the blankets in the cellar, Miss Joanna."

The child's memory surprised Joanna, for in truth she had forgotten all about the blankets they'd brought over that morning. She put the cups away and headed down to the cellar, where she'd spread out a blanket for each of them.

As she folded the last one a noise rattled from above her and she wondered if Sergeant Buckles had returned to help her with the load.

But Colt walked down the steps slowly, allowing his eyes to adjust to the dim light. "It's dusty down here," he commented as he reached her level. His eyes were still black with anger from their conversation hours before. "What did you need, Miss Whiddon?" The light outlined his frame, making him seem huge as he moved toward her.

"Me!" Joanna's word was drowned out by the sound of the cellar door closing, cutting out all the light in the tiny room. One moment she could see the captain standing only a foot in front of her, and the next, the room was as black as a starless night.

Colt's swear words were loud enough for anyone outside to overhear. He bolted up the steps and slapped against the door just after the lock fell into place.

"Open the door, Captain!" Joanna suddenly felt a kind of panic at being trapped in the cellar. "I don't want to be down here in the dark." She heard Colt's body slam once more against the door.

"I can't." Colt swore again. "Whoever closed the door threw the lock. We built this place to double as a jail if we ever needed one. There's no way out from the inside."

She could hear him feeling his way back down the steps. "Light a candle," he ordered.

"I can't," Joanna answered. "I sent them up top with the girls earlier. They were only stubs and I planned to send new ones over."

"Why'd you send for me?"

"Send for you? I didn't!" Joanna fought the urge to swing wildly through the blackness and see if she could hit him. His tone told her he considered this mess to be her fault.

"But Johnnie said you did." He shot the words at her with such anger she could feel them move across the space between them. "She said I had to come quick."

Light flickered inside Joanna's mind, if nowhere else in the room. "Can she lift the door to the cellar?"

"Hell, no." Colt seemed to follow her thinking. "But all three of them probably could."

"They wouldn't," Joanna whispered. "Why would they do such a thing? All we have to do is bang on the door and someone will let us out."

"No." Colt's laughter surprised her. "I told all the men except the sentries to go back to their barracks and get a few hours' rest."

Joanna fumbled her way along the wall until she reached the steps. She felt Colt jump as she touched his shoulder, but she held tight and sat down next to him. "Are you telling me that three little girls locked the commander of this fort away?" She didn't remove her hand from his arm. Even if she was angry at Colt, she needed to know he was near.

"Looks that way." Colt moved, scooting closer so that their hips touched.

Joanna leaned into his body slightly and somehow the blackness didn't seem as frightening. Despite their words something drew her to him, something stronger than just a need not to feel so alone in this place.

"But why?" Joanna tried to use logic. "Have you ever locked them up?"

Cold sounded offended. "Of course not. They're my daughters, not criminals. However, when I get out of here, I might give punishment more thought in the future." He absently slid his hand behind her, offering her back a rest.

Joanna tried not to think of how close Colt was. She could feel the light movement of his chest as he breathed. "Are they angry at you?"

"Of course not." Colt leaned back against the steps and pulled her with him. "No more than they're mad at you."

"We've been having a wonderful time talking about Valentine's Day tomorrow. Johnnie's been asking me questions all week about how people fall in love." Joanna sucked in her breath suddenly as an idea struck her.

"What is it?" Colt turned slightly, his knees bumping hers. "Are you all right?" His fingers brushed along her arm in more of a caress than a search. "Did you hurt yourself?"

"No." Joanna meant to push his hand away. Yet when their fingers touched, she had no desire to remove his nearness. "I just figured out why we're here."

Colt waited. He slowly turned his hand over and threaded her fingers through his. He knew if someone were outside the door listening, they'd have no idea how close he was to Joanna in the darkness. Or what their bodies were telling one another even while they spoke of other things.

"Remember"—Joanna squeezed his hand loving the game as much as he—"the other morning when Johnnie asked me how people fell in love and I told her by spending time alone together?"

Colt didn't comment but slowly circled his thumb across her open palm.

"So the girls are giving us some time alone . . . together." She could feel the warmth of Colt beside her, but he didn't speak.

"Did you hear me?"

"Of course I heard you," Colt answered. "You're trying to tell me my little girls dreamed up this plan. What about your aunt Etta? She's the one with the crazy stories. Maybe this is one she'll add to her collection."

"Maybe." Joanna realized she didn't want to believe her aunt would do such a thing any more than he wanted to believe his daughters were at fault.

"So what's the plan, Captain?"

"We have no choice but to wait here until the cook comes in to start dinner. My guess, since I can't see my watch, is that'll be in about half an hour, maybe more."

"And what do we do until then, talk about your lack of feelings?" Joanna knew she was being unkind, but cellars had never been one of her favorite places.

"I didn't say I don't feel." Colt's words were surprisingly calm. "I only said I don't believe in love."

"And how do you feel right now?" Joanna asked. "Are you angry, feeling betrayed, or only frustrated that you're trapped in here with me when you hoped by now I'd be on a train headed back east?"

"I feel"—his voice lowered—"like I want to break that promise I made to you this morning."

Before she knew he was moving, he pulled her into his arms. His hands gripped her shoulders and slid slowly up her neck to hold her head as his mouth lowered over hers.

Joanna closed her eyes and forgot all about the darkness. The musty smell of the cellar was replaced by the scent that always surrounded Colt. He smelled of fresh soap and spring water from his baths in the stream and wool and brass polish from his uniform.

"Kiss me back," he pleaded as his fingers plowed into her hair, destroying her bun.

"Is that another order?" she murmured as her hands slid up his shirt and wrapped around his neck. She ran her fingers into his thick hair and pulled his head lower. Joanna felt as if she'd been starving for his touch all her life and now she couldn't let go even if the door to the cellar were suddenly flung open.

"No," he whispered as his kiss grew more demanding, bruising her lips with his need as he held her in a warm embrace. "A request."

He loved the taste of her. Never had a woman felt so right in his arms. Colt found himself holding back for fear he'd frighten her if she knew how great was his need for her.

"I'm not dead inside, Joanna," he whispered, his lips brushing her cheek. "My guts twist every time you enter the room. Do you have any idea how many times I've thought I'd go mad these past few weeks from longing to touch you?"

Joanna couldn't believe she was in his arms. She felt she was living out a dream she'd had for years. A dream of a handsome lover longing for her alone.

"Tell me you don't want me to touch you and I'll stop." Colt's voice was so low it was almost a thought between them. "If you don't want to be this close to me, I'll pull back."

Joanna couldn't lie. She'd relived their first kiss every night in her dreams and had finally decided it couldn't have made her feel as wild as she'd thought. But now he'd kissed her again and she knew it was real. His touch made her feel that every part of her was alive. She was no longer waiting on a shelf, but living and loving as she'd always longed to do.

Sliding her fingers from his hair to his face, she touched his strong jaw and the roughness of his cheeks. Slowly she touched his open lips and felt his warm breath against her fingertips. This was the man she'd looked for all her life and she'd only been able to recognize him in complete darkness.

"I've never been kissed like you kiss me," she whispered honestly, wishing she knew how to be coy and play the game of loving so many women seemed to know how to play from birth. "I feel like I'm riding the wind."

Colt raised his hand to cover hers in the blackness. He pressed each one of her fingers against his lips. "I've never met a woman like you, Joanna." He moved her hands to his chest. "You make my heart pound and my blood feel like it's running double time."

He kissed her cheek and moved slowly across her face to her lips. This time his mouth was gentle, giving her great pleasure. She pulled at his uniform jacket, wanting to feel his flesh and not the wool that covered him.

Colt held the kiss as he unbuttoned his jacket and let her hands move inside. He loved the way she explored, hesitantly at first, then with a boldness that surprised him.

He leaned her back and slowly unbuttoned her blouse. With each button freed he felt her tremble, but she didn't move to stop him or turn away. He gently pulled her blouse open and lifted the cotton camisole. Then, with a feather-light touch, he brushed his rough hands over the softness of her breasts.

She heard his sudden intake of breath as he touched her so tenderly, and she knew there was much loving in this man despite what he said. With a knowledge borne deep inside every woman, she covered his hand with hers and pressed his fingers against her skin. He was still for a moment, then leaned and kissed her fully as his touch grew bolder.

While his hands roamed over her he kissed her with a passion that surprised them both.

Joanna relaxed to his loving, knowing it was right. No man had ever touched her so boldly, but she knew he was taking only what she freely gave.

Silently he moved her atop him and pulled her to face him. His mouth slid along her neck and lower, tasting her skin, warming her flesh to his need.

She dug her fingers into his hair and leaned back, loving the explosions of emotions setting fire to her body.

"This is what feelings are. Not thoughts and speeches, but real," he whispered, his voice husky with need. "Love is flesh and need, not spirit."

"No." Joanna didn't want to pull away, but she didn't believe his words.

"I want you," he returned. "But in my life there is no place for hearts and dreams, only reality. I want you like I've never wanted a woman in my life, but love is action, not emotion to be played with by poets and fools."

Joanna understood how he felt; she mirrored his desire. But love had to be more than just convenience or need. It had to be as vital as the pounding of one's heart. It had to be made up of more than just reality. Dreams and longings and desires also must be its substance.

With a cry of loss she pulled away, stumbling into the blackness and falling over the stack of blankets.

"Joanna!" he shouted. "Don't do this. Don't pull away from me."

Tears spilled from her eyes, but she crawled farther away.

Milton had offered a passionless love and now Colt offered only passion. Neither were enough for her.

Absently she buttoned her blouse as though she could close out the pain. "No," she whispered as she bumped into a corner.

"You know you want me." His words were low with anger. "Don't lie and pretend you bargained for only a kiss."

"Yes, I want you." She pulled her life back into order. "But your just wanting me is not enough."

"I have no more to give." Colt wouldn't break down the wall and allow another to hurt him no matter how much his arms ached to hold Joanna. Once in his life was enough. The scars were too deep to heal now.

"You have more to give," she whispered. She'd seen the depth of love in him when he'd danced with his daughters. "You're just not willing. Not willing to take a chance."

"Not again," he vowed. "Never again."

The silence in the tiny room seemed as thick as Mississippi mud. All that could be heard were footsteps in the distance. Footsteps coming closer.

Chapter Seven

The door to the cellar swung open with a powerful pop and light flooded the dusty room. Colt swore again to himself and stepped away from the stairs, allowing Joanna to leave first.

"Joanna!" Aunt Etta shouted. "Are you all right?"

Joanna climbed the steps, praying she didn't look as disheveled as she felt. "Yes," she answered as she climbed. "I fell over some of the blankets and hit my head." She knew her words sounded stupid, but she couldn't think of any other reason her hair would look such a mess.

She blinked away the darkness and glanced around. There, hiding behind Aunt Etta, were the girls, their cheeks crimson with mischief.

But before she could reach them, someone stepped in her path. "Joanna!" a male voice shouted. "Are you sure you're uninjured?"

"Milton!" Though she only whispered his name, it seemed to bounce off the walls and slam back into her ears. Standing before her, solid barrel chest and broad stocky shoulders, was the man she'd known and loved since childhood. But for the first time she really looked at him . . . his thinning hair . . . the hardness around his eyes of one who only saw the straight and narrow path. She also saw worry and an unsureness in his eyes that hadn't been there before.

Milton held her elbow as though she might need help in walking, but his voice was colored more with anger than concern. "We were so worried about you. No one seemed to know where you were, and what with wild Indians in this awful country—" He stopped suddenly as Colt stepped from the cellar.

"Sir." Milton straightened to his full height. "Am I to understand you were locked in that place with my betrothed?"

Colt's long legs were headed straight toward his daughters. "Not by choice, I assure you." He glanced at Milton, his eyes seeming to narrow at the hold Milton had on her arm. "But if you wish to take exception?"

Joanna could see the fire almost bouncing through Colt's body as if it were trapped inside and looking for a victim to vent itself on. There was nothing he'd like better than a fight. "Of course Milton understands. You couldn't very well have locked us in from the inside." Her head felt like she really had fallen and suffered a blow. "Come along, Milton. I've got to put a cold rag on my head."

As Milton backed away from Colt, much like a sensible farmer backs away from an angry bull, Colt turned his attention to his children, who giggled and ran toward home. Their lack of any real fear of their father told Joanna the punishment would probably not be stern enough no matter how angry the captain looked.

By dinnertime the confusion was about to drive Joanna mad. Milton had planted himself in the kitchen and refused to leave until he talked to Joanna. Aunt Etta had been cooking around him, telling him stories of Texas as though in her few weeks here she'd personally lived through every one of them.

Sergeant Buckles, for some reason, didn't think it was proper that Milton was in the house with the ladies without a chaperon, so he'd camped at the kitchen table as well.

The only one who had the sense to disappear was Colt. He'd talked to his daughters, then walked through the house without a word and simply vanished.

"I have to talk to you!" Milton had been saying the same thing for two hours, only now he was ordering, not pleading or asking.

"We have nothing to discuss." Joanna held the rag to her forehead as if there really was a bruise from a fall there.

"I wish to talk with you alone, dear Joanna."

"There is nothing you can say that can't be said in front of everyone in this house." She was afraid if they were alone he'd try to kiss her as he had so many times in the past. His lips were always watery soft, and after Colt's kiss she didn't think she could stand Milton's.

As Aunt Etta passed the plates out on the table, she looked at the farmer. "My advice is you'd better catch the next train back home, Milton Miller."

Milton's patience wore thin. "I don't remember asking you." He didn't even look at Etta, for like most of Joanna's family, he'd fallen into the pattern of not even realizing the woman had feelings.

Sergeant Buckles and Joanna were on their feet faster than prizefighters at the sound of the bell. As Joanna opened her mouth Buckles beat her to the draw. "I think you'd best be apologizing to Miss Etta, mister." His balled fists left no doubt he was issuing an order, not making a request.

Milton looked disgusted. "Are you kidding?" He flipped his hand as if to shoo the soldier away.

"No." Buckles pulled his breeches up and shoved out his chest. He might not have the youth of Milton, but there was still a great deal of fight in him. "I've been sitting here listening to you whine and beg all afternoon, but I won't tolerate you being rude to a lady."

Milton opened his mouth to argue just as Colt stepped through the backdoor. He was dusty from head to toe and his boots were caked with mud. "Evening." He slapped his hat against his leg casually, as if he didn't notice the air was charged as if lightning had been bouncing off the walls in the kitchen. "Supper about ready?"

Etta took his cue. "Will be by the time you get cleaned up, Captain. I made your favorite tonight—fried chicken. Guess you can see we're having two extra for supper."

"Chickens or guests?" Colt laughed and walked through the room without looking at anyone except Etta.

Etta smiled and looked at the two men at her table. "One guest and one I'm not too sure about."

Milton stood and stormed to the backdoor. "Joanna, I want to talk to you on the back porch. Now!"

Joanna turned back to Etta for help, but found the old woman wasn't even looking at her. Buckles was handing her aunt a piece of crumpled paper he must have carried in his pocket for some time. Joanna watched as her aunt slowly unfolded the paper and stared at it for a long moment before looking up at the sergeant.

To Joanna's surprise they didn't even seem to know she was still in the room. Etta raised her hand to cup Buckles's cheek and he kissed her palm softly, holding her hand in his as if holding a great treasure.

"Joanna!" Milton snapped from the porch. "I'm waiting."

Joanna stepped outside, more to allow Buckles and Etta privacy than out of any desire to talk to Milton. "What is so important?" she asked as she looked at Milton, wondering how she could have thought she loved him for so many years.

"I have some things that need to be said." Milton folded his arms over his chest. Out of his element, he didn't seem as strong and powerful as he had back in Ohio. "Your father thinks he may have acted in haste last month."

"May have?" Joanna suddenly found the conversation more interesting.

"He says if you'll come back home, he'll give you more time to decide before you marry me." Milton's manner left no doubt of how fair he thought her father was being. "I can go ahead come spring and farm the land like it was already ours, but you can take your time and set your own wedding date. He said you can even teach, if you've still a mind to."

"How generous," Joanna answered. "And what about Aunt Etta?"

"She'd keep house for your father, of course. Then when you have babies, she can come stay with us as long as she's needed."

"What about when she's not needed?"

"I know you care deeply for her and I'd be willing to say she'd always have a home with us if that's what you want." Milton looked at her like she was a child. "Someone else will probably let her live with them, though. You've got a large family."

"I suppose." Joanna looked out into the vast sunset of this land called Texas and realized she hadn't missed her home at all. "Why do you want to marry me?" she whispered.

"What a question!" Milton had the sense to look offended by her statement. "We're alike. I want to marry you and build a future together. In ten, maybe fifteen years we could have one of the richest farms in the state."

Joanna sighed, as if just realizing something was gone that had died a long time ago. He hadn't mentioned love.

"But you didn't always feel this way. I remember when we were in our teens, you used to spend hours telling me of your love for others."

Milton looked down at his feet. "I was a fool in love with first one then another before I realized what was best for me. Marry me, Joanna. I'll make you a good husband. Our families are alike. We were made for one another."

Joanna looked him straight in the eyes. "One important question. What day is it tomorrow?"

Milton smiled as if he never doubted the answer. "February fourteenth. The same day the train will pull out of the nearest station for home."

Joanna looked past him and saw Sergeant Buckles and her aunt holding hands across the table. He'd given her a paper valentine, Joanna realized. One he'd carried all day—waiting for the opportunity.

Joanna took a deep breath, clearing her mind. She wanted that kind of love. The kind that's willing to take a chance of being a fool. She wanted it so badly she was willing to wait until she was Aunt Etta's age to get it.

Milton was talking about the ride home, but she wasn't listening. Joanna was formulating a plan. She'd force Colt's hand tomorrow and one way or the other she'd know if it was meant to be between them. She was twenty-five and it was time she took full control over her life.

If Colt didn't love her, she'd go with Milton and tell him on the train that she would never marry him. Then she could go home and pull her life together.

Milton leaned and kissed her cheek, putting a wet period to any thought she'd ever had of marrying him.

Chapter Eight

An hour before dawn Joanna slipped from her bed. She'd heard Colt leave the house for his morning dip in the creek and knew she didn't have much time. She'd thought about her plan all night and knew she couldn't leave him without taking with her one last memory of his touch. Even when she'd told Milton she'd be going back with him on the morning train, she knew she'd spend one last time in Colt's arms. If he didn't declare his love, at least she'd have a memory to carry into her spinsterhood.

Silently she tiptoed across the room and opened her door. She moved without hesitation the few steps to Colt's room.

Once inside his private quarters, she felt suddenly cold and wished she'd brought her robe, but there was no going back now. She only had time enough to add a log to the small fire before she heard Colt returning.

He stepped into the room, drying his hair as he moved. Firelight danced off his bare chest and sparkled in his damp hair as he closed the door and turned to face her. At first he didn't react, but only stood staring at her as if seeing a dream take form.

She wanted to tell him how much he'd changed her life. She thought of begging him to hold her one more time and not send her back to her room without a memory. But Joanna couldn't make herself speak.

Even now his gaze touched her far more deeply than any other man's hands ever would. He was stubborn and cynical, and yet he made her feel not only wanted and needed, but loved.

Silently he moved toward her. When he was only a foot away, Colt pulled the towel from his neck and tossed it aside. Firelight danced in his dark eyes as he looked at her.

Joanna raised her chin slightly, as though steeling herself for his order for her to leave, but he slowly raised his hand and lightly touched her hair.

Colt wished he had the words to tell her that her hair reminded him of sunshine. He thought of a hundred things he wanted to tell her about how important she was to him and how she'd brought happiness into his life. But he'd heard her tell Milton she'd go back with him, and Colt was too proud to beg any woman to stay.

He moved toward her, loving the way her eyes welcomed him with growing need. Somehow in the predawn light the world seemed unreal and magical, made up of only the two of them. He knew if he spoke of his love, it would somehow shatter the perfect world.

Gently he bent and lifted her into his arms. In long strides he walked to his bed and laid her down on sheets still warm from his sleep.

With no other sound but the crackling of the logs on the fire, he removed her nightgown and lowered himself beside her. The night had been chilly, but neither felt the cold as he touched her gently with hands unaccustomed to gentleness.

Joanna didn't close her eyes, for she wanted to see him as she gave herself to him. At dawn she might leave with Milton and return home to teach, but she'd know passion once before she left. Colt might never say he loved her, but for once in her life she'd feel loved.

Colt felt as if he were dreaming. She couldn't have come to his room. But here she was stretching beside him. Touching him as easily as he touched her. He moved his hand over her body, feeling the excitement of a new love and the comfort and belonging, as if he'd already loved her for a lifetime.

He kissed her lightly, enjoying the way she moved at his touch. Slowly, silently, his touch grew bolder, his kisses deeper, until the stream of passion became a raging river that consumed them both and swept them ever faster and faster.

She cried his name as the world exploded around Colt and he clung to her as to life. They drifted slowly into quiet waters of fulfillment, and held on to one another like children afraid to let go of one perfect moment.

He pulled her close against him and fell asleep knowing he'd found heaven. A last thought drifted through his sleepy mind. He'd tell her in words what he'd told her with his body before dawn.

Joanna listened to his low steady breathing as she slipped from his arms. Tears ran unchecked down her cheeks as she felt on the floor for her nightgown.

"If he'd only said he loved me," she whispered. "If he'd only said my name, I'd stay forever." But he hadn't. He'd taken her body, but promised nothing, and she couldn't wait forever for him to believe in love.

Joanna walked slowly to her room and dressed in the early light. She could hear Etta already preparing breakfast in the kitchen and was thankful for a few minutes alone. She'd been a fool to believe her plan would work. First she'd thought she could push him into declaring his love by saying that she was leaving with Milton. When that hadn't worked, she was sure he'd tell her how much he loved her after he'd touched her again. But he'd fallen asleep without a word.

No other choice existed. She would go back to Ohio with Milton and stall her father for as long as she could. Maybe she'd answer another tutoring ad or become the town's old-maid schoolteacher. It really didn't matter. The only man she'd ever really loved didn't believe in love and she'd done everything she could to try to make him. If Colt Barnett wanted to spend the rest of his life alone, that was his choice. She'd done all she could to change him.

Slowly Joanna packed her carpetbag. Aunt Etta had told her after supper that she wasn't going back with Joanna and Milton. She planned to stay here and help the captain with his daughters until he could find another tutor.

Joanna wasn't sure how she could leave both Colt and her aunt, but she knew she couldn't stay in this house loving him and having him only needing her. Maybe pride was a flimsy armor, but it was all she had.

Aunt Etta appeared in the doorway, wiping her tears with the corner of her apron. "I cooked you some breakfast," she whispered. She'd already begged Joanna not to go. There was no use repeating.

"I'm not really hungry. We have to get an early start." Joanna hugged her aunt one last time, then turned and lifted her bag. "Tell the girls I'll write."

Aunt Etta nodded and followed Joanna to the door. "Are you sure, child?" Etta said as she handed Joanna her mother's Bible.

Joanna shook her head. "I've given up being sure of anything. All I know is that I can't marry a man who doesn't love me with all his heart, be it Milton or Colt."

Etta nodded as if she understood. She hugged Joanna tightly as Milton pulled the buggy up to the porch.

Joanna rode silently beside Milton as they crossed the empty land between the fort and the train station. He talked of the farm and of all that had happened since she'd left, and she tried to listen.

She wanted to scream that she'd never marry him, but there would be time for them to talk later. A month ago she'd ran from Ohio to Texas because she knew she'd never have the love she wanted and now she was running back for the same reason. If cowards could be rated, she surely would win a blue ribbon.

Milton turned his buggy in at the livery and they walked to the train station.

As the train pulled up Joanna fought back her tears. A couple of hours before she'd been in Colt's arms feeling more love than she thought she could ever hold. But love couldn't just be a physical thing. He had to believe it was more. But he hadn't said a word.

As the whistle blew to load the train she looked up and saw Colt's lean form storming toward them. "Joanna!" he shouted.

She turned and watched him grow nearer, her heart pounding in her throat.

When he was within a few feet, he stopped. Angry black eyes flashed fire as he stared at her. "You were just going to leave without saying good-bye?"

"You said one month, remember?"

"But there's still one more day in the month. Today's only Valentine's Day. You said you'd leave on the fifteenth. I thought you liked being a tutor?"

"I did."

Milton was saying something, but neither of them was listening to him.

"Then stay. The girls need you," Colt shouted.

Joanna closed her eyes. If he'd only told of his feelings; but, no, he would never allow love in his life again. He'd made that plain. "I can't."

Milton pulled her onto the first step of the train. "Joanna's going to marry me, Captain."

Colt's eyes never left Joanna's. He didn't have to ask her if it was true. No one but Milton believed the statement.

"Stay." Colt's voice was hard.

"Another order?"

"A request," he answered, but his voice still revealed no emotion.

Milton lifted Joanna's gloved hand and made the gesture of kissing it. Only Joanna knew that his lips never quite touched her glove. "We must go, dear."

She looked at Colt, his stance rigid, his face an emotionless mask. "And if I stayed, when would you have married me?" she whispered more to herself than anyone as she stepped onto the next step of the train. She knew he'd never talk of marriage. How long would he want her to wait? Until the children were grown? Until the thousands of miles of frontier were settled?

The train started to move.

"My answer's in that Bible you're so fond of toting!" Colt yelled above the noise as he turned to leave, knowing he'd lost her forever.

Joanna opened her Bible. Between the pages of the Book of Ruth rested a folded red paper cut in the shape of a heart. Inside, written boldly as though without hesitation were the words *I'd be yours in a heartbeat, and I'll love you one day longer than forever.* He'd signed his full name as though she wouldn't know who the valentine was from.

Joanna jumped from the moving train, clutching her carpetbag and Bible, before Milton had time to stop her. She ran toward Colt's back, not caring that everyone was watching or that Milton was yelling for her to come back.

Colt turned just as she reached him and caught her. As the train rattled by he held her tightly against his heart. "I love you," he whispered. "I will be yours in a heartbeat if you'll have me."

He was still kissing her several minutes later when Buckles pulled up with Aunt Etta and the girls. Etta took one look at her niece and knew the world had finally been set right on its axis.

"I knew she'd come to her senses." Etta smiled. "Good men are hard to find." She patted Sergeant Buckles's knee and he swelled with pride.

The three girls giggled in the back of the wagon as they scratched out Joanna and Colt's names on a tattered valentine they'd reworked several times and added the words *Mom and Dad.* "We did it all"—Johnnie patted the twins' shoulders—"even without Cupid."

GIFTS OF THE HEART

by
Colleen Quinn

Dear Reader,

Valentine's Day . . . the holiday makes one think of lace and ribbons, fancy cards and flowers, bon bons and cupids. The day is dedicated to romance, a time when everyone forgets practicalities and indulges in thoughtful gestures and flights of fancy.

And is there a woman alive who doesn't love it? What girl hasn't thrilled to opening that card from a special someone, and seeing the words engraved especially for her? Or discovering a bundle of pink roses placed shyly on her dressing table, or seeing a heart-shaped box of chocolates, sinful in luxury, waiting just for her?

Most of my friends can still recall their first Valentine, no matter how silly or awkward. It wasn't the gift that captivated them; it was the romance. Romance is as necessary as the air we breathe. Yet there are still many who approach courtship with the same cool-headed logic that they use for business. One of the men I know, a charming and brilliant technician, confided to me that he had chosen his wife because she met his proscribed criteria.

I stared at him, stunned. Sure, such an approach was fine in writing a proposal, but in choosing a life's mate? What happened to feelings, emotions, those indefinable things that make a Valentine? All I could picture was our absent-minded professor with his list, checking off qualifications.

Thus came the idea for this story. As a Victorian elitist attorney, Stephen is very certain he knows what he wants. The woman he marries must be pretty and intelligent; she must be of similar social standing; she must be able to converse with his friends and family; she must be of the same religion and beliefs.

What happens then, when a man like Stephen, despite his logic, falls in love with the wrong woman? Elizabeth Carey comes from the other side of town. Not only does she have no money or standing, she is a reporter, for God's sake, and is posing as a beggar in order to do a story about Philadelphia's poor. She doesn't fit *any* of the criteria, and yet, Stephen cannot resist her.

I loved these characters and I loved writing this story. It is a different type of Valentine story, yet I feel it is very appropriate to the true meaning of the day. We need this holiday to remind us what romance is really all about.

To everyone and their families, I wish you a happy Valentine's Day.

—Colleen Quinn

Chapter One

"Elizabeth, you cannot mean to do this." Horace Bierce stared disapprovingly through bushy white brows as the young woman ignored him and continued setting out vats of face paint and rags. "You have to know the risk you're taking. Even for a story, you cannot put yourself in danger. My God, think of what you're proposing!"

Elizabeth Carey grinned, then dipped a rag into the face paint and smeared a liberal amount of it over her cheekbones. "I have thought about it, and you know it's the right thing to do. You and I both agree that the *Record* will never be a first-rate paper if we only print fluff. Bill Singerly wants this paper to succeed, and so do you and I. Ever since he bought the paper, he's wanted to give it a more serious direction. That's why for Valentine's Day we decided to do a story that counts, one that will make a difference. And the poor immigrants will do it."

"I agree." Horace nodded, watching her sharply. "If we're ever to outsell the *Philadelphia Public Ledger,* we need to get a tighter focus. Hard-hitting news stories. Good editorials. Crusades against local abuses. But we aren't going to do it by endangering one of our best and brightest reporters."

"Oh, bosh. Stop being such a worry wart. After all, you are the editor. You want this as much as I do. And it's only for a couple of days.'' Elizabeth pulled back her chestnut-colored hair and wrapped it beneath her cap. Then, after dipping her hands enthusiastically into a dish of mud, she rubbed the blackened mixture over her face and arms. Finally she dipped a paintbrush into an inkwell, then darkened her front teeth until they seemed to recede within her mouth. Her makeup complete, she turned to the man beside her, suppressing a smile as his mouth dropped in astonishment.

''You look . . .''

''Terrible.'' She finished for him. ''And absolutely perfect. A little gin sprinkled on my clothes, a wretched overcoat, and even the beggars will be fooled.''

''I can't believe it.'' Horace stared in astonishment at the female reporter. Elizabeth Carey was not what one would call beautiful, but she had a kind of charm and intelligence that more than made up for flawless features. She had a lively face, with a turned-up nose that betrayed an Irish ancestry and a mouth that seemed to smile perpetually. Even her freckles were full of life, for they danced across the bridge of her nose and marched over her cheekbones with every twist of her elflike expression. But it was her eyes that captured the most attention: pure gray blue, they were like the ocean just before a storm, sparkling, changing, brimming with anticipation. Yes, even without the gruesome makeup, her eyes made more than one person look back, and stay.

But the transformation astounded him. Elizabeth grinned, then slumped in a chair, assuming the posture of a down-on-your-luck charwoman, one who drank too much and was the ruin of her own life. Her cheeks were properly reddened, to give the appearance of chapped skin, while her nose showed the broken blood vessels of the perpetual drunk. And it wasn't just the makeup. It was her expression, the doleful way she stared back at him, the way her mouth hung open as if she were simply too apathetic to close it, that really made her transformation complete.

"I'll have to admit, Lizzie," Horace said grudgingly, his voice containing a little pride, "the stage lost an actress when you took up reporting. You look wonderful. But still, when you consider—"

"I'll be careful." Elizabeth sensed the weakening in his armor and pressed home. "This isn't any more dangerous than the story we did on the mentally ill. Remember that? Or the one where I posed as a suffragette . . ."

"And wound up in jail." Horace scowled, but his sneer was less intense than a moment ago. Elizabeth could almost see him weighing the possibilities.

"We've got only a few weeks until Valentine's Day, Horace. And it's cold out there. Do you know how many people will sleep, huddled in a corner tonight, while you and I go to our beds? There are hundreds. Families with children. Men and women, unable to get work, sharing a trash-bin fire that will last for perhaps an hour. We have to do something, we have to wake up the people of Philadelphia. Do you know what I saw yesterday?" When the editor shook his head, she continued passionately: "A child, begging for food, right on the steps of St. Paul's Church. A woman with a fur overcoat brushed right past him and knocked him over. She didn't even look back. She didn't even see him." Elizabeth's eyes sparkled with tears and she leaned closer. "Horace, we have to make them see these people. And this is the way to do it. Remember when Dickens wrote *Oliver Twist*? He made the people of Whiteface see the plight of the poor when nothing else would."

Reluctantly he nodded, seeing the triumphant look on Elizabeth's face. "All right. You've got a point. And Valentine's Day is the perfect time to run the story.

Everyone is feeling generous, full of love, exchanging tokens of affection to celebrate the day. But you still have to do the society pieces. People want to read them, no matter what you and I think."

"All right." Elizabeth grinned. "But just think, we can help them give some of that love to those who really need it. Instead of buying flowers, they might provide a meal to a family that is starving. Money spent on candy or trinkets could buy shelter for a poor man in the snow. Mrs. Billington is organizing a Valentine's Day charity dinner to benefit these people. So far attendance is dismal. But we could change that. To do it, to get a decent reaction, to arouse emotion, I have to know what I'm writing about. I have to live it, even for a few short days."

"I hate to admit it, but you are the right person for the job." Horace sighed, aware that he'd been conned but unable to argue. "And I have to agree with what you're saying. But I don't like it, Elizabeth. It's dangerous. If you insist upon doing this, then I must ask that you take a few simple precautions."

"I've thought of that." Elizabeth indicated a map of the city of Philadelphia that was hanging on the editor's wall and stabbed with so many pins that it looked like a porcupine. "This is the location I've chosen. It's a law office, respectable people, close to the police station, and in full public view. I plan to sit there during the day with my cup and beg for money."

Horace rolled his eyes. "But what if there's trouble?"

"Remember old tin-armed Willy? You helped keep him out of jail one time by proving that he couldn't have committed that murder on Rittenhouse Square."

"He wasn't in town at the time." Horace nodded. "He was sleeping in a railroad car in South Carolina. I know, because he brought me back valuable information on the boxcar scandal of 1877. Great story."

"Right." Elizabeth glanced at the map once more. "Willy resides right here, on the steps of the church. He'll be just a few doors away, should I need help." She saw the editor's doubtful expression and continued quickly. "At the very least he can send for you or the police. Don't worry, Horace. It will be just fine."

"All right, Lizzie. You win. I'll take care of things here. But if there's trouble—"

"We'll call the whole thing off." Elizabeth hugged him, oblivious to the mud and makeup. "After all, what could possibly go wrong?"

"Mr. Brooks?"

Stephen Brooks stared out the window of his office on Rittenhouse Square, the four most prestigious blocks in the city, watching the snowfall. Normally he took the luxury of his office for granted, but today he was exceptionally glad to be inside. The wind whipped up through the granite walls, freezing the pedestrians who hurried along the sidewalk. Ice coated the naked walnut trees with a rock-candy glaze while thick clouds threatened to dump more snow onto the slick streets.

Frowning, he turned back to his painfully neat desk, where several contracts awaited his signature. All of them were success stories. At the age of thirty he managed to utilize his negotiating skills, helping the new businesses form liaisons and partnerships in a way that was advantageous to everyone involved. Any agreement was good if both parties benefited and prospered, John Tyler had taught him, so he structured his negotiations with that thought in mind.

And his clients loved it. They returned time and time again, recommended him to other businessmen, called on him for everything from a simple legal agreement to complicated proposals. He had a knack for cutting through technical terms and legal jargon, wording his documents so clearly that even the unsophisticated could understand them. The law firm was delighted with him, and there was even talk of a political future.

Why then wasn't he completely happy?

"Mr. Brooks? I have your schedule."

Stephen glanced up at the secretary and nodded as she took a seat. Mrs. Hudson had been with the office since its beginnings. Although she was getting along in years, Mr. Smith, the founding partner, wouldn't hear of replacing her. She gave Stephen a quizzical glance through her spectacles, then read aloud from her list.

"You have a meeting with Mr. Tyler this morning at ten, Mr. Magiotti to discuss his contract at eleven, lunch with the mayor at noon. Mr. Colley is meeting with you and Mr. Tyler this afternoon. You have a supper scheduled with Father Anthony regarding the church benefit at six, a tea with the chairman of the opera company at eight, then a late dinner with Miss Mary Logan to discuss the St. Valentine's dance. Oh, and don't forget breakfast with your mother tomorrow morning."

Stephen withdrew his calendar and nodded, checking to make sure he had everything listed. "Anything else?"

"Yes. You have five minutes to drink a cup of tea. I'm scheduling it for you." Mrs. Hudson rose to her feet, almost daring him to object. "Oh, and here's your mail. There appears to be another one of those . . . cards for you."

Stephen recognized the satin paper and the lush engraving on the cream-colored envelope that lay on top of his other mail. It was a valentine. He had already received several others, which Mrs. Hudson brought to him with a disapproving frown. She thought it shameful the way the local debutantes chased him, and even more shameful that he hadn't been caught. In her opinion it was high time he was married, for what good was money without family? She waited expectantly, then frowned in disappointment when Stephen placed the mail aside and picked up a contract. He glanced at her quizzically.

"Is there anything else?"

"No." She turned sharply on her heel, then walked out of the office, her boots clicking loudly on the hardwood floors.

Stephen hid a smile. He fingered the card, playing with the lovely seal, smelling the sweet perfume that clung to it. Mrs. Hudson acted as if it was so easy, or just a matter of deciding. It wasn't as if he didn't want to settle down . . . even for business reasons, it was time. He met all the right people at the functions he attended, including the wealthy daughters of the local gentry. It was strange, but he almost felt as if he was shopping for a wife. She had to be pretty, with the right social background, intelligent and knowledgeable. She had to be of his religion, educated, and with high morals. He'd met dozens of women who met those qualifications, but somehow he couldn't imagine himself married to any of them for the rest of his life.

He flipped open the seal and saw that he was right. It was from Helene Steadman, the daughter of a shipping merchant. He'd gone to college with her older brother. Helene had been a giggly thirteen-year-old and was now a giggly eighteen-year-old. He'd taken her out a few times and had tolerated her company. Maybe he'd call on her later in the week, if he could find the time. . . .

John Tyler, the senior partner, stepped into the office, his florid face even redder from the weather. He stamped his feet, ridding them of snow, then tossed his coat over a chair. "I didn't forget our meeting. Congratulations, my boy, on landing the Chester account. That and the railroad fund are nice feathers in your cap.''

Stephen put the card away, then nodded, obviously pleased. John Tyler's approval was extremely important to his future. He indicated the other contracts.

''Some of the other things we've been working on are coming along nicely. I'm hoping to wrap everything up by the end of this quarter so we don't have any loose ends. By the way, were you able to get financials for the Magiotti agreement?''

John patted his leather bag. ''Right here. We have everything we need for this meeting. We should be able to finish the contract this afternoon.''

Stephen nodded, then glanced out the window once more as the lawyer rifled through his bag. The snow had dusted the walk leading to the law offices. A black splotch marred the virginal blanket on the second step. Looking closer, Stephen frowned.

''Who is that huddled beneath the window?''

John Tyler glanced out and saw a woman dressed in a tattered overcoat, shaking off the snow. His jowly face grew tighter and he sighed in exasperation.

''That's the beggar woman. She started showing up yesterday. I think she cleans one of the local offices. Filthy, ragged mess. A drunkard, I believe.'' His nose wrinkled distastefully as he followed Stephen's gaze. ''I told her to find another place to sit, but she keeps coming back. It doesn't create a good impression for the law firm.''

''Where is she from?''

''How the hell do I know? But she seems determined to stay there. I'm thinking about calling the police. I don't think our clients will like having to deal with her when they come to the office.''

Stephen glanced out once more. There was something pathetic about the way the woman hugged the wall, as if seeking shelter from the relentless snow. And the police were likely to arrest her. He didn't know much about the state of the Philadelphia jails, but he doubted if they had much to recommend them. "I'll go speak to her. Maybe I can get her to leave."

John shrugged. He recalled the stream of invectives the woman had hurled at him when he suggested she move. He suppressed a smile, picturing Stephen's reaction. Oh well, the young attorney would soon discover that some people were immune to his charm.

No matter how noble his motives.

She heard him coming before she saw him. His footsteps made soft crunching sounds on the snow, then he stopped within a few inches of her, radiating disapproval.

Elizabeth sighed. She'd thought she'd had her last encounter with the elderly lawyer, that he finally understood that she didn't intend to move, but apparently she was mistaken. Her eyes fell on his square-toed boots, then the immaculate crease in his trousers, past the dark greatcoat that cost more than she earned in an entire month, and finally to his face.

Her mouth dropped. It wasn't the older lawyer—that was for certain. This man was extraordinarily handsome and young. She saw that his hair, naturally wavy, sparkled with snow, and that his nose, finely cut and aristocratic, was beginning to redden. His jaw was firm and decisive, his eyes, a peculiar hazel, were bright and penetrating. But his mouth . . . Elizabeth almost smiled in return. His mouth was full and sensual, betraying everything that his stern face sought to hide.

"Madam, I'm sorry, but I must ask you to leave. You cannot stay here." He took a step forward, his nose wrinkling in repugnance as he smelled the gin. "Can I help you to a cab?"

Elizabeth fought a grin. Handsome, he might be, but she sensed an arrogance about him that needed a set-down. He obviously saw her the way most businessmen saw beggar people, as something less than human. Wielding her tattered black umbrella, she spoke almost cheerfully.

"I ain't moving nowhere." She managed a coarse, rough voice, and she wiped her nose with her sleeve before continuing. "This here's my block, and this is my seat. Now you can just go back inside your office where it's warm and leave me be."

"Madam," he continued, obviously losing patience. "There is a law against loitering. If you don't move, you will be arrested."

"Call the police." Elizabeth got to her feet, twirling the umbrella menacingly. "That will look just fine in the morning papers."

"Give me that. . . ." He reached for the umbrella, determined to rid her of the weapon. A tug-of-war ensued, Elizabeth struggling to maintain her property while he tried to disarm her. Success rewarded him a moment later when he seized the umbrella, but Elizabeth cried out and slipped on the steps, falling to the ground. There was a strange buzzing in her ears and a throbbing pain above her eye. Blackness smothered her and she fainted.

"My God . . . John!" Stephen reached for her while the other attorney raced down the stairs. He was sickened by the sight of blood on the snow as the woman seemed to lose consciousness. The older attorney grasped her feet while he took her arms, and together they managed to carry her up the steep steps to the reception area.

She weighed much less than he'd thought. Puzzled, Stephen wondered when she'd last eaten. In spite of the bulky coat he could tell that she had a small body and slender legs, which were visible when her coat fell open. Even the upper part of her body seemed amazingly slender, and he wondered how she managed to fight off illness and the cold.

"Mrs. Hudson, get some water with a splash of brandy. John, let's get her to the couch. We should call a doctor." Stephen barked out orders while the secretary, who stared in amazement, rushed to do his bidding.

John gave his young partner a worried glance as he placed her feet, clad in broken boots, on the brocade sofa. "This could be trouble. All we need is a lawsuit and we'd be hung out to dry."

"For Christ's sake, John, she's a beggar, not a lawyer. She wouldn't know—"

"I wouldn't count on it," the older man said with a sigh. "It's amazing how many people know all about lawsuits. It reminds me . . ."

The secretary returned with the brandy and water, and to Stephen's relief the woman's eyes opened and she stared around the room in confusion.

"Where am I?"

"Here, drink this." He handed her the glass, aware of the smell of gin that clung to her. He could scarcely see her face for the dirt, and her hands, clad in torn gloves, looked chapped and rough. "You'll soon feel much better."

Stephen glanced at John in confusion, but the older lawyer didn't seem to notice anything wrong. The woman had spoken in cultivated English, not in the coarse accent she'd used earlier. Puzzled, he watched as she delicately sipped the beverage, then shuddered at the taste of the brandy. Choking, she sat up as the liquor fought its way to her belly. She reacted as if she seldom imbibed. Gasping at the effect of the drink, she wiped her eyes, oblivious to the dirt, then she looked directly up at him for the first time.

"I've got to go."

They were beautiful. Stephen stared in amazement at the gray-blue eyes of the charwoman. Urgent and compelling, they were completely out of character with her slovenly appearance, almost as if they were someone else's eyes, someone that he would like to know. And up close she seemed so young, much younger than he'd originally taken her for. Mentally he shook himself.

"Stay and rest. We'll get you something to eat. Surely you must be hungry?" Although he didn't really believe in the threat of a lawsuit, Stephen knew it was a possibility. The charwoman seemed to know exactly what he was thinking, for a small smile came to her. He could have sworn he saw a twinkle in her eyes.

"Yes, I think I'd like that," Elizabeth answered, keeping the hoarse scowl to her voice. "And hot tea, if you have it. I takes it with me gin, you know."

The two men exchanged looks of disbelief, but the younger nodded to the secretary and the woman procured a tray. All of them watched in silence as the charwoman, oblivious to the elegant surroundings, placed her snow-covered boots on the table and loudly slurped her tea. When Stephen cleared his throat, appalled, she gave him a toothless grin, then belched.

Sometimes it just didn't pay to be a gentleman. And this seemed to be one of them.

Chapter Two

"Damned-fool notion for a woman, working for that paper! When will you use the brains the Good Lord gave you and give it up? You're wasting the best part of your life, you are!"

Elizabeth sighed, knowing what would follow. She'd tried not to make any noise when she' entered the two-story row house, but the door, which perpetually squeaked, today sounded like a chime. Her father had instantly glanced up from the floor where he was playing stones with his three younger children, and his ruddy face immediately scowled with disapproval.

"I was just saying that you should have been home long ago. Heathen paper. Good Lord, lass, what's happened to you?"

Elizabeth removed her coat and shrugged as if the matter were of little importance. "It's nothing, just a cut. I slipped on the steps."

"Nothing!" James Carey got to his feet and brushed aside the soft brown hair that fell on her forehead. "It's hurt you are. Nothing! Mrs. Carey, Lizzie's hurt! Bring a soft cloth!"

"I lost a tooth today, Lizzie." A little one tugged on her skirt, oblivious to the noise. "See?" His tiny fist held out a molar, then a cavernous mouth displayed the newly formed gap.

"I see." Elizabeth smiled as another child examined her cut, arguing with a brother.

"I saw it first. He's touching me! Stop it!"

"Timmy, leave your sister be." Elizabeth's mother brushed past the tumbling children, then frowned at her husband. "Don't preach at her, Jim. She knows what she wants. Let me see, Elizabeth." She gently touched her daughter's forehead, frowning at the cut.

"And this is it?" James indicated Elizabeth's forehead, already swollen and bruised. "This is what she wants? Lord, woman, it's almost Valentine's Day! Lizzie should be receiving flowers and candies, being courted with roses and lace. Not this!" Disdainfully he picked up Elizabeth's notebook and pencil. "You're telling me that she prefers this to a man who would keep her, give her wee ones, make her happy."

"Bosh!" Elizabeth took back her precious notebook as the other children inspected her injury with interest. She faced her father with the resignation of one who'd lost the same argument over and over. "Papa, you know I love my work. And I could slip anywhere. It doesn't mean—"

"What about that nice Sean Ryan? He calls for you at least once a week, but you're never here. You're too busy writing those news things. Now, it's not that I'm not proud of you. You know that. It's just that I want to see you find true happiness, and you won't find it scribbling away for that penny paper."

The children gathered closer, giggling in anticipation. Lizzie and their father had wonderful fights, each one better than the last. But tonight they were disappointed. Irene intervened with the calm authority that they all respected. "Jim, don't start on her now. Can't you see she's hurt? Come now, Lizzie, let's go up to bed. We don't want the brain fever to settle in."

Elizabeth smiled gratefully as her mother led her past her fuming father, up the staircase to the quiet comfort of her room. Her mother silently helped her remove her dress with its annoying bustles and stays, then she slid into her nightgown, sighing in relief as the warm fabric enveloped her chilled body.

"Thank you," Elizabeth said to her mother. "I really wasn't up to a brawl tonight."

Irene nodded, then pulled back the quilts. "It's only because he cares about you. He doesn't understand."

Elizabeth saw her mother's chapped hands, her hair prematurely gray, her eyes red from sewing and taking in washing for the wealthy. Her mother had always been in her corner, had defended her when her father's rantings had become too stern. As if by tacit agreement, her mother bought her pencils with her hard-earned laundry money when she was little, helped her write her stories as a child, even assisted her with her first news story for the *Record*. She alone understood her daughter's determination to have something better, and quietly assisted that effort.

"Do you think he ever will?" Elizabeth asked softly, aware of the conflicting emotions on her mother's face.

Irene shook her head. "He's from the old school. It frightens him to think you might wind up alone, a spinster. But because you've chosen a different path, doesn't mean you can't marry. You will have to find a special man, one who understands you." Irene helped Elizabeth into the bed. She gave her a kiss and smoothed away the bangs that fell on her forehead. "Good night, dear."

Elizabeth watched her mother go, a strange feeling settling within her. How could she possibly find a husband and marry? Most men never saw her as a romantic possibility. True, they liked her, befriended her, admired her work and her mind. But they always moved on to court the soft and sweet women who giggled appropriately, gazed at them with wide-eyed admiration, and fainted at the mention of reality.

Yet Valentine's Day was coming. Elizabeth frowned as she thought of the society stories she was covering, of the dances, the courtship rituals, the lace-covered cards and richly decorated boxes of sweets. Much as she loved her work, there was a part of her that wanted the same things, that longed for a man to treat her nicely, but it just wasn't possible. Good Lord, as her father would say, no man would tolerate a newspaper woman for a wife. And she just couldn't give it up, not yet.

There was too much she had to accomplish. And no one was worth that sacrifice.

"Christ, Stephen, what does this mean? That she'll be camped out there forever?" John Tyler scowled as the charwoman assumed residence outside their window for the third day in a row. "I gave her some money to leave. Ten dollars! But she didn't move. She just grinned that toothless smirk, thanked me very kindly, and stayed."

"I don't think we have much choice," Stephen said thoughtfully. "We can't force her to go."

"But we have Douglass Colley coming for a meeting today! He's one of our most prestigious clients. How are we going to explain her presence?"

Stephen shrugged. "Maybe it won't be such a big deal. I'm sure Mr. Colley has seen beggars before. Surely he couldn't think it was our fault if one chooses to sit there."

"I don't like it," the older attorney continued. "Especially after that fall. What if something else happens? Damn it, we pay taxes . . . don't we have a right to our own property? There's got to be a way."

"Well, if you think of it, let me know. I really feel you're blowing this out of proportion. After all, she's just sitting

there. She isn't threatening anyone, or doing any damage."
Stephen tried to sound convincing, but even to his own ears
his reasoning was weak. He glanced outside. The woman's
presence *was* disturbing. And there were so many contra-
dictions about her. She hadn't always been poor—Stephen
would have bet his life on that, remembering when she had
spoken. So how did a woman descend to such a level that
she needed his steps as her bed?

"She may not do any physical damage, but she could hurt
our business," John remarked. "And what if she gets sick
or something out there? Surely there has to be help for these
people. Some kind of charity organization in the city." He
looked at Stephen and brightened. "You attend enough of
those functions. Why don't you find someone to help her?"

Stephen glanced sharply at the senior member of the firm.
John smiled benignly, then patted him on the back. "I have
every confidence that you can handle this, my boy. I'll leave
everything in your capable hands."

"Thanks," Stephen said dryly. As he glanced out the
window once more he realized that for some inexplicable
reason, this woman moved him. And John was right. There
had to be help somewhere in the city for women like her.

Now all he had to do was find it.

"I'm sorry, my son, but there's nothing we can do."

Stephen stared in disbelief as Sister Grace Madeline
wiped her slender hands on her robes and sat down beside
him. Inside this converted church basement, soup bubbled
constantly on the stove while a coffeepot spewed brown
liquid into the fire. The other nuns worked unceasingly,
their chapped hands handing out coffee and soup and an
occasional piece of stale bread to the poor and destitute.

"She is welcome to come here if she needs food or a bed

for the night, but otherwise there is nothing we can do. We have very little money, and few people willing to help.''

"But aren't there jobs? Can't these people work?''

The nun gave him a penetrating look and answered sharply: "I believe you are aware that the city is in a financial crisis. When such occurs, the mills have less work, the builders stop making new houses, the grocers demand payment. The unskilled workers, such as the immigrants, are hurt the most by these events. Surely as a businessman you understand these things better than I. I can only explain what I see.''

Stephen flushed, feeling as if his hands had been slapped with a ruler. Still he persisted. "What about the charities? Isn't money donated for these causes?''

Her look was even more chiding. "The poor are ignored unlike more fashionable causes such as the opera company. We are surviving on the pennies we collect at Sunday Mass.'' She gave him a stern look. "I don't suppose you have a few coppers you could spare?''

Somehow he found himself digging into his pocket and giving the woman his money. Guilt, he thought, good old-fashioned guilt. Relieved of his money, he walked back toward the law office, aware that he was behind schedule and still hadn't come up with a solution to their problem. If the newspapers ever got hold of this story, there would be no end to it. CHARWOMAN THROWS LAW OFFICE INTO A TIZZY. It was just the kind of thing that the *Ledger* would eat up, and the *Record* wouldn't be far behind.

He returned to his office, giving the woman a wide berth as he climbed the steps. He had wasted enough time on this and he was behind in his work. Scowling, he went into his office and closed the door, then tried to concentrate on the contracts that still adorned his desk.

A beggar woman. With a cultured voice. He forced

himself to concentrate, and to forget that she had the most incredible eyes he'd ever seen.

Elizabeth giggled as the young attorney stalked inside and slammed the door. She knew what was bothering him. Something odd had transpired between them when she'd looked directly into his eyes. She didn't know what it was or how to handle it, yet a strange fluttering began in her stomach every time she thought of their encounter.

Yet the story was turning out great. Even Horace had grudgingly admitted that when she turned in the first draft the previous night. He had read it with open admiration, commending her on her writing ability. Elizabeth had blushed, but was very pleased.

And she had come to know some of the other poor men and women who lived the way she pretended. Tears welled up in her eyes when she had spoken with tin-armed Willy and learned that he hadn't been able to find work for over three years due to his handicap. And Clara, the woman who begged on the steps of City Hall . . . Clara had long since lost her senses and trusted no one. Elizabeth found that by leaving a crust of bread or a cup of hot tea near the pavement, eventually, like a shy sparrow, Clara would take the food, then scurry away to a corner to eat in silence.

Then there were men like John, who had turned his begging into a kind of a business. John collected old books and newspapers that he found inside the waste bins of the City Tavern and the homes of the rich. These he positioned all around him, selling them to the passersby for a few pennies apiece. It was enough to provide him with spending money, and occasionally a new pair of shoes. The shoes he displayed to Elizabeth with shining eyes, more proud of his accomplishment than if he'd found a twenty-dollar gold piece.

Yet for the most part these people were invisible. Elizabeth scribbled inside her notebook, noting that they dressed the same color as the granite, as if wanting to blend, chameleon-like, into their surroundings. They didn't want to call attention to themselves, for there was danger in doing that. Instead, as unobtrusively as possible, they just wanted to survive, drifting in and out of the city's consciousness like living ghosts.

She grinned. Stephen Brooks may not like her presence on his nice clean steps, but that was unfortunate. She had a job to do, and she wasn't about to disappear.

Not by a long shot.

"I can't believe that in the entire city of Philadelphia there isn't any real help for this woman." Stephen Brooks refilled his punch glass and turned to the silver-haired society woman beside him. They were at the final planning meeting for the St. Valentine's dance. Women in beautiful silk dresses and satin bustles glided beneath the gaslights while the elegant gentlemen of the city stood apart in their dapper-looking suits, smoking cigars and sipping brandy. Champagne flowed freely, and a serving woman offered trays filled with punch glasses and sugared almonds. All of the important people of the city attended these meetings, and this one was no exception.

"I've tried everything," Stephen continued, his voice betraying his frustration. "Almshouses. The Mission for Rescuing Fallen Women. The Franklin Home for Reformation of Inebriates. All of them had the same story. They have too many people in need right now, and unless she does something violent, there is nothing they can do."

Flora Steadman nodded sympathetically. "I saw that wretched woman. Filthy, isn't she? It is amazing that she is allowed to wander in such a state."

Stephen looked at her for a long moment. Something about the woman's attitude bothered him, but before he could react, Flora smiled and held his arm. "It is good of you to be so concerned. In fact, some people are wondering just why you are." When Stephen sent her a sharp look, she continued in the same sweet tone of voice. "Well, you have to admit it does look odd for a man of your station to be so worried about a beggar woman."

"She is camped on my steps," Stephen said, feeling the blood rush to his face.

"Yes, I know." Flora sighed as if tired of the conversation. She brightened as she spotted two beautifully gowned young women sampling the tea cakes. "Come, you must speak to my daughters, Emily and Helene. I believe you are acquainted."

Stephen rolled his eyes but said nothing as he was forcibly escorted to the reception table. He had to forget the beggar woman anyway. Lately she'd been taking up too much of his time and his thoughts. He smiled charmingly as Flora stopped before two young women who blushed and giggled uncontrollably.

"Stephen, you know my daughters. Emily has just come out, while I believe you and Helene are old friends. Say hello, girls."

The two young women broke into renewed laughter. Emily, sixteen and pretty in a frothy sort of way, looked embarrassed and refused to meet his eyes while Helene extended her hand with the confidence of a woman who is sure of her charm.

"Stephen." Helene's voice was soft and tinkling. "I was hoping to see you here. Did you get my card?"

He stared at her, uncertain for a moment as to what she was talking about, then he recalled the lacy valentine that he'd received just a few days ago.

"Yes, I did. I'm sorry I forgot to acknowledge it. That was very nice of you."

Helene giggled, then looked flirtatiously at him once more. She was pretty, Stephen realized, prettier than he remembered. With blond hair and soft blue eyes, she had classic features and an elegant carriage that went far to offset the fact that she'd never entertained an original thought in her eighteen years. Maybe he expected too much, he thought. She wore a rose satin gown that enhanced her coloring, and she fluttered behind a lace fan. Forcing aside his impatience, he indicated the gathering.

"Seems like a nice event. I think they're planning for a dance."

Helene nodded, obviously relieved that he'd brought up the subject. "The St. Valentine's dance. You *are* going, aren't you?"

The question was rich with invitation. Stephen toyed with his glass, then shrugged. Why shouldn't he ask her? After all, Helene met all of his qualifications for a woman. She would definitely be an asset to him. He reached into his pocket and withdrew his book, flipping through the pages until he reached February 14. "It doesn't look as though I'm occupied. . . ."

Laughter broke through his thoughts, bright and full, unhindered by social conventions. Stephen glanced up and saw a woman standing nearby, surrounded by men. She certainly wasn't anyone he knew. About five feet three inches tall and with a dusting of freckles across her face, she looked decidedly Irish and brimming with amusement. Her eyes met his, and for a moment he felt an odd confusion, as if he'd seen this woman before. There was something about her. . . .

"Who is that?" Stephen asked.

It was Flora who answered, her voice thick with disapproval. "It is the press," she whispered, as if accusing the woman of being a harlot. "That is Elizabeth Carey!"

Her daughters gasped, but Emily glanced with interest at the young reporter. "Isn't she the one who wrote that story about the suffragettes?"

"Yes." Flora sniffed, then spoke sharply to the girls. "I hope neither of you reads that trash! It isn't good for a woman to read too much. It gives her ideas."

"What is she doing here?" Helene asked, trying to recapture Stephen's attention.

"I don't know," Stephen said thoughtfully, putting down his glass. "Probably writing a society piece. I'll ask if she disturbs you."

"Please. The organization needs publicity, but only of a certain kind. And Elizabeth Carey! Wanting the vote, as if we didn't have enough to worry about! It's just . . . unfeminine is what it is!" Flora gathered her girls closer beside her while Stephen approached the woman.

"Miss Carey, do you have an invitation to this meeting?" he asked quietly, ignoring the disappointed glances of her admirers.

Her face lifted and she looked directly at him. She was younger than he'd thought and surprisingly different. He had pictured a martinet, devoid of femininity, but Elizabeth was dressed prettily in a bustled emerald gown that complemented her coloring, and her chestnut hair was beautifully upswept. She reminded him of his own mother, a woman who believed in the value of education and insisted on completing college when such a notion did not enjoy great popularity. Elizabeth had an ink spot on her sleeve and a pencil poised over the notebook she held, but Stephen noticed that her practical manner didn't detract from her appearance in the least. In fact, she looked damned interesting, and her expression clearly indicated a vital and intelligent mind that enjoyed every odd moment of life. She didn't seem at all upset by the encounter but acted as if she'd expected it, and she gave her audience a shrug before returning her laughing gaze to him.

"No, I'm afraid I don't. It seems they must have forgotten the Careys when making out the guest list." Her audience chuckled appreciatively, then Elizabeth shrugged again. "But as the press, I don't need one. Thank you anyway."

The inflection in her voice was unmistakable, amused and mocking, but with a sense of humor. Yet there was something else about her, something that compelled him. She reminded him of . . . the beggar woman. Stephen shook his head. It couldn't be. Yet even as he admired Elizabeth Carey's figure as she retreated to accept a glass of punch, he couldn't stop thinking of the similarities. Her height. Her weight. Her voice. And most important . . .

"Good God!"

She had hardly returned when he looked into her eyes and cursed himself for being ten times a fool. He couldn't ever forget those eyes. They gazed at him with a mixture of amusement and disbelief even as he mentally peeled away the beggar woman's disguise. It was all there. The same smirk. The same knowing grin. The tiny cut on her forehead. And the eyes that were his conscience. They bored into him, reminding him that nothing was ever what it seemed.

"I beg your pardon?" Elizabeth said, though she couldn't keep the laughter from her voice.

"It is you! You are the beggar woman!"

Chapter Three

He hauled her away from the others, ignoring her splashing punch glass and her squeal of outrage. When he'd gotten her to the outer perimeter of the room, he let her go and glared at her. "I know I'm right. My God, how could I have been so stupid! It was you posing outside as that . . . charwoman!"

Elizabeth laughed, seeing his incredulous expression. "I confess, it was me. I thank you for helping an old drunkard into your office. It was so kind of you."

Stephen was about to explode. He saw her laughter, then winced as he thought of all the time and effort he'd expended to find her a home. Worse still was the guilt she had made him feel. My God, if he'd have only known!

"Just answer me one question." He could barely contain his outrage. "Why?"

"Why what?" Elizabeth asked innocently. "Why am I doing the story? Or why was I dressed as a beggar? Or why your steps?"

"All of the above."

Elizabeth shrugged. "You've seen it yourself. I've heard you've been asking around town. There really isn't enough help for these people. I'm trying to change that, and so is the *Record*. Rittenhouse Square is the logical place to start. There's no sense dramatizing the story to those who already live it."

"I see. So you didn't single me out purposely. My steps were simply . . . convenient." When she nodded, wide-eyed, he grew even more angry. "And how long do you plan to continue this charade?"

"Don't worry." Elizabeth smiled sweetly. "The story is almost done. You won't see me adorning your steps again. I promise."

The twinkle in those incredible eyes didn't help. Stephen nodded, somewhat relieved to discover that she would soon be gone. But he still didn't entirely trust her. "So, if I understand you correctly, you thought to use me as a tool to write your yellow-journalism rubbish. And tonight?" He indicated the society crowd. "Is this more of the same?"

"Not at all." Elizabeth shook her head, then paged through her small notebook. "I do have other stories to cover, you know. Important stuff, for the society column. Your name does occur rather frequently, however. Let's see . . . the Benefit for the Walnut Trees of Philadelphia, the Society to Preserve the Billiards Club, the reception for the First Federal Bank . . . Have I missed anything of importance?"

He walked away from her, furious. He could hear her laughter behind him, like the tinkling of a bell, and knew it was at his expense. Downing another drink, he forced himself to concentrate on what a colleague was saying and not on the soft chuckles and conversation of the woman behind him.

Elizabeth Carey had to be the most infuriating woman he'd ever met.

Thank God she'd soon be out of his life.

Elizabeth couldn't help the laughter that bubbled within her. Stephen was so handsome and so charming that it almost seemed a shame that she'd chosen his steps to sit on. Still, in her mind, he was representative of what was wrong in the city.

She was sorry the story was almost finished. Elizabeth realized that she would miss her encounters with the attorneys, especially Stephen. There was something about the way he looked at her that made her blood run thicker. True, he had every reason in the world to be furious at her, knowing that he'd been tricked, but there was an attraction between them that she sensed and didn't have the slightest idea what to do about.

Elizabeth sighed. There was no sense thinking about it anyway. Stephen Brooks was from the Main Line. He had everything: education, money, a prestigious job, a good family, and a position in society. The debutantes were infatuated with him, the wealthy matrons encouraged him, and their fathers looked on him favorably. Stephen Brooks would marry well, then continue his success.

She was a newspaper woman from the wrong side of town, and she didn't have any of those things. Her education had been borrowed from the *Record* and had been reinforced by experience. An original thinker, Horace had called her, but Elizabeth didn't have any choice. All of her ideas came from what she saw, and this gave her stories a freshness that others lacked. She had learned to be independent, to make her own way, to take risks, and to live life to the fullest.

In short, she was everything a society gentleman would avoid. And Stephen Brooks was no exception.

"This is incredible, Elizabeth. I've got to hand it to you. With every installment you just get better." Horace Bierce put the story down and shook Elizabeth's hand, his gruff face beaming with pride. "You've got everything here. Human interest. Social issues. Hard-hitting facts. Possible solutions. I really think you may start an uproar within the city."

Elizabeth blushed with pleasure. "Do you think so?"

"No doubt about it," Horace replied, tapping his pipe against the wall. He relit it and puffed thoughtfully. "In fact, there's only one thing that might make it stronger. It occurred to me as I read that the most interesting part of the piece is the young attorney. His reaction to finding a beggar adorning his steps, then his frustration upon not being able to procure help for this woman."

"Do you mean Stephen?" Elizabeth asked, wondering if her own interest in the lawyer was obvious.

The smoke made a wreath around his face when he glanced up, a small smile crossing its center. Elizabeth braced herself. She'd seen that look before. "I've got an idea," Horace said, chuckling gleefully as he rubbed his hands together. "I want you to do another piece, a sidebar, if you will, covering the story from the attorney's viewpoint. I want everything—names, dates, you know. I want to know his background, who his friends are, what they think of him. It will be sensational."

Elizabeth gulped. What Horace said made sense—even she couldn't deny it. And it would make fabulous reading. Still . . . she thought of Stephen's face when he'd recognized her. He hadn't taken too kindly to being fooled before. She had a feeling that he would take even less kindly to being featured by name in a piece of "yellow-journalism rubbish," as he called it.

"Are you sure you want to do this?" Elizabeth questioned softly. "He is an attorney, remember. The last thing this paper needs is a lawsuit."

"On the contrary." Horace grinned. "A lawsuit would be perfect. He would play right into our hands, since any trial would be public news. And as the defendant, the *Record* would have the jump on all the other papers."

Elizabeth nodded. The story would be sensational. But every time she thought of Stephen's face . . . She just couldn't think about it now.

"I know you're right," Elizabeth admitted. "And it is definitely the right thing for the paper."

"Good." Horace nodded. "Then it's settled. And with you covering the society pieces, you are in the ideal position to get information about Stephen Brooks. There are several more Valentine's Day events coming up that you are covering."

Elizabeth groaned. "I will. But I need to be in costume once more." When Horace raised his bushy brows, she hastened to explain. "Tin-armed Willy has disappeared. As a reporter, none of the beggars will tell me anything. But in disguise I can at least make sure he is all right."

Horace frowned. "He may have just moved to another location."

"Yes, but I just want to make sure. The others will help. They seem to know exactly what's going on in all parts of the city and where each of them has taken up residence. It's almost proprietary, the way they claim street corners. Still, living like that is dangerous. Willy may be sick or hurt."

"Be careful," Horace said. "It's dangerous for you as well."

"I will," Elizabeth promised. "Just one more time, and I'll put the makeup away forever."

Twilight descended as Elizabeth resumed her perch on the granite steps. She could see the business people rushing home, hear the shrill whistles of the men for a cab, and smell the acrid smoke that a thousand fires spewed into the night. The steps felt like ice beneath her, and she struggled to tuck her battered coat around her slender body in a feeble attempt to keep out the cold.

It was a miserable night. The gaslights gleamed with frozen halos as a thick mist settled on the city, making her bones ache with the chill. Sniffling, Elizabeth reached inside her pocket and fished out a ragged handkerchief, then wiped her reddened nose.

She couldn't stay out too long. She could tell that already, and although she wanted to help Willy, she wouldn't jeopardize her own health. Yet the snow that had fallen earlier had driven the beggars into shelter, and only now would they quietly emerge, looking for food and a bed for the night.

Shoving the handkerchief back into her pocket, Elizabeth thought of the crippled man. She had become familiar with Willy's ways and knew that if everything was all right, he would make an appearance just after sundown and beg from the city people who were on their way home. It was the most lucrative time of day for Willy, and he often collected enough coins to provide a warm meal and a pint of gin. And if he didn't show up . . .

She couldn't think of that now. Her fingers ached from the holes in her gloves and she rubbed them together in an attempt to stay warm. She would wait one more half hour. A smattering of light shone from the attorney's office behind her, not much but enough to illuminate the square. She was just about to give up when she saw Willy's familiar form appear on the church steps, and with a glad cry she rushed down the cobbled street, her feet slipping on the stones.

"No!" Elizabeth's breath froze in the air as she saw a darkly clad ruffian grab Willy and fling him against the ground. He was joined by another, and Elizabeth gasped helplessly as Willy tried to fight back. With one arm mangled he was like a turtle on its back, squirming and frustrated as the two men rummaged through his coat.

"I told you he'd got money. They all do, these beggars. Look, here's a couple of greenbacks as well."

"No, that's mine," Willy croaked, but the one man hit him contemptuously while the other laughed, a horrible sound that echoed in the cold night.

"See what he's got in his pants pockets."

Without thinking, Elizabeth rushed forward and yanked at the man who held Willy. Startled, the thug turned toward her, but seeing her pathetic figure, he laughed, then flung his hand back, knocking her against the wall. Dimly Elizabeth was aware of Willy shouting, of the other man running, of footsteps on the granite, then of the intercession of strangers. Gathering her wits, she clambered to her feet and gasped in astonishment as she saw Stephen Brooks with one of the thugs at his feet.

"Summon the police!" he shouted to a wide-eyed pedestrian, who hastened to do his bidding. He rubbed his knuckles as if he'd been hurt, then glared at the other passersby, who hastened to leave. There was something so formidable in his manner that when he turned to Elizabeth and recognition dawned, she froze.

"You! I should have known. Haven't you the sense God gave an ant? Stay right where you are." Before she could retort, he indicated Willy. "The police may need to ask a few questions. And I have a few of my own."

Elizabeth nodded, shivering in the cold. She saw the beggar fumble around on the ground, and without looking at

Stephen, she went to Willy's assistance. The poor man rose unsteadily, then gave her a rueful smile as he rubbed his injured arm.

"Gave them a run for the money, didn't we, Lizzie? Aye, but your friend here was a help. Thought they had me for a moment."

"Don't talk." Elizabeth's eyes filled as she saw the pain on Willy's face. Reaching to the wet ground, she found his flask and brought it to his lips. "Here. Maybe this will help."

Willy drank the liquor gratefully, then put it back in his pocket. "I've got to go. Can't have police . . . they put me away."

"You can't leave," Stephen said, still watching the groaning thug on the street. "The police will need to hear—"

"Sorry, lad," Willy said, wrapping his coat around him. "I can't stay. Thanks." He sped off, disappearing into the shadows.

Stephen swore under his breath as the police arrived and loaded their quarry into the wagon. A ruddy-faced officer approached, giving Elizabeth an odd look, then turned with more respect to the young attorney.

"I understand there's been a mishap." He jerked his thumb toward the body in the wagon. "Bad lot, that one. We've been looking for him."

Stephen nodded. "He's working with some other man. I saw them from my window. They seem to be preying on the beggars and the poor immigrants. I think you need to keep a closer watch."

The policeman gave him an incredulous look, and Elizabeth could almost read his mind. He'd only answered the summons because of Stephen's name. Nodding, the policeman knew better than to voice his opinions, and giving Elizabeth a curious look once more, he turned and retreated to the wagon.

"Will do, sir. Good night, Mr. Brooks. And take care of that cut."

It was then that Elizabeth noticed that Stephen had been hurt in the scuffle. As the wagon pulled away she saw him touch the corner of his lip, where a trickle of blood formed. She gasped, reaching for her handkerchief, but before she could withdraw the flimsy cloth, he grabbed her arm and hauled her toward the office.

"And now I want to hear what the hell you think you're doing."

Looking up into his face, Elizabeth saw that he was more than angry. He was furious.

Chapter Four

Elizabeth thought it wiser not to comment when Stephen led her firmly into the building, then slammed the door shut behind them. Broken icicles tinkled to the steps outside, but he ignored the sound and propelled her into his office.

"I suggest you make yourself more presentable." He indicated the washbowl, his voice barely controlled. "I don't think you intend to play the charwoman anymore this evening."

Elizabeth was about to protest, but his glare silenced her and she decided she should do what he said. She dipped the cloth into the bowl and washed her face, removing the dirt and the makeup, until her own complexion shone forth. Then, seeing his glance, she removed the gin-drenched coat and waited.

Practically growling, Stephen looked into a small mirror above the washstand and grimaced. He touched the bleeding corner of his mouth and winced, then wiped away the blood with a cloth. His manner was rough and angry, as if with himself as well as her, and he only seemed to damage his lip more.

"Let me." Elizabeth took the cloth, ignoring his scathing look, and walked outside to the icy steps.

"Where do you think you're going?"

Ignoring his tone of voice, she returned a moment later,

the cloth packed with snow. His eyes locked with hers, obviously not trusting her, but his swollen mouth helped her to keep her nerve and approach him confidently.

"I was just getting some snow for the cut. It's swelling. The ice will bring it down and clean it."

He snarled. That was the only word for it as Elizabeth pressed the cloth against his mouth. Stiffening in pain, he narrowed his eyes even more and she realized that his cold anger was even more intimidating than all her father's rumblings.

"Ouch! Damn it!" he muttered. "Give me that. This is all your fault." He tried to snatch the cloth away, but Elizabeth held on to it tightly.

"No one asked you to rescue me," she said firmly, ignoring the hot anger in his eyes. "You could have stayed in your safe little office."

"And let you get killed or worse." It was hard to maintain his anger with her so close and so . . . solicitous. From this perspective he could see past her soft mouth that for now wasn't laughing, past the ridiculous nose, right into those incredible eyes. They seemed bottomless, luminous and changing, as fascinating as the woman. For some reason he grew even more annoyed. "I should have stayed inside, but I thought it might have been you. Would have served you right. What kind of woman are you anyway, dressed like that, and taking every kind of risk? Good God, don't you realize what could have happened to you?"

"It was for Willy," Elizabeth protested. She refused to let go of the compress and kept the cloth pressed against his skin, removing it occasionally to press a new square of the material on the injury. "He'd disappeared. I couldn't find out anything as the reporter, so I looked for him as the charwoman. I didn't think . . ." Her voice trailed off as he continued to glare at her.

"No, that's the problem. You never do. If I didn't know better, I'd think you were sent deliberately to ruin my life. Ouch!"

Elizabeth gazed at him innocently. "You know why I'm doing what I'm doing."

"Yes. I know. For the betterment of the world." He looked at her quizzically, as if seeing her as a real person for the first time. "Don't you have any family? A suitor? Who lets you get away with this? Doesn't any man care about you?"

He was getting too close to the truth. Elizabeth felt the color rise to her cheeks and hated him for it. Involuntarily she thought of the pretty women that surrounded him at the meeting the previous night, and she couldn't help but compare herself unfavorably. She snatched back the cloth. "Look, if you hate me that much, then I'll go—"

His hand caught her wrist, preventing her from leaving. He looked surprised at her words and answered quietly, almost apologetically: "I never said I hated you. In fact, I sort of admire you. I just wondered why you don't have some protection."

Dumbfounded, Elizabeth stared at him, realizing that he was sincere. Where other men were intimidated by her work, he admired her. It was hard to believe, but it was true. "My father doesn't approve of the newspaper business," she explained slowly. "He doesn't know that I'm doing this."

"My God." His expression turned incredulous. "Then you mean that all the time you've been writing this story, dressing up as the beggar woman, no one even knew?"

"My editor did," Elizabeth said. "And Willy. He promised to look after me. I knew he wouldn't shirk his duty. That's why I was so concerned when he disappeared." She took a deep breath, then said what she'd wanted to say for the past half hour. "Thank you. You may have saved my life."

"You're welcome."

His eyes met hers and held her gaze for a brief moment that seemed like an eternity. Elizabeth was stunned by the warm understanding she saw. It was as if his defenses were gone, punched away, as it were, by the ruffian's fist. A dim recognition grew within her that she had made some of this difference. He had come out, not because of some altercation he'd heard from his office, but because he was worried about her.

Suddenly they both seemed aware that he was still holding her hand. He was almost caressing it, his fingers warm and sensuous as they traced hers. Quickly he let it drop, then ran his hand through his hair as if distracted.

"I suppose you need a ride home." He glanced outside at the velvety blackness, which was barely illuminated by the gas lamps.

"I can find my own way," Elizabeth began, but at his glare, forced down a smile. "A ride would help tremendously."

"Fine. I'll call my carriage. It's time I went home myself. As it is, I missed my seven-thirty meeting." He reached for her coat and, to Elizabeth's surprise, helped her into it. He didn't even cringe at the smell of the gin, but simply fetched his own coat and started for the door.

"Are you coming?"

Elizabeth nodded, swallowing hard. It was a long ride home to the Irish quarter and she would be alone, in a carriage, with Stephen Brooks.

God give her strength.

* * *

The clomp of the horses' hooves on the street was the only sound that broke the silence in the carriage. The drive through the well-to-do neighborhoods of the city into the poorer sections seemed endless. Even the wheels were quiet as they sliced through the newly fallen snow.

Elizabeth shivered as she stared straight ahead, not daring to look at the man beside her. Stephen saw her wrap her gin-sodden cloak more firmly around her and tuck her hands inside the enormous pockets. In the dim light of the carriage, she could still pass for a charwoman, but up close, any resemblance was impossible. Devoid of the mud and makeup, her face positively glowed. Her slightly tilted nose was red from the cold but attractive like a kitten's. And her eyes, easily her most remarkable feature, glittered with intelligence and humor.

Stephen frowned, aware of the implication of his thoughts. God, she'd taken a terrible risk that night, and obviously this wasn't the first time. She'd dressed as a beggar at least three times that he knew of, courting disaster each time. And all for the sake of a story. He wanted to feel superior to her for that, yet he couldn't, for her motive could almost be called noble.

If he had any doubt about her sincerity, her actions this night dispelled them. It was only concern for Willy that brought her out into the cold and made her don her costume once more. The fact that she'd risked her own life barely seemed to matter to her—she was worried about a friend, and if the friend happened to be a ragman who had disappeared, he was still a friend.

She was easily the most remarkable woman he'd ever met. Stephen couldn't take his eyes from her. She stirred something within him that bothered him. Elizabeth Carey had spelled trouble from the first time he'd laid eyes on her, and he had a feeling that it wasn't about to end.

"Are you cold?" he questioned softly as she shivered again.

Elizabeth nodded, but fished inside her coat with a grin. "I can have a swig of me gin, you know."

"I have a better idea," he said dryly. He reached beneath them and withdrew a lap robe, spreading it over her knees and legs. Elizabeth looked at him in surprise, but he shrugged and indicated the road. "We have a ways to go yet, and I don't want you getting ill."

She nodded, but something about their close proximity seemed to disturb her as well as him. She was careful not to touch him in any way, and when his hand accidentally brushed hers as he spread out the lap robe, he noticed her slight shiver. That was interesting, and for the first time since they'd entered the coach, he wondered if she felt the same attraction for him that he did for her. Ridiculous, he told himself, remembering her surrounded by men at the meeting. Elizabeth Carey was well-known throughout the city and spent most of her time in the company of men. He had no doubt that she had plenty of callers and wasn't interested in him in the slightest. Still . . . he couldn't help noticing the trembling of her mouth.

"Elizabeth." He broke the awkward silence once more. "I'm sorry I've been so curt with you. It's just that I was worried about what could have happened to you, out there alone. I didn't mean to shout at you."

She nodded once again, this time more carefully, as if really listening to his words.

"I also think we've gotten off on the wrong foot. I really would like us to be friends. Good friends."

"You would?" Elizabeth turned to him, incredulous.

"Yes," he answered, puzzled. She'd moved closer to him, so close he could see right into those bottomless eyes, and could touch that remarkable hair if he only reached up. . . . Good God, did she know what she was doing to him?

"Your . . . approval would help a good deal," Elizabeth said guiltily, her beautiful eyes softening. "It would make the story that much easier."

"Then I'm glad." He didn't understand what this had to do with some story about the beggar woman, but he didn't care. For the first time since he'd known her, they were facing each other, not as antagonists, but as two people attracted to each other and alone together.

His breath caught in the back of his throat as she smiled at him. She looked so innocent, so damned charming, and so different from what he'd expected that he couldn't help the way he felt, nor what happened next. Without forethought he leaned closer to her and kissed her, his mouth barely brushing hers.

Her eyes closed and she sighed. He heard a breathless little sound in the back of her throat, and to his amazement he recognized it as one of desire. Elizabeth Carey, famous reporter, apparently felt something for him . . . the thought was intoxicating. He deepened the kiss, feeling the warmth seeping over him, drugging his senses, making him want her the way he'd never wanted any giggling debutante. Logic meant nothing; reason was just a word. His blood positively pounded in his veins, and for the first time in his adult life, he lost all control. He pulled her closer, forgetting his injured lip, wanting nothing more than to taste the hot satin of her mouth. Suddenly he cried out in pain as the throbbing returned with unbearable sharpness.

"What's wrong?" As if recovering from a deep sleep,

Elizabeth stared at him in confusion as he retreated quickly, then fumbled for his handkerchief.

"I forgot . . . my cut." He pressed the cloth to his face, then looked at her with such chagrin that she broke into laughter.

"I'm sorry. Does it hurt?" She attempted to help him, aware of his embarrassment, but her eyes danced with amusement.

"Yes," he snapped, obviously humiliated, but within a few moments the humorous side of the situation struck him and he began to chuckle as well. "Ouch." He replaced the cloth again and glared at her accusingly as the pain increased. "It hurts when I laugh."

The carriage pulled up to the row house and the two of them, helpless with laughter, almost stumbled out as the coachman found the door. "I really am sorry." Elizabeth tried to sound sincere, but her mirth broke out, making the coachman scratch his head as his overly serious employer joined her.

"Get out of here. I'll see you soon, all right?" he called as she walked up the steps toward the forbidding door.

"All right." Elizabeth grinned, wiping the tears from her eyes. She laughed again as he reentered the coach, the cloth still pressed against his mouth.

Stephen shrugged as the carriage rumbled away. It may not have been the most graceful wooing he'd ever done, but it was a step in the right direction. Elizabeth hadn't rejected his passion.

And that, in his mind, more than made up for the rest.

Elizabeth entered the row house and closed the door behind her with a sigh. She couldn't wipe the grin off her face and didn't even want to try.

If anyone had told her how the past twenty-four hours would end up, she'd have said they were out of their mind. But Stephen Brooks, the up-and-coming Philadelphia attorney, wanted to be friends with her. She made him laugh, when she sensed that he seldom laughed, especially at himself. And when she thought about that kiss . . .

The color rose in her face, but she also experienced a delicious sense of excitement, the same excitement she'd felt when his lips touched hers. Good God, was it possible that she really meant something to him? It seemed impossible, and yet the facts were there. Like any good reporter, she knew how to piece together a story, and all of her instincts told her she was on track.

Taking off the gin-drenched coat, she stuffed it in a broom closet and glanced around the house. Her heart sank. Although her father had tried to keep up the repair of the house and it was immaculately clean, it was still poor. Her mother's lace shawl bravely covered the back of a sofa that had worn through, a simple vase bore the signs of mended cracks. The wooden floors had long since lost their sheen and bore testimony to the dozens of little shoes that marched across its surface. Although they lived better than most of their neighbors, they were still in Kensington, which was a far cry from the Main Line.

He couldn't possibly see her as an equal. The only reason he could want her was . . . color inflamed her face and the kiss in the carriage took on a new meaning. Although she hadn't been courted by many men, she knew that most did not attempt to take liberties until well into the courtship, and even then they were firmly rebuffed. No lady allowed such things to happen or, worse, openly encouraged them! No wonder he had been so bold. She'd practically swept him into her arms herself.

Her throat grew tight. Elizabeth forced herself to face facts. There was no way Stephen Brooks could be interested in her, the daughter of a good man, but a shopkeeper. She didn't live in the fashionable part of town, she wasn't invited to the fancy teas and receptions, she hadn't gone to college or associated with society people. Why did she waste a minute feeling guilty for writing that story about him? She was a newspaper woman, a reporter, for God's sake. Stephen Brooks would go on to marry a woman of his milieu.

She was a fool to think anything else.

"Lizzie, darlin'. Is that you?"

She wiped her eyes quickly, not wanting her father to see that she had nearly made a fool of herself. "Yes. I just got home. It was a late night at the paper."

"So I see." James gave his daughter a searching look, with an odd smile playing on his face. "And who did you get a ride home with? Now, now, don't be fooling me. I looked out me window and saw that fancy carriage outside, and a young man escorting you."

Elizabeth turned away, embarrassed, but her father chuckled lightly. "It's not angry with you that I am, but I don't want you keeping things from me. So you've got a gentleman caller. It seems he is well-to-do from the look of him."

Elizabeth cringed. Her father would be relentless now, especially if he thought her would-be husband had money. She had to nip this in the bud. "No, Papa, he isn't a caller. He's . . . a resource, you might say. Horace wants me to feature Stephen Brooks in a story. Unfortunately, that means that I'll have to spend some time in his company."

"Ah." James's face fell, but a moment later he brightened. "Well, surely after seeing the man awhile, he might get to know you. You're not a bad-looking girl, Lizzie, especially when you want to be. Maybe with a bit of that perfume and a new dress . . ."

"That man will never be anything to me but a story," Elizabeth said firmly. "Not now or ever. If you'll excuse me, I really have to get to bed. I'm tired."

She marched past him and up the steps, leaving her father to stare at her back. James Carey tapped his pipe on the banister, then refilled it. Taking a seat by the fire, he smoked thoughtfully.

Elizabeth had sounded more emotional about this Stephen Brooks than any other man she'd ever known. Yet she seemed resigned to see him just as a news source. He could have sworn she looked like she'd been crying, but his Lizzie never cried.

The pipe smoldered as another thought occurred to him. It was just possible that Elizabeth was in love with this man. That would explain a lot, especially her actions tonight. James puffed harder, aware that his daughter was unhappy, and perhaps he'd been partly to blame. He practically nagged her to find a husband since her sixteenth birthday. And now she cared for a man who apparently didn't return her feelings.

And there wasn't a damned thing he could do about that.

Chapter Five

Percival Kent wiped the sweat from his brow and settled into a leather armchair, grinning with good humor. "Good game, Brooks. I hate to admit it, but you become a better billiards player every year while I just get worse. What's your secret?"

"Lack of discipline," Stephen replied dryly, knowing the opposite was true. He poured two drinks of water and splashed some whiskey into each glass, then handed one to his companion. "Actually I've been practicing, and I think I've finally seen some improvement. Now if I could just do better at cricket, I'd be happy. That damned Saunders took over a hundred from me last year."

"Two hundred from me." Percival shuddered. "He wants me to join the Germantown Club this year. I think I'll have to wait until my finances improve."

Stephen grinned, then sipped from his glass. The library at the billiards club gleamed with polished cherrywood and the light from a fire. Other gentlemen talked quietly from sequestered corners while servants unobtrusively replaced ashtrays and refilled glasses. Busts of Pallas and Athena watched the scene before them from a massive bookcase, and overhead a chandelier glittered restlessly with every breeze, sending dancing prisms over the sedate furnishings.

Swirling the liquor in his glass, Stephen glanced at his

friend curiously. "How is business, then? I thought it had improved."

"It has." Percival shrugged. "Earnings are up over fifty percent from last year. The mills are doing very well, production is increasing, especially since we made some improvements to the working conditions and equipment. But you know how my father is. Nothing is ever enough."

Stephen nodded. Jared Kent was known as a taskmaster and, like many of the industrial leaders, strove to increase his profits relentlessly. Thankfully Percival was not as ruthless as his father and, much to the latter's dismay, sought to balance his life with equal measures of work and recreation.

Stephen remembered the last time he had visited the mills. He had been working with Percival on a contract and had met him at the factory. Unlike many of the other mills, the shop had been clean, well lit, and comfortable. And Percival, who was attuned to the workers' needs, introduced breaks and lunch meetings that allowed his employees the opportunity for social contact. Overall, the Kent mills enjoyed a low rate of turnover and high satisfaction among its workers. In fact, it just might be the perfect solution for a problem that had been troubling him for the past few days.

"Perce, do you think that a man with one arm could operate your looms? I mean, if he really wanted to work?"

Percival shrugged, looking surprised. "I don't see why not. He might not be able to finish as much as a person without such impediments, but he should be able to earn a living. Why, do you know someone like that who needs a job?"

"Yes." Stephen briefly described tin-armed Willy and the attack that had occurred outside his office. "The man seems bright enough, and from what I've been told, he is

oyal and trustworthy. I would like to let him have a
hance.''

"Sure." Percival nodded. "I can put him on the Kens-
ngton mill. I need a few more workers right now, anyway.
and the supervisor there is a little more patient and
understanding than some of the others. I think it might work
out fine." He glanced at his friend curiously, a small smile
playing on his face. "Why the sudden interest in helping
his man?''

"I felt sorry for him when he got hurt," Stephen
explained uncomfortably. "And a friend of mine, who is
working with the beggars, pointed out his plight. I've tried
other sources, but there really isn't much help available in
the city. This man is an easy target for the gangs due to his
infirmity. And without a job he'll never get off the streets.''

"I see," Percival said, although he didn't sound entirely
convinced. He stared at Stephen in amusement. "This
wouldn't have anything to do with a certain reporter that
ou've been seeing lately, would it?''

Now it was Stephen's turn to look surprised. He glanced
at his friend, but Percival's expression was innocent
enough. "Are you talking about Miss Carey?" When
Percival nodded, Stephen continued: "I'm not seeing her
he way you think. We happen to be friends. And she is
doing a story on the beggars.''

"I see."

"And what does *that* mean?" Stephen persisted, aware of
the other man's tone.

"Nothing!" Percival protested. "I think Elizabeth Carey
is charming. It's just . . . interesting, that's all." When
Stephen's expression didn't change, Percival grinned. "Oh,
come on, Steve. You know how Philadelphia is. This is a
small town still in some ways, and there isn't much better to

talk about. By the way, I ran into Helene the other night at the Concourse. She seems set on going to the valentine dance with you.''

Stephen winced. He'd forgotten that conversation, where he never quite got the opportunity to ask Helene to the ball. He really had to make a commitment one way or the other.

"I haven't spoken to her since the night of the planning meeting. I suppose I should call on her.''

"Helene is not a bad catch for someone in your position,'' Percival remarked. "Her family has considerable standing and money. She could probably help you tremendously.''

"I know,'' Stephen agreed. "And she is very sweet. Still . . .'' He looked almost embarrassed, then finished the thought: "If she could only stop that giggling.''

Percival broke into laughter, and even Stephen's serious face relaxed. After a moment he joined him. Percival rose and slapped his friend on the back. "Well, it looks like you can't have everything. Call on her, Steve. The girl adores you.''

Stephen grimaced. "You sound like Mrs. Hudson. All right, you've done your duty. I'll think about it.''

". . . and the young attorney, finally understanding the charwoman's plight, lifted a hand to assist her from the cold and icy steps and, in doing so, found his own salvation. . . .''

Elizabeth crinkled her nose and tore the piece of paper into shreds. Even to her eyes it was rubbish. The problem, she admitted to herself, was that she didn't have enough material. She needed to spend some time with Stephen Brooks and learn more about the inner man. Only then could she write a decent story about the effect the beggar woman had on him.

But that was easier said than done. Frowning, she recalled Stephen's busy schedule. He always arrived at his office on time and always left on time. He spent his lunch with colleagues, his supper with prospective clients. During weekends he improved and maintained his social standing, and the few spare hours he had were no doubt spent with the debutantes, who loudly sang his praises. Elizabeth frowned more deeply and chewed on her pencil as she checked her notes. He was also proficient in cricket, billiards, riding, and bicycling. In fact, he had less free time than Horace when the paper was going to bed. Elizabeth wondered why he didn't have gray hair.

To get him out would require a major deception. That part didn't bother her—a story was a story, no matter what. Yet she'd already tried his patience considerably, and they were just starting to be friends . . . her thoughts drifted to that kiss in the carriage, but she hastily caught herself. Men like Stephen Brooks didn't think of her that way. Still, she was reluctant to antagonize him.

Shrugging, Elizabeth hid a grin. She would just have to think of something. After all, he couldn't stay in that office forever. He needed a break.

And she was just the girl to see that he got it.

"Mr. Brooks, a Miss Carey is here to see you."

Stephen glanced up from his documents, his pen still scribbling. "Send her in." He didn't miss the curious look on Mrs. Hudson's face, but he didn't respond to it, either. He returned to his work, ignoring her indignant huff and the tap of her boots on the floor.

Elizabeth entered a moment later and he put down his

pen with a smile. In a soft gray dress with a matching jacket, she looked elegant and businesslike, a far cry from the aggressive reporter. His eyes traveled over her searchingly, then he sat back in his chair, apparently intending to enjoy the meeting.

"Elizabeth. This is a surprise. What can I do for you?"

Elizabeth started to smile, then checked herself with an effort. God, he was so handsome, it was difficult to keep to her plan. Instead she fished out a handkerchief and tried to look as pathetic as possible.

"I had to see you," she whispered, dabbing the cloth at her eyes and sniffling. "Only you can help me."

He instantly looked concerned. "Of course. You know I'll try to help you—we are friends, after all. What's wrong?"

"It's . . . my father," Elizabeth said quickly, crossing her fingers under his desk and reminding herself to say three Hail Marys for a penance. "He's in trouble and needs help. I hate to impose, but—"

"No, you did the right thing. I'm glad you came." He rose from behind the polished oak desk and sat beside her, taking her hand. "Now tell me what the problem is. Is it something legal?"

Hazel. They were definitely hazel. His eyes were a swirling mixture of blue and gray, green and gold, all shot with sherry and sparkling with intensity. Elizabeth almost forgot her purpose, then hid behind the handkerchief once more.

"Yes, that's it. He's in . . . legal difficulty. I don't understand it myself, and he's too embarrassed to tell me much. But I know it must be bad. Do you think . . . no, I just couldn't ask that of you."

"What?" He moved closer, obviously interested and concerned. "Elizabeth, tell me what it is."

She almost felt guilty enough to call it off. Almost. But the reporter within her couldn't pass up the opportunity, and the woman within her wanted to be with him as well. She sniffled, then turned to him weepily.

"If you could spare the time . . . do you think you could come out to see him? I know where to find him, and he can tell you all the details himself. But no, it would take most of the afternoon, and I know you're busy."

"That's all right, of course I'll come. Mrs. Hudson?" Stephen rose and opened the door, and within a moment the bespectacled secretary, who had been at the keyhole listening, nearly stumbled into the room.

Stephen gave her a stern look. "Mrs. Hudson, would you mind rescheduling my afternoon appointments? You have my calendar."

"But . . ." The older woman looked as shocked as if he'd announced he was going to set sail immediately for the East Indies. But Stephen seemed little concerned by her reaction.

"I know a messenger may not reach everyone in time, so please extend my apologies. I have something important to take care of."

Mrs. Hudson peered at Elizabeth while Elizabeth feigned innocence. "Of course, sir. I'll take care of it."

"Fine." Stephen picked up his muffler and coat, then turned to Elizabeth. "Shall we go?"

"Thank you," she said sweetly, beaming with gratitude. She hoped he didn't notice the rising color in her face, and she hoped he wouldn't be furious when he found out what she really wanted.

After all, the only legal difficulty she had was in securing a route to take a sleigh ride.

And the driver she'd selected, a sturdy Irishman named Murphy, assured her he'd take care of that.

"I could cheerfully strangle you," Stephen said, fighting to sound indignant as the truth dawned on him. He stared at the woman who tricked him as she pulled the robe over his legs and chuckled gleefully at his expression.

"Oh, come now. It was the only way to get you out and you know it. Now tell me honestly—if I had come into your office and suggested a sleigh ride, wouldn't you have found a million reasons not to go? Admit that I'm right."

He chuckled, unable to hold back his genuine mirth. "All right, I admit it. But don't do this again. One time you'll really need something, and I'll think you're crying wolf."

"Mea culpa." Elizabeth grinned, then nodded to the driver. "I think that means we're off."

Murphy smiled, then slapped the reins of the horses. "It's a fine day to be riding, an excellent choice, sir. When the lady came to me this morning and explained what she wanted to do, I was right jealous. She must think a lot of you, laddie."

Elizabeth said nothing but blushed hotly as Stephen looked at her with a wry expression. Unable to bear his grin, she reached beneath the robes and produced a basket covered with a blue-checked cloth.

"I took care of lunch," she explained. "I figured you hadn't eaten."

He shook his head. "No, not since breakfast. In fact, I'll have you know that I canceled lunch with an important politician, a meeting with a wealthy client this afternoon, and a dinner with the Friends of the Chamber Music Society.''

Elizabeth sighed. ''They'll just have to do without you for one day. My God, isn't it beautiful?''

She glanced at the hillside. The brown hills broke through the snow, gleaming like the shoulders of a woman in an ermine cloak. Pine trees glittered in the distance, their icicled branches seeming to jab the ground like disdainful fingers while the silver river threaded its way through the lustrous blanket. It was beautiful, magical, and breathtaking.

It was also blissfully still.

Stephen nodded, entranced by the scene. The ruddy-faced Murphy glanced back at the couple and grinned.

''This is Fairmount Park. The Water Works is straight ahead, as well as the gardens. They're all froze now, but in the summertime they're nice. Folks like to come from all over.''

He talked as if they were strangers to the area. Stephen grinned, relaxing in the sleigh. In a way the Irishman was right. He'd never taken a day off and just enjoyed life . . . since he didn't know when.

''I have to admit,'' he said quietly. ''This was a good idea.''

Elizabeth grinned, looking so relieved that he wanted to kiss her again. When he'd first discovered her deception, he'd been torn between feeling flattered that she desired his company and outraged that she'd tricked him once more. But it was difficult to stay angry at her, especially with her sitting so close and looking so beautiful. No woman had a right to appear that way, especially outside with the cold and the snow. But unlike so many of the delicate women he knew, Elizabeth actually looked invigorated by the weather. It was hard to understand.

The sleigh stopped, the blades crunching in the snow, when they reached the most scenic part of the ride. Here, enveloped in a grove of snow-covered chestnut trees, Murphy leaped out and withdrew a bundle of wood.

"For the fire," he explained cheerfully, then he removed a flask from his pocket. "And this is to keep meself warm." He drank down a prodigious quantity of the whiskey, then offered Stephen the flask. "Want some, lad? It's whiskey, God's ambrosia."

Ignoring Elizabeth's laughter, Stephen accepted the drink, surprising even her. When he handed her the flask, one brow lifted as if daring her to do the same, she willingly complied. Wiping her mouth with the back of her hand, she handed the tin back to Murphy.

"My God," Stephen said, stunned to realize that she drank as well as any man. "Is that part of the job?"

"No, at-home training," Elizabeth explained. "My father drinks it, and so I got used to it at an early age. He always said whiskey was invented by the English to keep the Irish in their place."

Murphy chuckled in agreement, then proceeded to build a fire in a miraculously short time. The crackling flames warmed them, sending a soft column of smoke into the sunlit sky. Stephen rubbed his hands over the fire, turning his back to Elizabeth. Suddenly he felt a soft thud on his shoulder and turned to see her laughing.

"That's one for me," Elizabeth said, wielding a snowball and smoothing it into icy perfection. "Here goes two."

Ducking, Stephen couldn't stop laughing as her snowball zoomed over his head to land with a plop. "So it's going to be like that, is it?" He grinned, then reached down and scooped up a handful of the white powder. "I think it's time I evened the score."

Shrieking, Elizabeth started to run, but the snowball caught her square in the back and she dissolved into chuckles. Before he could resume his attack, she dipped into a drift and scooped some more snow. The air was filled with flying pellets of snow, and the ruddy Irishman shook his head at the spectacle of the prominent young attorney and the hard-edged lady reporter in the midst of a very fine snowball fight.

"Do you give up?" Stephen asked, laughing as Elizabeth collapsed into the snow.

Nodding and gasping for breath, she looked up at him and burst into laughter as she saw his expensive coat, spattered with blotches of snow. Clambering to her feet, she shook the glistening powder from her hair and clothes, then joined him beside the fire.

"You look ridiculous." She grinned, bringing the picnic basket from the sleigh.

"What do you mean? I think I look grand. You're just mad because you lost." He helped her with the basket, placing it on the ground where the snow had been cleared.

Elizabeth grinned cheerfully. "You're right. As loser, I get to serve. What would you like? There's wine and cheese, bread and apples."

He stared in appreciation at the sight of the food, then indicated a round parcel. "What's this?"

"Soda bread. My mother makes it. And there's tea in the flask, and sandwiches beneath."

"It's enough for a feast," Stephen said appreciatively. "Here." He put the napkin on her lap, then accepted a sandwich and a steaming cup of the tea.

She looked so pretty, sipping from her cup and openly enjoying his company. He'd forgotten how to just play, to relax, to enjoy life without worrying. He'd been driven for the last few years, and never realized how badly he needed a break until this moment. He felt like a child again.

Elizabeth shivered, then moved closer to the fire and to him. She was so different from any other woman he'd ever known. Her hair, tucked inside a warm winter hat, tried to escape and only managed a few curls that framed her face. He wanted to touch them, to run his fingers along her face and trace that profile that had captivated him from the beginning.

He had to stop thinking like this. They were friends, nothing more. She was a reporter, for God's sake. Still he had to look away when she smiled at him; there was only so much he could take.

And only so much he could give.

It was like a dream, Elizabeth thought. The scenery, unbelievably brilliant, added to the feeling, and having Stephen treat her like a woman whose company he enjoyed was wonderful. She reached across for a sip of the wine, and he refused to let her, insisting on getting it himself and serving her.

The entire experience was heady. It was almost embarrassingly pleasant, having this much attention. As one of a brood of children, Elizabeth wasn't used to receiving anyone's full notice, especially a man's and certainly not someone like Stephen Brooks. She had to stop this and quickly. Forcing her thoughts back to the story, she managed to think of a few questions.

"Did you always live here? In Philadelphia, I mean?"

He nodded, seeming more relaxed than ever. "I grew up here, went to school here. I never wanted to live anywhere else. I love this city, I really do."

Elizabeth knew he meant what he said—she could hear it

in his voice. For a brief moment she wondered what it would be like to have him feel that way about her . . . ridiculous, she chided herself. It was only the romance of the moment that made her feel that way, and yet there was something about his expression that made her breath stop.

Putting aside the food, she leaned closer, amazed when he pulled her beside him to cuddle before the fire. "Stephen Brooks, if you could be anything you wanted, what would it be?" He looked startled, then glanced down at her curiously. "No, I mean it. Would you be the best attorney the city ever saw? Or something different?"

He shrugged, his expression thoughtful. "I don't know. I really didn't want to be a lawyer, it just sort of happened. Actually, if money wasn't a concern, I sometimes think I'd like to be in politics. Really do something important."

Elizabeth looked at him in surprise. She'd always thought of him as intelligent and ambitious, but self-serving. To discover that he had a desire to do something greater stunned her. She nodded, then snuggled beneath the quilts.

"I think you'd make a good politician." She saw his expression, then continued quietly: "And I heard what you did for Willy. Thank you. There aren't many people who would take the time to help a poor beggar."

He glanced away, as if embarrassed by her discovery. "It wasn't anything. I knew the right people. It was just a matter of asking."

"I think it was noble."

He stared at her, amazed to see that she wasn't joking. For once her face was serious, and her eyes were filled with admiration. Swallowing hard, he stared out at the snow once more. But even that didn't seem to help. Shifting uncomfortably, he indicated the dimming fire.

"I guess we should get going. It's getting late."

Elizabeth nodded, then called to Murphy. He got up from his perch a few feet away, obviously more comfortable for the whiskey, then clambered aboard his sleigh and grinned.

"All right, we'll have you home in no time. Hold on!"

Elizabeth climbed in beside Stephen, encouraged by his arm tightening around her. Desire. That was what she had seen in his eyes, coupled with restraint. Yet she had almost concluded that he saw her as a conquest. But his actions were in direct contradiction to that theory. It was almost as if . . .

As if he wanted her.

Chapter Six

They stopped at his office after returning the sleigh to a local farmer. The carriage rolled up to the pavement and Stephen turned to Elizabeth, who was snuggled against him drowsily, the robes tucked practically beneath her chin.

"Are we there?" she asked softly.

Stephen chuckled, then reached across and opened the door. "Yes, at least I am. I have some work to finish up, especially since I've played hooky all day. My carriage will take you home."

Elizabeth sighed, a contented smile spreading across her face. She was obviously well fed, warm, and comfortable. Stephen laughed, then leaned over and placed a small kiss on her forehead.

"I'll see you soon, all right?"

She nodded, then curled up inside the robes. Grinning, Stephen slammed the door and gestured to the driver, watching with some regret as the carriage rattled off.

It had been a magical day. It was ridiculous for a man of his age and standing to have such a thought, but it was true. He felt young, revitalized, and . . . happy. As odd as it sounded, one simple sleigh ride, a snowball fight, and a picnic had brought him more pleasure than all of the society dinners and fancy teas he'd ever attended.

He was still grinning when he entered the building. After

tossing his coat on a rack to dry, he went into his office, aware of the stacks of paper that cluttered his desk. He took a seat, then started to sort through the law briefs when John Tyler entered the room and gently closed the door behind him.

"Stephen. I thought I heard you. It's a little late to be returning, isn't it?"

Stephen glanced up and shrugged. The older man had taken a seat and put his hands behind his head, as if embarking on a long conversation. Something was going on—he could tell by John's guarded expression. "I work late often—you know that," Stephen replied. "And I was out most of the day and I wanted to catch up."

"So I heard." When Stephen's expression turned speculative, John explained: "Mrs. Hudson told me about your visitor, Elizabeth Carey. Attractive woman, I've been told."

"Yes, she is," Stephen agreed. "She's doing a story on the poor immigrants of the city."

"How very interesting." When Stephen didn't respond, the partner continued in the same probing tone: "I understand you were with her most of the afternoon. Something to do with her father?"

Sighing, Stephen put down his pencil and leaned back in his chair. "I took the afternoon off. John, you know how little time I've taken for myself. I haven't had a vacation in years, I put in long hours, and I stay whenever I'm needed. I really don't think it's a crime if one day I decide to spend some time away from the office."

"No, I agree," John Tyler said quickly. "And I didn't mean to imply that you don't deserve it. You are one of the hardest-working attorneys I know. You are very successful and making quite a name for yourself. That is why I'm concerned."

Stephen frowned, forcing down his anger. "Concerned about what?"

"I'm just worried about your association with this Miss Carey. Now, don't get upset," John said quickly, seeing the angry flush come to Stephen's face. "I don't mean anything by that, and I know you aren't the type of man to behave in anything other than a gentlemanly manner. It's just that you're acting different lately, and I think it has something to do with that woman."

"Such as?" Stephen gritted.

"Such as today. The Stephen Brooks I know would never have taken off to gallivant about with a reporter, especially not when he has appointments lined up and work that is due. The Wetherby contract is expected tomorrow, and the Miles account needs a review. Again, you are perfectly justified, but it's uncharacteristic behavior."

"I don't think—"

"And there's the story about that beggar. I heard you were brawling in the streets, defending one of these people. Good God, man, that is for the police to take care of. You could have been badly hurt."

"The man is handicapped," Stephen said, openly outraged. "I couldn't just stand there and let those thugs rob him."

"No, instead you had to procure him a job. Have you turned reformist or something?" When Stephen didn't answer, John Tyler sighed. "Son, I'm not trying to interfere with your life. You're old enough to know what you want and what you're doing. I just sense an influence on you that perhaps you aren't aware of."

"Are you suggesting that my friendship with Elizabeth is corrupting my views?" Stephen asked, incredulous.

John shrugged. "I just want to give you some friendly

advice. I think a lot of you, Stephen, you know that. And you have a wonderful life ahead of you. You know we've considered you for a partnership in the firm, and you are enormously popular in the city. Your choices are unlimited. I'd hate to see you lose any of that or jeopardize your ambitions by foolish decisions. Miss Carey is a wonderful woman, bright and energetic. But she is one of these new women, wanting the vote and reform within the city. And she's a reporter. She is not the kind of woman you could share your life with.''

''We are friends, John. Nothing else,'' Stephen said angrily. ''And her politics don't concern me. She has a right to her own opinion, no matter who agrees with it. This is America, you know.''

''I know, and I'm not suggesting that you sever the friendship. Actually, having a reporter on your side can be helpful. I just want you to be careful. You wouldn't be the first man for whom friendship has turned, unexpectedly, to something else.'' When the anger seemed to leave Stephen's face, John Tyler smiled thoughtfully. ''I noticed that Miss Steadman stopped by earlier today, when you were out. I think you'll find her card among the rest. Why don't you call on her? Her father has a tremendous influence in Philadelphia society. And I hear the girl is delightful.''

Stephen said nothing. John got to his feet and departed, quietly closing the door behind him. Stephen started to say something, but John had already gone.

''. . . and I need you to do a story on chocolates. You know, the kind men buy for Valentine's Day. I'm sorry, Lizzie, but you're the only man, I mean woman, I have to do the job.''

Horace waited expectantly for Elizabeth's protest. She

hated to write fluff, and he knew she'd especially despise this kind of a story. But the readers loved holiday themes, and for Valentine's Day the men wanted to know which stores had the best selection and prices to buy treats for their lady loves. It was the kind of thing that would sell papers, but it was well-known that Elizabeth could barely tolerate such an assignment.

"Chocolates? Oh, I know what you mean. And flowers. We should do flowers, too. And maybe trinkets, you know, fans and the other things that women like to receive. That's a cute idea, Horace. Glad you thought of it."

The editor stared openmouthed as Elizabeth hummed to herself, then went back to her writing. Scratching his head, he decided that she must not have heard him right.

"Lizzie, I mean I need *you* to write the piece, to run along with your beggar story. Not that it's less important, but Valentine's Day is a time when ladies receive lacy cards and presents from their menfolk. People like to read this kind of thing."

"Of course." Elizabeth smiled beatifically. "Valentine's Day is really a sweet holiday, don't you think? It's so nice to celebrate people in love. And the chocolates angle will be perfect. I'll work on it this afternoon."

"Lizzie, are you feeling all right?" Horace actually put a hand to her head. "You've been working so hard and your face looks flushed. Maybe you should take some time off."

"I'm fine." Elizabeth grinned. "Better than fine. In fact, I feel wonderful." Scribbling the last sentence with a flourish, she handed the papers to the editor. "Here's the rest of the beggar story. I still have to finish the sidebar, but I don't foresee any difficulty with that." She smiled dreamily, putting her pen into the coffee cup to stir it.

Horace stared at her in amusement. His hard-hitting

reporter was acting more like the love-smitten suitors she was supposed to be writing about than herself. He saw her rise from her seat, still gaily humming, then put her coat on backward. It took her a full minute to realize her mistake, but instead of making a joke or a sarcastic remark, she merely laughed and turned the coat the right way. More confused than ever, Horace nearly collapsed when she planted a kiss on his forehead, then started for the door.

"I'll get the chocolate story for you right way. Have a wonderful day." Nearly dancing out of the office, she closed the door behind her.

Horace frowned. Either Elizabeth was taking gin in her coffee, or he was losing his mind. He sniffed the brew, then looked worriedly into the mirror overhanging the hall.

The coffee had smelled fine.

They were right. Much as he hated to admit it, they were right.

Stephen cursed himself as he fingered the cream-colored card embroidered with roses that was lettered *Helene Steadman.*

Percival had tried to talk to him. Mrs. Hudson had seemed shocked at his association with Elizabeth. And finally John Tyler had explained to him in the most explicit way possible that Elizabeth was having more of an effect on him than he'd realized.

He hadn't slept at all the previous night, his conscience keeping him awake long after midnight. He couldn't escape the truth, and it was that which kept him awake. It wasn't that anyone thought Elizabeth was a terrible person. On the contrary, Elizabeth had more intelligence and determination than any other woman he knew. It was just that she wasn't

the kind of woman they all pictured him with. And he was
becoming more involved than he'd ever intended.

And that was unfair to everyone. His eyes squeezed shut
and his throat tightened as he pictured Elizabeth laughing,
her incredible eyes sparkling, Elizabeth throwing snowballs,
Elizabeth turning to him with a kiss that sent his senses
aflame. . . .

No, he especially couldn't do this to her. She was starting
to care for him—he sensed it in the softening of her face, the
warmth in her eyes, the passion in her kiss. Who was he
fooling? Everyone else could see what he'd been blind to,
and it stung to know that they were right.

He had to get things back into perspective. Elizabeth
deserved better, and the last thing he wanted to do was hurt
her. He needed to distance himself, to involve himself with
other people, to see other women.

Crumbling the card, he thrust it into his coat. He would
call on Helene this afternoon. It was the right thing to do.

But he didn't have to like it.

". . . And here, miss, you must try one of these.
Chocolate heaven, I call it."

Elizabeth took the proffered candy from the shopkeeper,
then slipped it into her mouth. "Oh, this is wonderful," she
admitted, groaning with pleasure as the chocolate melted.
There was a brandy-flavored bite to the confection, and she
savored every bit of it.

"I am so glad it pleases you." The shopkeeper, a
Frenchman with a glossy mustache that he obviously waxed
with great pride, beamed at Elizabeth. "I have another you
must try. These are vanilla cream and they are perfection!
And the mint, and the orange truffle . . . oh, and you must
sample this."

He extended another candy, this one covered in the darkest, richest chocolate imaginable. Although Elizabeth knew she shouldn't, she couldn't resist the tempting morsel, and she plopped it into her mouth, then gasped with pleasure.

"Raspberry! That's what it is. And something else . . ."

"A liqueur." The shopkeeper grinned proudly. "Especially for Valentine's Day. Now you tell me, mademoiselle. Would you be able to resist the man that gifted you with these?"

"Not for a moment," Elizabeth admitted, finishing up the sweet. This one was even better than the last, rich and thick, with a tangy aftertaste. It was a benefit she hadn't expected with this assignment, but it seemed that every candy shop she visited insisted that she sample the wares, just to prove their confections were the best.

Scribbling in her notebook, she marked down her impressions, almost laughing at the shopkeeper's earnest attempts to sway her in his direction. In truth, she was enjoying this much more than she'd anticipated. It wasn't gritty journalism, but it was a welcome break from some of the heavier stories she'd been working on, and she found the theme refreshing and upbeat.

She didn't hear the door open, but she was aware of a cold breeze and she heard the shopkeeper excuse himself to help the customers who had entered the store. Elizabeth didn't look up, concentrating instead on her work. It wasn't until she heard the tinkly giggle of a woman's voice that a curious dread ran over her.

"Oh, come on, Stephen, let me show you those bonbons we were talking about. There is no other shop that has anything quite like them."

Somehow, she knew. Long before she looked up and met

his gaze, she knew what she would see. Her throat tightened with unshed tears and her heart pounded as she did exactly that, and looked straight into the eyes of Stephen Brooks and his lovely female companion.

"Sir, let me have a tin of those sweets . . . you know, the ones you showed me the other day? I'd like the gentleman to see them."

The woman giggled incessantly. The sound, like a brook in wintertime, was not unpleasant, but to Elizabeth it was like chalk on a blackboard.

"Helene . . ." Stephen spoke in the same familiar voice, his eyes pleaded with Elizabeth, but his hand was held possessively by the woman beside him.

She couldn't stand this, not another minute. Yet somehow, in the dark recesses of her mind she knew this day would come, that somewhere she would see Stephen with the mate of his choice. Her eyes went desperately to the woman, wanting to see her, wanting to torture herself as if probing a new wound in order to cure it. She was everything Elizabeth was not. Dressed in a stylish gown with an elaborate bustle and a soft edging of lace at her wrist and neck, Helene looked like a society lady of leisure, all soft and feminine and full of girlish giggles. Elizabeth couldn't help but notice the ink splotches on her own dress, the untidiness of her hair, the lack of attention to her own appearance, while Helene was flawless.

"Stephen, you promised me you'd look. After all, Valentine's Day is just a few days from now, and you wanted to give me something."

As if finally realizing Stephen's distraction, the woman glanced behind her and, with another giggle, nodded to Elizabeth. "Oh, I remember you. Elizabeth Carey, isn't it?" When Elizabeth managed a nod, the woman giggled again.

"I saw you at the meeting. My mother isn't very approving of what you write . . . well, she isn't, Stephen." She glared accusingly at her companion, then retrieved her hand and rubbed it meaningfully. "Anyway, it's nice to see you again."

Elizabeth nodded, wanting to be anywhere but here. Her happiness of a moment ago faded into the dismal conclusion that she'd been a fool. This woman, with her elegant dress and hair, belonged with Stephen, and not someone like her. She had been ridiculous to imagine anything else, and to think that perhaps she meant something to this man.

"Elizabeth," Stephen said, his voice filled with emotion. Elizabeth barely noticed. Somehow she managed to close her notebook as if none of this mattered, and she started for the door.

"Mademoiselle! Please! You haven't tasted my heart-shaped bonbons! They truly convey the meaning of love!"

"Why don't you give them to him," Elizabeth said sweetly, putting the pencil behind her ear in a deliberate gesture. "They seem appropriate. Good day."

Her heart breaking, Elizabeth strode out of the candy shop, fighting the tears that threatened to spill forth. She wouldn't cry, she couldn't.

Because if she started, she just wouldn't stop.

Chapter Seven

"What on earth is the matter with her?" Helene said, puzzled, while the shopkeeper berated himself in dismay.

"This is wrong, all wrong! Now the newspaper will not recommend my shop! I am ruined!"

"Don't worry," Stephen reassured him. "Miss Carey will give you a fair review. She always does. Come on, Helene. Let's go."

"But we haven't purchased chocolates," Helene protested as Stephen took her arm and led her firmly from the store. Entering his carriage, she pursed her lips and then sat far from him in a huff, clearly disappointed.

Stephen hardly noticed. Giving the driver his signal to go on, he felt the lurch of the carriage as they started toward home, his brow furrowed in thought.

He was upset about running into Elizabeth like that, yet he hadn't the faintest idea why. He had done nothing wrong—he had the right to entertain any woman he wanted. Just because he and Elizabeth had spent one day together and had gone on that sleigh ride didn't obligate him to her in the least.

Yet the pain in her eyes had been real. He hadn't mistaken that, or the tremor in her voice when she'd spoken to him disdainfully. She had been hurt, seeing him with Helene, and though she tried valiantly not to show it,

Stephen would have been a fool not to recognize the signs.

His eyes closed tightly, shutting out the rich leather interior of the carriage. God, he'd tried to prevent this, to keep emotions uninvolved, but somehow it had happened anyway. Maybe it was for the best. Maybe Elizabeth needed to see him with another woman to put things back into perspective.

Yet even as he tried this rationale it left a bad taste in his mouth. The worst part was that he genuinely liked Elizabeth and admired her. He didn't want to see her unhappy, or to know that he was the cause of her pain, no matter how brief. He opened his eyes, observing Helene's indignant pout, and wondered desperately why it wasn't she who engaged him so completely.

Somewhere Cupid was laughing. He could hear it in his heart.

"Come on now, Lizzie. You're making the rest of us look bad. Take a half hour off, will you?"

A cigar-smoking reporter grumbled in the newsroom while his apprentice grinned in agreement. The wire hummed on a scarred table in the center of the room while the reporters scribbled their notes, arranged their copy, and fed the results to the typesetter. Another man in a grimy apron laid out the finished stories, trimming the columns with a razor and pressing them onto a table for Horace's inspection.

"You'd think she wants to put the paper to bed by herself."

"For Christ's sake, Elizabeth. Lay off."

"You aren't a one-man army, you know. Horace'll see you and expect us all to slave."

Elizabeth scribbled the final notes on her copy, then put

down her pencil and faced the men with her hands on her hips.

"I'm sorry, but I want this done and done right. I'm a newspaperman, just like you all are. I've finally realized my calling. I'm no society woman, no man's wife, but I can be the best damned reporter this paper ever saw. And that's what I aim to be."

The men continued grumbling as Elizabeth took another swig of coffee, then examined the notes from the telegraph for copy. Horace watched them from his office, a frown creasing his face as Elizabeth dug into the papers, obviously intending to make a night of it.

She'd been doing just this for the past three days, working feverishly around the clock, almost as if possessed. It hadn't escaped the editor's notice that she seemed to want to hide from something, perhaps her own thoughts. Whatever it was, it wasn't healthy. Clearing his throat, Horace called out into the newsroom.

"Elizabeth! Get in here!"

Annoyed, Elizabeth had no choice but to obey him. Putting aside her work, she ignored the scowls of the men and crossed the littered floor to the office.

"Have a seat." Horace watched closely as Elizabeth took a chair and faced him. He could see the circles beneath her eyes and the paleness of her complexion. Worse, he knew that he was right. Every reporter's instinct told him that this was more than mere dedication, and he was determined to get to the bottom of it.

"The candy story turned out well," he began. "You did a nice job covering the local stores."

"Thank you." Elizabeth looked at him expectantly. "Is that it? I have a new piece I'd like to finish tonight, and there's some good stuff on the wire—"

"Elizabeth, you know I'm not one to beat around the bush," Horace said carefully. "So I'm going to ask you outright. What the hell is wrong?"

It was Elizabeth's turn to look confused. "What are you talking about? Nothing's wrong."

"You've been working thirteen hours straight with hardly a break. You are up to date on every feature you've been assigned, yet you've taken on more work. I know you came in last night and finished editing the Valentine's Day story, when we have three more days. The only thing I'm waiting for from you is the sidebar on the young attorney, and there's time for that. So I'll have to ask you again. What's going on?"

Shrugging, Elizabeth toyed with the paperweight on his desk. "Nothing. It's just that I've come to realize what this job means to me. I'm a reporter, and that's what I intend to be. You and I both want to make this paper the best thing in print. I just want to work hard and make sure that happens."

"You don't succeed by exhausting yourself," Horace said firmly, ignoring Elizabeth's protest. "Now look, you and I have been friends for a long time. I respect your privacy, so if you don't want to tell me what's wrong, I understand. But I'm not going to stand by and let you work yourself into an early grave. Take a few hours off. See a show. Do whatever you have to do, then come back fresh."

"I feel perfectly fine," Elizabeth insisted. "Just because I've finally realized my calling doesn't mean anything is amiss. You work around the clock a lot of times."

"When it's called for. And when necessary, I expect you to do the same. However, when it's not necessary, I enjoy myself. That's the secret of leading a successful work life. Otherwise you can become ill. I've seen it happen before." Horace held up his hand, forestalling the next protest.

"Now I want you to take the rest of the day off. Do whatever you have to do. And I'll see you tomorrow morning, bright and early."

Crestfallen, Elizabeth got to her feet. "This is so ridiculous. . . ."

"Tomorrow morning. That's an order. And I expect to see you rested."

It was more of a question than anything else. Frowning, Elizabeth snatched up her coat and hat and started for the door. It seemed that no one wanted her.

Outside, it was cold. Elizabeth signaled a cab, and as the shabby horse-drawn carriage approached she felt an ache in her head and a burning in her lungs. Climbing inside, she had barely settled in the seat when the wind blew, making her gasp with the chill. Shivering, she wrapped herself in the robes and tried to snuggle in a corner.

The approaching nightfall gave the city a sinister look as any welcoming warmth from the sun was quickly obliterated. The wind howled, and from the seat in the cab she could see people scurrying to their homes, unable to endure even the slightest exposure to the cold. Ice coated the cobbled streets, lending them a frosty sheen that resembled waxed paper, and was as treacherous as a banana peel beneath an unsuspecting foot.

The wire. There was a story . . . Elizabeth remembered reading that the frigid northern winds were expected to arrive that evening, winds that would cause the temperature to drop abruptly. She'd noted the article with little interest at the time, since her father had brought in a good supply of coal. But there were others less fortunate, others who didn't have the luxury of a fireplace or wood or even a piece of coal. They were out there tonight, alone. . . .

She'd been so wrapped up in Stephen and that society woman that she hadn't thought of the beggars, of the people she'd come to know in the last few weeks, some of whom she regarded as friends. There were church shelters, that much she knew, but she knew as well that the poor often didn't use them. Some of them, their minds long since lost to gin, wouldn't even realize that the wind had changed, or that the temperature had dropped. They would stay outside, wrapped in a torn overcoat, battling the chill with nothing but liquor and a prayer.

She had to help them, no question about it. The nuns had enough to do and didn't have the resources to scour the city looking for the poor. No, if she managed to bring in even a few of the people this night, she would save their lives. It was as simple as that.

"Cabbie! Pull over." Elizabeth dug into her pocket and paid the disgruntled cabdriver his fare, then stepped out into the frosty night. She was near the square. That thought made her cringe, but she didn't have much choice. Willy was one of the first people she needed to find, and this was the place to start.

Stephen rubbed his hands before the fireplace, aware of the increasing chill. It would be a damned cold night—he could tell that already. He was looking forward to his warm muffler, his good wool coat, and a hot cup of tea when he reached his luxurious town house.

Glancing outside, he remembered the man Willy, who used to beg a few doors down. Willy was now working for Percival and was doing extremely well. But Stephen would see him occasionally at his old haunt, as if he really thought of the church steps as a home.

Surely the man wouldn't be there tonight? Ice crystals

coated the window, preventing his view, but the thought wouldn't leave him. Then there was that woman Clara. Elizabeth had told him all about her, and how she no longer had her wits. Would she even know enough to come in? And what of the others?

A month ago he wouldn't even have noticed, let alone cared. And tonight he had plans. He was supposed to go to Helene's for a late supper. Yet he just couldn't bring himself to do this, not until he'd checked and made sure the beggars had shelter. Wrapping himself in his coat, he started for the door.

He would be delayed maybe an hour or so. And Helene, he was certain, would understand.

"What are you doing here?"

Elizabeth glared at Stephen as he stepped from his elegant carriage and reached down to assist her with Clara. Choking back an angry reply, he managed to ignore her until he got the beggar woman into his coach.

"I'm helping you," he said evenly. "I believe it is a free country. You aren't the only one who can make a difference."

"Bah!" Elizabeth shivered involuntarily, then wiped her nose with her handkerchief. "I can manage just fine by myself. I've already gotten Willy to the shelter, and I can get Clara there as well. Now why don't you just mosey on back to your town house, where I believe a fire and a butler are probably waiting? I have work to do."

Stephen fought the impulse to either shake or kiss her. There was something about this woman that aroused his emotions more than he cared to admit. Fighting his temper, he reached closer and wrapped her scarf against the chill, then tried to speak with patience.

"I want to help. I have the carriage . . . you can round them up much more quickly that way."

She stared at him, her eyes measuring. He could almost see her thinking through his strategy, seeing his logic, but doubting his intentions. He forced a smile.

"It's also much warmer inside for you as well."

"I'm not worried—"

"Elizabeth." His patience at an end, he glared at her. "You won't help them much if you freeze yourself. Now, you're coming with me, and we're taking this woman to the mission."

She hesitated a moment, but one more gust of wind seemed to convince her and she climbed reluctantly into the vehicle. Stephen joined her, and as the carriage lurched forward he wrapped the old beggar woman in a blanket while Elizabeth settled her onto a seat.

Neither of them spoke as the carriage skidded on the ice, then continued to rumble down the street. Stephen started to speak several times, but remembering her expression in the candy store, he just didn't know how to begin. And Elizabeth did nothing to encourage him.

The mission, thankfully, was only a short distance away. The carriage slowed to a halt and Stephen climbed out, ignoring Elizabeth's indignant expression as he hoisted the older woman out of the coach and into the mission. The sisters, harried and overworked, approached the young couple and took Clara by the hand.

"Bless you both. She looks near freezing. . . ."

Stephen watched as Elizabeth and the nun brought a shivering Clara to a potbelly stove that belched smoke and flames. They pressed a cup of hot soup into her hands, and he could almost see the color rush into her face, replacing the gray pallor she'd had when they'd first brought her into the coach. Clara stared about her in bewilderment, as if gradually realizing that she was safe. She lifted her lined face to Elizabeth and there was a faint glint of recognition, and something close to gratitude.

It made him feel humble.

"There are so many more. Some of the priests are out looking, and a few of the neighborhood people, but there are just so many."

"Don't worry," Elizabeth assured the sister. "I'll see who else is out there."

The nun nodded, her sternness gone. She glanced at Stephen in confusion, obviously wondering at his part in all this, then a child called for more soup and she hastened to refill his bowl. Stephen joined Elizabeth at the door and she stared at him questioningly.

"Thank you." The words seemed to stick in her throat. "Look, I know you must have other things to do. You were right—the carriage did help. But I don't expect you to give up your plans to help me."

"Where next?" Stephen spoke as if she hadn't said a word. "I was thinking the Spring Garden ward. I noticed a lot of poor people there this morning, huddled around a fire."

Elizabeth hesitated, then grinned at him, her beautiful eyes sparkling with mirth. "All right then, Senator. You've got it. But I'm warning you, this isn't going to be easy. It's no fun facing the real world when you've lived in an ivory tower."

He grinned back. "It's time I came out of it. Now are you ready?"

She nodded. "Yes. Thank God there isn't a single candy shop on the way."

"It's a good thing," Stephen agreed. "I almost wore

those raspberry delights. I swear I thought you were going to dump François's entire collection in my lap.''

Elizabeth followed him into the coach, wisely refusing to comment. Stephen pulled the door shut, then shouted to the driver. And if the man thought it odd that his fashionable employer directed him to one of the roughest parts of town, he didn't show it.

After all, it was almost Valentine's Day. And everyone was feeling generous.

''It was work,'' Stephen said, ignoring Elizabeth's laughter as they entered his home. Exhausted and chilled to the bone, they had delivered the last unfortunate to the mission. The occupants of the place were barely aware that they had been saved from frostbite, pneumonia, or death. Only the sisters seemed to know, and they thanked him and Elizabeth so profusely that Stephen was embarrassed.

''What did you expect?'' She looked up at him, and in spite of her exhaustion her eyes shone. ''Philanthropy doesn't come cheap.''

''I noticed.'' Grinning wryly, he planted her on the couch in front of the fireplace. ''Now I want you to take off those boots and warm your feet. It won't do any good if you get sick.''

''But—'' Elizabeth started to protest, but one glance from Stephen convinced her it was useless. Grinning, she removed her boots and stretched before the fireplace while he managed to get a good fire going.

It was wonderful, warm and comforting. The town house was as beautiful as she'd imagined it would be, done in rich shades of hunter green and russet. Cherrywood furniture was everywhere, and the rugs were so thick and soft that her feet sank into them. Stephen returned with two glasses of brandy, gave her one, then sipped from his own. "For the chill," he explained, shuddering when she tipped back the glass and drank freely of the liquor.

"That's so good." Placing her glass aside, Elizabeth curled beside him like a kitten, letting the heat from the brandy and the fire warm her.

It was incredibly pleasant to be alone with him like this. Stephen had insisted they stop, just to get warm, before continuing to her home. Truthfully she had wanted to spend some time with him, especially now. Somehow his actions this night didn't fit the image she still had of him. The man was a mystery, and she was just beginning to wonder if she hadn't judged him too quickly.

He stared at her and she smiled, wanting to share the tremendous feeling of satisfaction she had. No one else would have understood this evening. She needed to touch him, to feel his arms around her, to share the unfamiliar emotions that overwhelmed her. Looking into his eyes, she saw the same need reflected there, astonishing in its intensity. Something was happening, something illogical and wonderful. Without forethought Elizabeth spoke, her voice barely more than a whisper.

"Stephen. Could you, I mean, just this once. Could you hold me?"

She saw the surprise on his face, then he gathered her in his arms. Neither of them spoke; neither had to. What had happened this night had changed their relationship. Elizabeth couldn't explain it, but it felt so right to have his arms around her. She couldn't help that, nor could she help what happened next.

Lifting her face to his, she saw his mouth, so close to hers, and she pulled him into a kiss. She needed this man, the one man she fought with, struggled against, then lastly felt a companionship with that she'd never experienced before. No one else had made her feel as beautiful as he did, nor did they ever approve of her the same way, especially going out of their way to help her.

"My God, Elizabeth, you are so special." His kiss deepened, and she tasted passion and a longing that matched her own. A gasp came from her throat and she felt an overwhelming desire for him that was almost frightening.

He wasn't hers; she knew that. But she needed him, needed to touch him, to feel him, to know that he wanted her. The thought was dangerous, forbidden. She had always been told that this was wrong, that the sharing of physical passion without the blessing of marriage was a sin. And yet, with his arms around her, her heart told her it wasn't. For this one night God had given her this gift, this sharing, and it was hers for the taking.

"Stephen. Please. I want you. . . ."

He stared at her, smoldering desire ignited into flame at her words. "Elizabeth, I can't take advantage of this. You know I want you, more than anything else. But I don't know if I can promise . . ."

"Just tonight," Elizabeth whispered. "Stephen, I don't want empty promises. But tonight I need you. Please."

He groaned, unable to resist. She looked at him so honestly, so lovingly, that even if he had wanted to, he couldn't stop himself any more than she could. Clothing became a hindrance. He unfastened her coat, then the buttons of her dress. When his fingers touched her bare skin, she shuddered with pure, primal pleasure, wanting him so badly she didn't think she could stand it.

"Are you all right?" he questioned softly. "I don't want to hurt you, I want to be sure."

She knew what he meant, but she no longer cared.

"Please. Stephen, I just want to touch you, to love you. Oh God, please."

She couldn't help the urgency in her voice, or the passionate response she felt when his lips lightly brushed her throat, then lower. Her body seemed alive, every pore crying out for him as he teased her into oblivion, his hands artfully arousing her to the point where she could no longer think, only feel. All of the emotions she'd tried to keep hidden enveloped her and culminated in this one moment, when he was finally hers. . . .

"Elizabeth." His voice was strained. "I want to be gentle with you, but I don't think I can. . . ."

She pulled him into her, wanting to be a part of him. Emotion overwhelmed them. Stephen heard her slight gasp of pain, then she nearly sobbed with pleasure as she wrapped her legs around him, wanting to experience everything. In a communication older than time, they shared what they'd felt all along, their bodies saying what their hearts could not. Frantically they built to a climax, their feelings so powerful that Elizabeth could only cling to him, holding him as closely as possible. For that one moment Elizabeth Carey knew what it was to have, to hold . . .

And to love.

Chapter Eight

The log broke in the fireplace, sending crackling cinders up into the chimney. The unexpectedness of the sound brought them both back to reality, to the flurry of clothes that lay about them, hastily discarded, to the sofa cushions that were haphazardly tumbled around them.

"Elizabeth." Stephen pressed a kiss on her forehead, smoothing back her hair and touching her with a reverence that made her feel incredible. "Stay with me tonight. Please."

She smiled, nearly overwhelmed with emotion. "I can't. My family is probably worried to death as it is. I've got to go."

He watched her slip into her clothes. She was obviously unused to such a situation and extremely self-conscious. He reached for his own garments, turning his head and allowing her privacy to dress. When she was ready, he turned back to her.

"I'll take you home then. If you want, I can speak to your family, explain—"

"No!" Elizabeth said so suddenly that he stared at her in surprise. She saw his expression, then explained her outburst. "If I came in with you at this time of night, my father would have heart failure first, and kill you second. No, I think it's better if I go alone."

The implication of her words didn't escape him. He'd dishonored her; it was that simple. Yet his own intentions were vague. Obviously confused, he reached for her, but Elizabeth smiled and withdrew from his embrace.

"Stephen." She touched his face with her hand, as if memorizing every last detail. "I just want you to know that I don't expect anything from you. I don't regret what happened between us, but I know that you can't make a commitment to me. And I think it better if we don't see each other again."

He stared at her, his mouth parting. "What are you talking about? Elizabeth, it's obvious that you mean something to me, and I you. . . ."

Tears glistened in her magnificent eyes, and she squeezed his hand the way one would comfort a child who didn't want to face the truth. "We are from two different worlds, and you and I both know it. What would your fancy friends say if they thought you were seriously involved with me, Elizabeth Carey, reformist reporter? I don't think very much. And your family, the law firm . . ." She wiped at her eyes with the back of her hand, then smiled with a wisdom far past her years. "Don't you think I know what goes through your mind when you see me? I don't fit, Stephen. I know that. And so do you."

"But we can get through it." He couldn't deny her words. Yet he couldn't believe this was happening, that she would just walk through that door and disappear from his life. "We can make adjustments."

"Can we?" Elizabeth shook her head ruefully. "You can't change who you are any more than I can. And even if we could make the adjustments, could everyone else? Stephen, you know I'm right. Someday you'll thank me."

"Elizabeth, I can't let you go—"

"Don't do this." She choked, then refused his hand when he tried to clasp it again. "I've got to leave now. I won't forget you. Ever."

Before he could stop her, she had turned and run. Stephen stood in the formal foyer, seeing the door close before him, and feeling that all of the life was extinguished from his heart.

She was gone.

The row house was, thankfully, quiet when Elizabeth returned home. Her mother, no doubt, she thought gratefully, noticing that her father was fast asleep by the fire, covered with a shawl and the remains of a big dinner beside him. Irene knew when Elizabeth was working late, and she often distracted her husband so that James would not berate his daughter when she walked in the door.

Her bed was never so welcome as it was this night. The simple furnishings were strikingly different from the elegant home she'd just left, but they were familiar and comforting. After removing her clothes, she put on her nightgown, aware that her body felt different, special. Stephen Brooks had made a woman of her, and though she felt as if her heart was breaking, she had no regrets.

Whatever else happened in her life, this night would always be special to her. She knew now that she loved him, for all his faults, all of his differences, all of his strengths and complexities. She couldn't alter the fact that she didn't belong in his world. Stephen would go on to be an important politician, perhaps a congressman or senator, and she would still be scribbling away at the newspaper, making headlines and dazzling Horace.

"You can't change a man's soul, Lizzie," James Carey had once said. "If he's a fool, he's that whether he's clothed in rags or fine wools. But you'll never change him from what he is.''

And Stephen was a gentleman. He would have wanted to do the right thing, even though it would have never worked. She had to be the one to do it, to break it off with him, for both their sakes. Yet she wouldn't give up this memory for the world. Happiness, she realized, was like the shiny coppers her father kept in a jar, then took them out one at a time, remembering. She would always have this night, the one night when a man held her, caressed her, and loved her.

And as she'd promised Stephen, she'd never forget.

Horace put down his cigar and held up the newspaper, looking at Elizabeth with so much compassion that she was embarrassed. ''This is absolutely your best work,'' he stated, the words coming slowly, as if inadequate to express his true feelings.

''Thank you.'' Elizabeth smiled. Once she would have been tremendously flattered, but something had changed. She had more confidence now and knew the piece was good. Still, it was nice to hear.

''I mean it, Lizzie. This is beyond journalism. This piece has literary merit.'' He shook his grizzled head, then glanced at the story once more. ''Are you sure you want me to print this?''

''Of course.'' She looked at him in some surprise. ''It is what you wanted, isn't it?''

''It's fabulous. You've got it all, the subtle change in the young attorney from a good man, oblivious to the need around him, to a caring, compassionate person who actually makes a difference. It is moving, real, and compelling. I don't think we'll have a dry eye at any breakfast table in Philadelphia come Valentine's Day.''

"Then that's what we wanted," Elizabeth said, picking up her files. "If it's all right with you then, I've got to finish my work. Tomorrow is Valentine's Day, and I have to cover the dance. I think attendance will be way up, thanks to the story."

"Elizabeth." Horace clasped her hand in a gesture so uncharacteristic that it surprised the both of them. He paused for a moment, clearly uncomfortable, then spoke quickly: "He really meant something to you, didn't he?"

She nodded, aware of the pain in her heart. But she wasn't unhappy for knowing Stephen, and the emotions that filled her were as complicated as the story.

"It's all right," she told Horace, then managed to smile back. "Really."

He watched her go, wishing there was something he could say or do. For the first time since he'd known her, Elizabeth Carey had fallen in love.

And no matter what she said, he knew it wasn't all right.

"Stephen." John Tyler entered the office with a serious expression on his face. "Have you seen this?" He indicated the morning *Record*.

"No," Stephen responded dryly. "I don't read the newspaper these days."

"I think today you should make an exception." John slid the paper across Stephen's desk and indicated the marked column.

Frowning, Stephen picked up the paper as John Tyler discreetly left the room. The last thing he'd wanted to think about was Elizabeth. In truth, he hadn't been able to get her out of his mind, even though he was convinced she didn't give a damn about him. How could she make such exquisite love and then just walk right out of his life? But she'd done exactly that, and even though it hurt, he had to accept facts. Elizabeth didn't want him.

His eyes scanned the paper and he found the article. It didn't take him long to realize why the senior partner had acted as he did. He read the main story, BEGGARS: PHILADEL-PHIA'S INVISIBLE PEOPLE, and he had to hand it to her. She'd done a terrific job of conveying the plight of the poor without being overly sentimental. He couldn't help the surge of pride he felt for her, regardless of everything else, then his eye fell on the sidebar: ATTORNEY'S PLIGHT: WHEN THE POOR LAND ON YOUR DOORSTEP.

He couldn't believe his eyes.

Fury and humiliation raged through him. She'd written about *him*. No one in the city would fail to recognize him as the young lawyer, plagued with a beggar on his steps. She'd used him to write this, to explore his reaction to her presence as the beggar woman. He'd meant nothing to her, nothing except a story to be exploited. Forcing aside his reaction, he read the article.

It was all there. His resistance to the beggar woman. His realization that she was a human being. His transformation from a self-serving lawyer to a man full of understanding and empathy. His anger faded as he realized the story was nothing like he'd envisioned. True, she'd written about him without telling him. Yet there was nothing exploitive about the piece, nothing that disparaged him or made him appear ignoble. Instead she portrayed him as a man to be emulated, a good man, a man who was guided by an inner strength and compassion.

It made him feel humble.

His heart began to pound as he reread the story, this time between the lines. Every sentence glimmered with emotion, raw and unveiled. Elizabeth had spared no detail, nothing.

Her own feelings toward him flowed from her pen, and she had exposed herself in a way that left him astonished.

". . . This proud man, this attorney who had never known poverty, helped a shabbily dressed immigrant from the snow, and carried her, heedless of his fine garments, into his own coach. When confronted with a person in need, he responded in a way that touched the heart of everyone who observed it, including this reporter. . . ."

The paper fell from his hands.

Elizabeth Carey, coldhearted reporter, loved him and didn't care who knew it. Emotion tightened his throat.

He had been the one with all the experience, the sophisticate. Yet Elizabeth had shown him, in the most dramatic way possible, that she thought him worthy.

Suddenly his heart lifted and he grinned, joy flowing through him. My God, but he had been blind. Shoving the paper into his pocket, he grabbed his coat and raced past the gaping John Tyler toward the door. Elizabeth didn't fit any of his criteria. She wasn't a society woman, wasn't from his circle, didn't have connections, and came from the wrong side of town. She was a reporter, happiest when digging into some social problem and exposing it for the world to see.

Yet she had the most important qualification of all—his love.

And it seemed that it was returned.

"You're going to the dance, are you, Lizzie?"

James beamed with pride as his daughter descended the steps. Clad in a rose-colored gown that was trimmed demurely in lace, she looked every bit the lady. Her hair had been upswept into a charming style that enhanced her eyes and brought out the best of her features. She smiled at her father's expression, then indicated her reticule.

"My notebook. This is a story, you know."

"Yes, but I don't think the paper will fire you if you enjoy a dance with a man or two," James said. "You look lovely. Every man there will want to waltz with you."

Her mother nodded, but Elizabeth saw the worried expression on her face. In truth, she knew her parents had been concerned about her the last few days. There was a wistfulness about her that neither one of them could explain, yet it wasn't as if she was unhappy. Instead of arguing the point with her father as she once would have, she picked up her wrap and started for the door.

"I won't be late. I'm looking forward to the dance. From what I've heard, the tickets are selling well. It seems the story was a success."

She closed the door behind her and her parents looked at each other with some concern. Elizabeth was being her usual practical self. But it was Valentine's Day after all.

And if anyone deserved a little romance, it was she.

The hall was covered with paper hearts, pink and white streamers, paper lace, and satin ribbons. Cupids grinned, hanging from the ceiling, their sharp arrows aimed at unsuspecting hearts, while a fountain gurgled with pink punch. Music filled the hall, and women dressed in every shade of rose danced beneath the twinkling lights like fairies at a ball.

Elizabeth sipped the punch and watched with satisfaction. Everything was perfect. The heart-shaped cake was a masterpiece, intricately decorated with candy roses, while trays of chocolates tempted the guests from every corner. It was beautiful, the event had been a sellout, and everyone was having a good time.

"Miss Carey. Your article this morning was wonderful. But we all want to know . . . who is the attorney?"

"Come on, Elizabeth. You can tell us."

"If we guess?"

Elizabeth grinned, enjoying the company of the society men who flocked around her. She refused to tell them anything, yet they continued to ask, delighted with the game. Although they wouldn't think to ask her to dance, they seemed genuinely interested in her work. They went out of their way to be kind, and yet she was forcibly reminded that she wasn't one of them, wasn't of their station. None of them took her hand, or introduced her to his family, or escorted her to the table for some punch. In truth, the only man who didn't treat her this way was . . .

She had to stop thinking like this. She couldn't keep comparing every man to Stephen Brooks. She had to go forward with her life, perhaps take a risk and allow another man to get close to her. There was that new reporter. . . . For some reason, the thought was distasteful. Excusing herself, Elizabeth was about to retreat to the punch bowl when a voice behind her made her heart stand still.

"I believe this is our dance. Miss Carey?"

The flood of happiness she felt was ridiculous. Turning, she saw him, looking so elegant that her breath stopped. He was wearing a dark suit and a sparkling white shirt that enhanced his handsome good looks, but it was more than that. His expression was one that she'd only seen in her dreams, filled with joy and . . .

Love.

Somehow she took his hand and he led her to the dance floor. She heard the whispers of the society folk, for the implication of his action was startlingly clear. He was showing the people that she was his choice, publicly demonstrating his affection. When his arm went about her waist and the dance began, she was floating, unable to believe this was really happening.

The music enveloped her and she looked at him, her eyes full of love. They fit perfectly together, and as the lights twinkled softly around them she could see nothing but him, was aware of nothing but his arms around her, and the way his body felt, warm and close beside her. It seemed the most natural thing in the world when he bent his head to kiss her, and it was only when the crowd, politely clapping their approval, brought them back to reality that they broke the kiss, embarrassed at the display.

"Happy Valentine's Day, sweetheart," he whispered.

Elizabeth grinned. "Happy Valentine's Day."

PAPER HEARTS

by

Kathleen Kane

Dear Reader,

I wasn't always a "saver," or as my family likes to call me, a "packrat."

In the fourth grade, my true love Paul, a handsome blond with black horn-rimmed glasses, managed to elude our teacher, Sister Lourdine, and deliver my very first Valentine gift. Of course, I almost missed it. He walked past my desk and slapped his hand over the ink well. (Yes, I'm that old.) After a few minutes of frantic hand waving from the back of the room, I got his message and looked in my desk. He'd dropped a roll of Lifesavers down the hole in the desk.

Pleased and excited, I raced home, bragged to my mother, then promptly ate my Valentine. Quite a romantic. But Paul continued to be my hero for four more years. Especially after he used a "dodge-ball" to slay the evil, teasing dragon of St. Marianne's school.

By the time I met my husband Mark, I saved everything. From movie ticket stubs from our first date, to every card he ever gave me. (Mark entering a store is still quite an occasion.) And now my old hope chest is filled to overflowing with souvenirs of my children's lives. Crayon drawings, misshapen lumps of clay, heart-shaped cards fashioned from doilies, report cards, and even the occasional note begging to be released early from a grounding sentence. And there is nothing I like better than sifting through the memories and embarassing my kids with my "oohs" and "aahs." In fact both the kids and my husband tend to head for the high country as soon as they hear me say, "Do you remember . . ."

In my story, J.T. has his own special memory tucked safely away and all he has to do is convince Emma of just how special it really is.

All of the characters in my story are real only to me. Except for three of them. My grandparents, George and Myrtis Hartsfield, and my aunt Nell Frampton have all left us now. No doubt they are, even now, attending a huge family party somewhere, tipping a cup of "shine" to those of us left behind. But in the pages of my story, they live again—just the way I remember them.

I hope you enjoy your visit with the folks in Buckshot, California, as much as I did.

And to Paul Martin . . . thanks for the Lifesavers.

—KATHLEEN KANE

Chapter One

Emma Taylor stood uncertainly on the wide boardwalk tapping her fingernail against her chin. There were so many things to do, she didn't know where to start. Her gaze moved over the main street of Buckshot, California. It still amazed her to think how little her hometown had changed in the two years she'd been gone, when so much had happened to her.

Gently she ran her hand over the front of her lavender day gown and smiled. In the two weeks she'd been back home, she hadn't worn the same dress twice. Quite a change from the days when dressing up meant wearing her faded yellow calico and brushing her hair.

Her tomboy days were well behind her now, though. And she would prove it to everyone with the Valentine's Day dance.

Unconsciously her gaze drifted to the sheriff's office. It was high time, Emma told herself, that *some* people in Buckshot found out that she wasn't a silly little girl anymore. Her chin lifted and she reached up to pat her perfectly smooth honey-blond hair into place.

Of course, she told herself, if she kept on avoiding J.T., how would he ever notice the change in her?

The sheriff's door opened and Emma looked away quickly.

* * *

J. T. Phillips stepped out of his office and stopped dead. Emma. He inhaled sharply as he watched her. Damn, she was beautiful. Of course, he'd always known she would be.

There was no sign now of the skinny little girl with flyaway braids who used to chase after him all the time. She was full-grown now, and as far as he could see, she'd done a right nice job of it, too. Her soft blond hair was pulled back from her face and fell in a heavy mass down her back to her narrow waist. Her gently rounded figure filled out one of the new eastern dresses she'd brought home with her, and he knew without looking that her sherry-colored eyes were sparkling and the light dusting of freckles across her small, straight nose looked like flecks of gold in the afternoon light.

Self-consciously he glanced down at his own rumpled appearance. He'd spent most of the night before squatting under a tree, trying to catch the fella who'd been stealing Maybelle Hawken's chickens. Now his black pants were dusted with molting chicken feathers, his vest was crumpled and mud-stained, and his long-sleeved white shirt was ripped and torn. Oh, he was a *fine* sight.

J.T.'s hands balled into fists of frustration. He'd been trying to get Emma alone for two weeks now and this was his first real chance. Ever since she got home, she'd been avoiding him like he had smallpox or something! He pulled his wide-brimmed hat down low over his eyes and frowned. Enough was enough!

This time she *was* going to talk to him. J. T. glanced down the street then stepped off the boardwalk and marched toward her. With every step, though, his mind tried to remind him that he'd made a vow to be patient. To let her settle in . . . get used to being back home again. But damn it, it was no easy task bein' patient.

This was all her pa's fault anyway. He never should have shipped Emma off to that fancy ladies' academy back east. She was bound to come home with all sorts of fancy notions from those fast-talkin', faster-movin' city folks. J.T. had tried to tell the man that no good would come of it . . . but nobody could tell Frank Taylor anything.

Well, now he was findin' out what was what. The first thing Emma did when she came home was toss out her pa's spittoon and tobacco. Told him it wasn't *re*-fined.

J.T. snorted and kept moving.

It wasn't just her pa's tobacco, either. Ever since she got home, she'd been hell-bent for changin' things around. Forever talkin' about how things were done back east.

Like the Valentine's Day dance.

He stepped up on the boardwalk and came up behind her silently. "Hello, Emma."

She jumped and spun around. "J.T." Her face paled then flushed with color.

He snatched his hat off, sending his black hair tumbling over his forehead. "Didn't mean to scare you."

Emma's heart pounded so heavily she could hardly hear him. Lord, she thought frantically, why hadn't she heard him coming up? She might have had time to get away if she'd only been paying attention. For two weeks she'd managed to keep from being alone with him and she'd hoped for still more time before facing him. Emma looked up into his dark, fathomless eyes and knew she was good and trapped. She recognized that look of determination. J.T. wasn't about to let her escape.

Deliberately Emma took a few long, deep breaths, trying to steady the nervous flutter growing in the pit of her stomach. Her nose wrinkled. What was that smell? *Chickens?*

She laced her fingers together to keep from reaching up and smoothing his hair back. Just like always. He needed a good haircut.

And, she noted as her gaze swept over him, his shirt was missing a button and his black vest looked as though it'd been under a herd of stampeding cattle. Emma shook her head slightly. Just like the town, J. T. Phillips hadn't changed a bit.

Well, she *had*. And maybe now was just the time to start showing him how much.

"I wasn't scared, J.T.," she said, straightening her gloves. "Only startled."

His eyebrows quirked. "Emma, I've been meanin' to get out to your place. . . ."

"Of course." Emma forced a smile. "We have a lot to discuss, don't we?"

J.T.'s face brightened a little. "Yeah, you could say so."

"After all, the Valentine's Day dance is only a couple of weeks away. We'll have to get our groups busy."

"What?" He cocked his head and stared at her. "Our groups?"

"Well, yes." She opened her string bag and pulled out a piece of paper. "Reverend Jeffries said he told you all about it. You're to be in charge of the men. I'll handle the ladies' end."

He snatched the paper from her. "In charge of what? It's just a dance. We have one every year."

"But that's just it," Emma retorted happily. "Everything's going to be different this year."

"Different?" J.T.'s eyes narrowed. "How different?"

"Well, for one thing," she said, straightening her shoulders, "there won't be any of Dutch's home brew floating around the crowd."

J.T. threw his head back and laughed. "Dutch's been bringing his moonshine to every shindig we ever had for years. How do you plan to stop him?"

"I haven't decided yet." Her eyes narrowed dangerously as he continued to chuckle. "But I will. Mark my words."

"Even if you do figure out a way to stop Dutch"—he shook his head slowly—"the saloon'll still be here."

She'd forgotten all about that. "Well, for heaven's sake, J.T., you're the sheriff. Make him close up for the day!"

"I can't do that, Emma."

"I don't see why not," she challenged, "After all, it's for the good of the whole town."

"Accordin' to you. But Tom Hill's got to make a livin' same as anybody else, and he ain't about to shut down his saloon on the day when everybody for miles around comes into town!"

Emma started to argue, then thought better of it. How would bickering with the man like a child prove to him that she'd finally grown up? She'd spent two years at that blasted academy learning how to control her temper. Now, five minutes alone with J. T. Phillips and she wanted to find a rock and pitch it at him.

She glanced up at him covertly and groaned silently. Wouldn't you think, she asked herself, that in two long years she'd have been able to learn how to overcome the flood of feelings that raced through her body anytime J.T. was near? But she hadn't. If anything, the feelings seemed to have gotten worse. Even when she was angry with him, her body responded to his presence.

Well, she'd just have to get used to it. Buckshot was *her*

home, too, and she wasn't about to leave town just to avoid *him*!

"If you won't do your duty, J.T.," she said finally, her voice shaking only a little bit, "I'll speak to Tom myself." She turned and walked toward the saloon.

Now, how in the hell did *that* happen? J.T. wondered. He hadn't meant to get her all het up. All he wanted to do was *talk* to her!

J.T. slapped his hat against his thighs in disgust and sneezed violently when chicken feathers floated up to his nose. He turned, jumped down from the boardwalk, and headed back across the street to his office. Shaking his head, he remembered that one moment when he'd spied the old Emma underneath all the prim starchiness. For just a second J.T.'d thought she was going to shout at him. When he refused to close down the saloon, those eyes of hers had lit up like a brushfire in summer. He sighed and wearily climbed back up on the boardwalk in front of the jailhouse. But, he told himself, it prob'ly wasn't *re*-fined to raise your voice.

He leaned back against the wood-framed building and stared at the saloon across the street. Something had to be done. Somehow J.T. had to find a way to get the old Emma back.

Chapter Two

Couldn't anyone in town see what she was trying to do? Emma left the saloon in a rush, sending the batwing doors flying. On the boardwalk she stood for a moment, her hand at her breast, trying to calm her breathing. For heaven's sake. The way Tom Hill talked, you'd think she'd asked him to burn his saloon to the ground. When all she wanted was for him to close up for one day.

She glanced over her shoulder toward where she'd left J.T. He was gone. Good, she told herself. She didn't want to see him anyway.

Emma sighed and shook her head slowly. She'd so wanted to show J.T. how much she'd learned while she was away. To prove to him somehow that she was no longer the pigtailed little girl who'd adored him and followed him all over town. That she was a grown woman.

But it appeared that it wasn't going to be easy. She frowned and glared at the buildings lining Main Street. Especially with the folks in town treating her the same way they always had . . . like a nice girl who sometimes got too big for her breeches.

Emma squirmed uncomfortably for a moment and found herself wishing that she *was* in breeches. The dang stays in her blasted corset were about to cut off her breathing altogether! She glanced down and frowned at her new shoes as she shifted from one foot to the other. The knife-sharp points on the dainty footwear held her toes in an agonizing grip. It was all she could do not to stoop and pull the hateful things off right there on Main Street. Emma smiled softly at the thought of walking home barefoot like she used to before she became a lady. Oh, it would be wonderful to feel the soft dirt sift between her toes again.

She straightened up suddenly. No, she told herself. She'd spent two years in that fancy academy learning how to be a lady. And by thunder, lady she was going to be . . . even if it killed her!

She stiffened her spine and lifted her chin. She'd show all of them. Everyone who'd ever thought that Frank Taylor's little girl would never be anything but a wild-haired hoyden would soon know how wrong they'd been.

A flash of color caught her eye and Emma turned quickly to see Myrtis Hartsfield darting back into the alley behind the Hartsfields' blacksmith shed and corral.

Instantly Emma leaped down from the boardwalk and started for the woman. She had to find out if Myrtis had finished making the list of foods for the dance and party. Ignoring the painful pinch of her shoes and only limping slightly, Emma kept moving, fervently hoping Myrtis would invite her in for tea. At least then she could sit down for a bit.

J.T. stepped out from behind the newel post and chuckled helplessly as he watched Emma. He'd seen the way Myrtis tried to duck out of sight and he knew it wouldn't do the woman any good. Once Emma's mind was set on something, she was as hard to move as a wagon load of rocks.

Ever since the town council had named Emma the head of the Valentine's Day dance committee, she'd been hounding the other ladies half to death with her plans. Everything had to be just so. And the menfolk were starting to complain about the whole thing.

He snorted, turned toward his office, but stopped outside the door and glanced back down the street. Emma, gripping Myrtis's arm, was hurrying toward the church. As he stared after the retreating figures J.T. told himself that maybe he was going about this all wrong. Maybe instead of giving her time to settle back into town life, he should just up and ask her to marry him. After all, hadn't he been waiting five years already?

No. He shook his head at his own impatience. He'd loved her for years and he'd go right on loving her. But he was going to do this right. And that meant giving Emma time. Time to realize the feelings she'd had for him as a girl could be returned now that she was a woman.

His body tensed and J.T. groaned. He only hoped he could survive the wait.

He grabbed the door latch and gave a mighty shove. The heavy plank door swung wide, crashing into the inside wall.

"Dammit all to hell!" The young blond man seated at one of the two desks jumped, swore, and threw his pen down. "See what you made me do?" he shouted, then looked up. His jaw snapped shut. After a few moments of stony silence the blond mumbled, "Sorry, Sheriff. Didn't know it was you."

J.T. moved into the room. He tossed his hat onto a nearby peg and walked to his own desk. He plopped down heavily onto his chair and glanced at his deputy. "You best be glad it *was* me! Suppose you'd cussed the preacher like that?"

Deputy Danny Hanks smiled sheepishly. "Reckon then he'd be most convinced that I'm a lost cause and give up tryin' to reform me."

J.T. laughed shortly then ran his fingers through his thick black hair. Absently he answered, "Danny, you know the Reverend Jeffries ain't the kind to give up that easy!"

"S'pose not," the younger man agreed. Then his eyes narrowed as he looked at his boss. "What's eatin' you?"

"Nothin'."

"Humph!" Danny shook his head. "Yeah. And I know what her name is. Emma Taylor." He leaned back in his chair. "What's she done now?"

"Nothin'. That's the trouble." J.T. pushed himself up from the chair and crossed the room to the nearest window. He stared blankly at the town outside and continued, "Hell, she hardly talks to me anymore."

"Things sure have changed, all right." Danny grinned at J.T.'s back. "Why, I remember all the times we had to chase that girl outta here so's we could get some work done!"

J.T. smiled at the memory and, not for the first time, wondered if he'd made a mistake by ignoring her childish advances so long ago. But no, he told himself. She was just a girl then. No more'n fifteen when she started in following him around. But even then he'd seen the woman she would become. Even then he'd loved her outspokenness. Her hardheadedness. Her unswerving loyalty to those she loved.

But he'd waited. Five long years. And two of those with her back east surrounded by city men. It had about killed him waitin' for her to get back home. And when she did, she couldn't see him for dust.

"Yeah. I remember," he said softly.

"You know, boss," Danny added, "she's about to drive everybody in town loco with all her high-falutin' plans for the dance!" He sighed heavily. "Hell, she's got all of us runnin' around in circles. Never had to work this hard

before to throw together a wingding. And I'm purely sick to
death of hearin' about the way things are back east.''

J.T. didn't stir.

"Why, do you know what she said just yesterday?"
Danny all but screeched in outrage. "Says all us men got to
wear suits and ties to this here dance. Says it won't hurt us
none to at last *look* like gentlemen! She says if we ain't
dressed up proper, we can't come!" He threw his arms
wide. "You ever hear the like? I mean, her tellin' us we
can't go to our own dance?"

J.T. turned around and walked back to his desk. Nothing
Emma did would surprise him. As he sat down he said
offhandedly, "So, quit workin' for her."

"Hah!" Danny shook his finger at J.T. "I'd as soon try
to grab a rattler by the tail as try to tell Emma Taylor I quit.
I swear, boss, once that woman's got you hog-tied, there
ain't no gettin' free." He frowned slightly. "You say she
ain't talkin' to you?"

"Nope."

"Then you're about the only one in town with any peace.
Can't figure how you're gettin' out of all this. You're
s'posed to be in charge of the men! And, Sheriff"—Danny
shook one finger at the other man—"the boys is kinda
wonderin' when you're gonna take over. The men're gettin'
right tired takin' orders from Emma Taylor. Hell, most of
'em remember wipin' her nose when she was a young'un."

J.T. stared at his deputy. "How is it everybody in town
knows that I'm in charge of the men's committee and
nobody bothered to tell me?"

"Reckon we all figured Emma would tell you." Danny
shrugged. "Hell, she's tellin' everybody *somethin'*."

"Well," J.T. said, and pushed himself to his feet, "I ain't
got the time to bother with a dance."

"Can't say as I blame you, boss. Why, spendin' this much time with Emma's about to wear me out!"

J.T. stopped and then slowly grinned. "You know Danny, you're right. It's my duty to help out the menfolk of Buckshot. I think what I gotta do here is march right on over to the church and have me a little talk with Emma."

"Boss, I think you're touched," Danny said softly.

"Nope." J.T. crossed the room and grabbed his hat. Jamming it onto his head, he said, "You said it yourself. The men don't want to work with Emma. So me and her will just have to work this all out between just us." He yanked the door open. "Thanks for the idea, Danny."

"Hey, boss?"

J.T. stuck his head back inside. "Yeah?"

"Maybe you best stop by your house first, huh?" Danny grinned. "You smell like the wrong side of the coop!"

"Good thinkin'!"

Danny Hanks sat openmouthed, staring at the door long after J.T. had slammed it. Yep. The man was touched.

Emma smiled as she tried to assemble her notes into some kind of order. She was thankful that Preacher Jeffries had no objections to the town ladies using the church as a meeting place. Of course, with his own wife on the committee, he could hardly refuse.

"So," Emma said firmly, trying to regain the ladies' wandering attention, "you all see what I mean, then."

The women threw glances at each other for a long moment before Priscilla Jeffries, the preacher's wife, spoke up.

"Yes, Emma dear. We do see, but . . ." The too-thin young woman twisted her handkerchief nervously in her lap. "Really, I don't think you can expect the folks here in Buckshot to put on a fancy ball like they do in Boston."

"Oh, but—" Emma started, but Nell Frampton interrupted.

"That's right, dear." The older woman pushed her graying hair out of her eyes with a paint-stained hand. "Why, most of us come out here to escape all that fall-de-rall. Now, if the meetin's over, I've just got to get back and finish my painting."

"It's not over yet, Nellie," Emma broke in quickly. "Please stay." She knew very well that if Nell were allowed to leave, it might take days to pry her away from her easel again. Besides, if Nell left now, she could very well start a stampede!

Nell settled back down reluctantly. "Oh, very well, Emma. A moment longer then." The older woman's sharp blue eyes narrowed slightly. "You know, Emma, you might stop by one day soon. I'd like to do your portrait."

Emma hurriedly groped for something to say. Nellie was a sweet woman, but no one in their right mind *volunteered* to pose for her. She had the oddest knack of painting what she called the inner truth. Emma still remembered the scandal that swept through town when the last preacher's wife had posed for Nell. The sanctimonious woman had been a thorn in everyone's side with all her righteous talk about virtue and the wages of sin. Then Nell finished her portrait.

You had to look hard to see it, but it was unmistakable. Softly worked in shadow colors, far in the back of the painting, was a couple, embracing lovingly. The preacher's wife and Loftus McKenzie, a hog farmer who lived outside of town.

Now, no one else had known anything about the woman's

fondness for Loftus. No one but Nell. And no one was quite sure *how* she knew. But at least something good had come out of that old scandal. The preacher's wife ran off with Loftus and the dried-up preacher left for parts unknown.

Still, ever since then Nellie had had a hard time finding anyone willing to pose for her.

Thankfully Myrtis Hartsfield spoke up before Emma was forced to answer. "That's enough about your paintin', Nell. We've got to get this thing settled. Now, Emma, honey, I know you're tryin' real hard and all . . . but folks in Buckshot like the sound of a good fiddle. We like toe-tappin' music. We don't want to hear it played like it was a cat dyin'."

"But . . ."

Maybelle Hawken raised her voice over the din. The seventy-year-old woman was hard of hearing and shouted as if everyone else was, too. "Don't know what the fuss is all about. Buckshot ain't gonna change, young lady. Not for you nor nobody. 'Sides. I figure any hoo-rah folks wear shoes to is high-tone enough for most around here!"

Priscilla and Myrtis turned on the older woman, both of them shouting to be heard. A couple of the other ladies started in commenting on the goings-on and Nellie leaned back and studied Emma, as if planning a portrait.

She'd lost control. Somehow it had all gone wrong. Emma looked helplessly at her audience and saw her lovely plans disappear. She'd only wanted to try something special. Like she'd seen back east. Why, last year's valentine ball had been simply elegant. With the faint droning of violins played the way they were meant to be played, fine wines, candlelight, and the men and women dressed in the height of fashion. It was all so magical. Was it so wrong to want to share a little magic with her friends?

She glanced at the familiar faces surrounding her and smiled helplessly. Even with all the aggravation, Emma wouldn't want anything about her hometown changed. *Permanently,* that is.

The arguing women had each, in her own way, tried to fill the hole in Emma's life when her mother had died. They'd loved her, comforted her, scolded her, and on more than one occasion swatted her backside for her. And though she wouldn't have them any other way, Emma *did* wish that they could bend just enough to see that a little change once in a while was a good thing. And that an elegant dance could be just as much fun as a good old-fashioned barn dance. Emma knew they would all enjoy it so!

But she realized that all Myrtis asked for was a bright red dress with a couple of stiff petticoats to rustle during the square dance. Priscilla Jeffries only wanted the men to spit into spittoons instead of the floor. . . . Emma sighed. And Maybelle only expected folks to wear shoes. It was hopeless.

"Well now, looks like I came at just the right time!"

Emma's breath caught. That deep voice set little spirals of delight dancing down her spine. Slowly she turned to see J.T. standing in the open doorway. The ladies' loud arguments ceased immediately as they all turned to look at the tall, handsome sheriff.

But J.T. only had eyes for Emma. "I'm here to help, Em." He smiled. "What do you want us men to do first?"

Chapter Three

J.T. filled the doorway and Emma stared at him. He'd changed clothes. The long-sleeved gray shirt tucked into a neatly pressed pair of black pants suited him perfectly. Her heart thudded painfully in her chest. It didn't seem to stop, this fascination with J. T. Phillips. For years she'd watched him, followed him, dreamed about him, and he'd treated her as he would a pesky little sister.

From the summer of her fifteenth year to that last humiliating St. Valentine's Day before she'd left for the east, Emma had loved J.T. to distraction.

She looked at him now and felt the same, familiar quickening of her blood, the curl of excitement in her stomach. He was tall enough for three men, with long legs, broad shoulders, jet-black hair that needed trimming, and eyes as dark and fathomless as a winter night's sky.

Emma forced a deep breath into her lungs and pointedly looked away. No. She wouldn't start that up again. She was a lady now, an adult, not a love-struck child. So why was it she asked herself, that the sound of his voice affected her the same way it always had? In fact, the only way she seemed able to control her reactions to J.T. was to avoid him completely. And that's just what she'd been trying to do. Besides . . . that Valentine's Day memory still hurt. It probably always would. Emma repressed a shudder. Never again, she silently vowed.

But she *would* accept his help! She knew very well that if
⌐T. became involved, the other men in Buckshot would
⌐llow.

⌐"Emma! Emma girl!"

She jumped, startled to find that she'd been staring at J.T.
⌐ hard she'd forgotten about everyone else. Emma spun
⌐ound quickly and faced Maybelle.

The older woman frowned at her. "Where'd your mind
⌐, child?"

The other ladies exchanged knowing looks and soft
⌐niles.

"Uh . . ." Emma said, feeling a flush of embarrassment
⌐veep her.

Maybelle shoved her large body out of the creaking chair.
⌐Well, if that's all you got to say, I'm goin' home. Still got
⌐ead to bake and Hollis's long johns to wash."

As if she'd rung the school bell for dismissal, the other
⌐omen rose and followed Maybelle to the door. J.T. stepped
⌐side nimbly to avoid the rush. Emma hurriedly stepped in
⌐hind them and shouted heartily, "All right, ladies! We'll
⌐eet again tomorrow. Same time. Right here at the
⌐urch."

No one answered, but Emma did see Maybelle's hand lift
⌐ightly in acknowledgment.

"Didn't mean to bust up your meetin'," J.T. said quietly
⌐hen they were alone.

"Oh, you didn't," Emma answered as she closed the
⌐oor. Why did everyone have to leave at once? "They were
⌐ itchin'—I mean ready to go anyway. I couldn't have held
⌐em much longer."

He held his hat in his hands and watched as she gathered
⌐ her bonnet and gloves. Afternoon sunlight streamed
⌐rough the stained-glass window, covering her in soft

patches of color. "Did you decide on anything yet for the dance?" he finally managed to say.

She glanced over her shoulder at him as she slid her string bag over her wrist. Her hands were shaking. "Not really. But we still have two weeks. I'm sure I'll manage."

"Yeah," he agreed.

Emma straightened and told herself firmly that she had to stop reacting in such a ridiculous manner to J.T.'s presence. Her childish adoration of him was in the past. And that's where she was going to keep it. He'd made it clear enough before she left town that he just wasn't interested.

"Well," she said with forced brightness, "thank you for your offer, J.T." She took a few quick steps to the front door.

He reached it ahead of her. "It was more than an offer, Em. Like you said, I'm supposed to be in charge of the men's contributions to this little get-together."

Her gaze shot up to his. "Get-together?"

"Yeah."

"J.T."—she pulled her gloves on with a sharp tug—"this dance is going to be much more than a 'get-together.'"

He grinned and leaned his shoulder against the door preventing her from opening it. "Not if you keep on ordering the men around like you've been doing it isn't."

"What's that supposed to mean?"

"It means, Em"—he chucked her under her chin—"that folks who remember you in pigtails with a runny nose don' take kindly to you all of a sudden bossin' 'em."

"I am *not* bossing anyone," Emma countered, stepping back just a little.

"Wasn't it you who said that they had to wear coats and ties?" He crossed his arms negligently over his chest.

"That's not being bossy," Emma argued. "It's simply informing them what kind of clothing would be appropriate."

J.T. laughed. "Appropriate? Imagine Emma Taylor worried about 'appropriate'!"

A hot wave of humiliation washed over her as she remembered what he was referring to. She grabbed at the doorknob but couldn't quite get it. "I don't know what you're talking about."

"Well then," he said leaning toward her, "I'll help you recall. Wasn't it you who sneaked into the church and rigged a bucket of honey so's it would fall onto our old preacher's wife when she came into services?"

Emma came up short and looked up at him. Maybe she was wrong. Maybe he wasn't thinking about that last Valentine's Day. *Maybe*, she told herself, it was such a small thing to him, he'd forgotten all about it.

"And wasn't it you who smeared axle grease all over Deacon Barnes's spectacles when he was drunk?" J.T. went on, shaking his head. "Poor fella woke up and thought he was blind!"

Emma's lips twitched and she covered her mouth with her hand to hide the smile. Then she realized how close J.T. was. The laughter in her died, swept away by a more powerful emotion. She swallowed nervously and forced herself to meet his gaze seriously. "That was a long time ago, J.T. I was a child."

"That's what I'm sayin', Emma." His breath brushed her cheek and her heart stopped. "Folks around here think of you as that child."

"Everyone?" She watched him closely.

"Just about."

For a few long moments neither of them moved. Just as

she'd thought. J.T. still saw her as the little girl of the past. Probably expected her to moon and sigh over him like she used to. Well, she wasn't about to do that again!

Emma reached out, brushed J.T.'s hand away, and grasped the doorknob. He jumped aside when she yanked it open. "Well, J.T.," she told him stubbornly, "it's high time folks around here learned that Emma Taylor's all grown up now. And this valentine's dance is one way to prove it."

He opened his mouth to speak, but she cut him off.

"If I have to drag every man in town to this dance, that's just what I'll do!" She turned away and started walking. Over her shoulder she added, "With or without your help, J. T. Phillips."

As she hurried quickly down the boardwalk she heard him chuckling behind her. Her mind's eye quickly drew up an image of J.T.'s smile and her heart stopped. But she reminded herself sharply of what had happened the day she'd taken him a token of her love. She felt again the wash of embarrassment. The sharp sting of discomfort. And she would always remember Dixie Murdoch's laughter.

Straightening her shoulders, Emma recalled the solemn vow she'd made on her trip east. That she would never again force herself on J. T. Phillips. That she would pretend the years of her adoration hadn't happened. That she would find a man to marry who didn't stir up every sense in her body so that she wouldn't again make a fool of herself for love.

The trouble was, the only man she'd ever wanted to marry was J.T.

But perhaps it was time to realize that she never would. And maybe it was better that way. She didn't want to feel again a driving need to be with someone. She didn't want to be the fool again.

"Hey, Emma!"

What did he want now?

She stopped and waited for him as he trotted up to her side.

"Just curious, you understand," J.T. said, "but what did you have in mind for the men to do?"

Emma thought for a moment then smiled. "You could build a dance floor, J.T."

"*Dance floor?*"

"Yes."

"What the hell, I mean, why do we need a dance floor?" He put his hat on and looked down at her in amazement. "We always hold the square dance in the meadow."

Her spine stiffened and she glared back at him. "Didn't you just say that you were going to get the men to help?"

"Well, yeah, but . . ."

"This year we won't be having a square dance."

"Why the hell not?" J.T.'s balled fists rode his hips. "Hollis Hawken is the best fiddle player in the state. Most folks come special just to hear him play. And Deacon Barnes practices all year to call the squares on Valentine's Day!"

Emma smoothed the front of her pale lavender gown. "This year we're going to dance the waltz."

"The what?"

She frowned at him. "The waltz. It's a lovely dance that I learned—"

"I know. Back east."

"Yes." Emma smiled softly. "It's a smooth, elegant dance where couples glide across a polished floor together." Her smile disappeared as she remarked, "We could hardly glide in the meadow with all the gopher holes out there. Not to mention the horse . . . er . . ."

"*Leavings?*" he suggested.

She cleared her throat and ignored his grin. "Exactly."

"And who besides you knows how to do this dang dance anyway?" He wasn't ready to admit that he'd seen the dance before, on a trip to San Francisco.

"Well, no one yet . . ." She held up her hand to cut him off. "But it's easy to learn, I can teach—"

"Of all the harebrained—"

"If you don't want to help," Emma cut in.

"Hell," he groaned softly, "you don't need help. *I* will. I'll prob'ly have to hold a gun on the men for this one."

"For heaven's sake, J.T." Emma's temper boiled up and overflowed. "I'm not asking you to *hang* anybody! It's just a dance!"

"No, Emma!" he shouted back at her, "what we have every year is a dance! I got no idea what *this* is!"

She inhaled deeply, color staining her cheeks. But before she said another heated word, Emma suddenly spun around on her heel and stomped off.

J.T. kicked a nearby hitching post and winced.

Frank Taylor sat in the kitchen of his hotel and watched his daughter move between the stove and table, carrying and serving supper.

"How's the dance comin' along?" he finally ventured.

"Not very well, Pa." Emma sat down opposite him and picked up her coffee cup. She looked at her father over the china rim and noted, not for the first time, the deep wrinkles in his suntanned cheeks, the receding gray hair, and the soft brown eyes. "I can't seem to get folks to try anything new."

"Ain't surprised, hon." He lifted a forkful of mashed potatoes to his mouth, then talked around them. "You come home with a lot of big-city notions that just ain't' gonna

work in Buckshot. Folks here do things the way they like
'em done. Why should they want to change?''

Emma glanced at her father's overalls and knew he spoke
the truth. He hadn't once worn the beautiful suits she'd
purchased for him while she was away. She moved her gaze
around the familiar kitchen and realized that since her
father'd hit that pocket of gold a few years back, he'd not
spent a penny of it on himself.

Oh, he'd built the boardinghouse, but only because he
liked company and figured that with his own hotel he'd
always have someone to talk to. And he'd sent her to a
finishing school, but only because he'd promised Emma's
mother that he would do all he could to see that Emma
became a lady.

But he wasn't interested in anything else. Like the rest of
Buckshot, he liked things just the way they were and saw no
reason to change.

Emma sighed and pushed her potatoes around on her
plate with her fork. If she were forced to tell the truth, she
supposed she would have to admit to feeling pretty much
the same. There was a lot to be said for just bein' yourself.
And yet she recalled clearly the snide remarks made by the
eastern women whenever they thought she couldn't hear.
They'd criticized her hair, her clothes, her way of speaking,
even the way she walked.

But by the end of her two-year enrollment she was every
bit as good as any other female in that blasted academy.
She'd learned her lessons well, and by heaven all that hard
work was not going to go to waste.

She was going to give the town of Buckshot at least *one*
day of elegance. One day of splendor where they could
enjoy what other folks had. Then, if they still wanted the old

way of doing things, at least Emma would know she had
tried.

Besides, she wanted J. T. Phillips to see what he had
missed by dismissing her love.

"Can't figure out why you'd want to do such a thing,
J.T."

J.T. stared at the man on the porch swing and ground his
teeth together in frustration. Hadn't he already explained his
position three times? Tiredly he rubbed one hand over his
jaw and started again. This was proving harder than he'd
thought.

"What's wrong with givin' the women one fancy day,
Deacon?"

"Ain't nothin' wrong I s'pose." Deacon Barnes leaned
over the porch rail and spat a stream of tobacco juice into
the dust. "But what about the square dancin'? Hell, I even
worked up a few new calls this year!"

J.T. sighed and tried to make a deal. "How 'bout if we
have a few squares called in between these waltzes Emma's
plannin'?"

"Well . . ."

"Now, Deacon." J.T.'s voice deepened. "You know as
well as me that you're always takin' breaks anyway."

"True, true. Throat gets dry." He coughed and patted his
throat. "A little sip of Dutch's brew clears it right up,
though. Well, all right then." Deacon narrowed his gaze.
"I'll help with the dang floor." The thin man's scraggly
beard split when he grinned. "'Sides, this way I'll get more
time to visit with Dutch!"

J.T. took off his hat. This wouldn't be easy. "Emma says
this year no jugs."

"*What?*"

Chapter Four

Emma moved slowly in the afternoon sun. She was in no hurry. She wasn't even sure if the other ladies would show up at the meeting. Somehow nothing seemed to be working out the way she'd planned.

"Thunderation!" She kicked a stone in her path and sent it skittering across the road.

"Well, Emma. What's the trouble with you?"

Emma jumped nervously and spun around in a circle. "Nell? Where are you?"

"Up here," came that voice again.

Emma leaned her head back and stared up into the branches of an ancient elm tree. "Where?"

"Right here, girl." Something moved and Emma squinted into the leafy darkness. "For heaven's sake. Are you blind?"

Finally Nell's face came into view. The older woman blended into her surroundings beautifully. She wore an old green shirt and a pair of beige men's pants. She was straddling a thick tree limb, her back against the wide trunk. Munching on an apple, Nell could have been a child on a summer day instead of a woman closing in on sixty.

"Hello, Nellie, what are you doing?" Emma asked, not surprised at all to find her friend up a tree.

"I climbed up early to wait for the sunset." Nell tossed

her apple core to the ground and wiped her hands on her pants. "You get a real nice view from up here."

"I remember." Nell had the best climbing tree in the county.

"Why the long face, girl? Your party not working out just right?"

"No, Nell, it's not. But it's not *my* party. It's for everyone."

"Is it?" Nell shifted her weight slightly and a few leaves floated to the ground. "I wonder."

"We have a Valentine's Day dance every year, Nellie. You know that as well as me."

"Yeah . . . but it ain't never been this much work before."

"I just want it to be special, is all," Emma said defensively.

"Now, why's that, do you suppose?"

"Well . . ." Emma looked up and met the older woman's steady gaze. "Is it so wrong to want something special, Nell? Just once?"

Nell leaned forward, her arms folded on the tree limb. "No. It ain't wrong, Emma. But you should try to figure out why you want it so bad." She smiled and the leafy shadows played over her face. "You maybe tryin' to show somebody a thing or two?"

Emma lowered her gaze and stared down at the town at the foot of the hill.

"Maybe that handsome sheriff you used to follow around?"

Emma stiffened. "No, Nellie. I'm not."

"Hmmm . . ." Nell cupped her chin in her hands. "Anyhow, folks're sure talkin' about this dance of yours."

"Imagine so," Emma murmured. "What are they sayin'?"

"Well, the women are pretty much on your side of the whole thing." She leaned back again, stretched her legs out along the limb, and crossed her ankles. "'Course it don't take much to talk a woman into gettin' all spruced up once in a while. But the men . . ."

"Yes?"

"I haven't heard so much grumblin' and complainin' since Tom Hill's saloon ran out of beer one Saturday night."

Emma crossed her arms in front of her and frowned thoughtfully. "And I'll just bet that J.T. is right in there with them."

"Well now, that *is* a funny thing. Ordinarily I would've figured that, too. But it appears ol' J.T. ain't as predictable as we thought." Nell smiled down at the younger woman. "He's got a whole slew of men down in the meadow buildin' that dance floor."

"He does?"

"He does. And from what *I* hear, it wasn't easy."

Emma stared silently down at the town, her mind whirling. J.T. was *helping*? Why? Last time she'd talked to him, he hadn't seemed any too anxious. Then her friend spoke up again and Emma shook her head.

"You know, Emma," Nell said in a different tone, "I've started a portrait of you."

Emma looked up into the tree and saw that Nellie had leaned back into the shadows. Her face was hidden from sight. "You have? But how? I haven't posed."

"Don't always need a body to pose for me," Nell said vaguely. "I keep my eyes open. Then I just paint what I see."

Emma squinted hard, desperate to try to read Nell's features. It was impossible. If she didn't want to be seen, Nell could practically disappear.

"Yeah, Emma," the woman said. "I think this painting is gonna be one of my best. You should stop by and take a look sometime soon."

A chill crept up Emma's spine, but she fought it down. It was ridiculous, this superstitious nonsense about Nell's paintings. Why should Emma worry about what Nell painted? It didn't mean anything. Did it? She shook her head. No. It didn't.

"Maybe I will, Nellie," she called as she started down the hill for town.

"Oh, you will, dear," Nell whispered, and leaned back against the trunk again to wait out the sunset.

In the meadow on the other side of town J.T. had his own problems. Deacon Barnes, Hollis Hawken, George Hartsfield, and a few of the other men had all showed up to help build the dance floor. But they were doing a lot more talking than building.

"I can't understand what all the hoo-rah is over this Valentine's Day anyway," Hollis grumbled. "Ever' female in town is abuzz with what they're gonna wear and, worse yet, what *we're* gonna wear!"

"Know what you mean," Deacon chimed in. "Why, it's gettin' so's a man ain't safe in his own bed no more. Just yesterday, Dove Charles come by first thing with a big ol' cake." He curled his lip in distaste. "Just passin' by, she says. A-carryin' that big cake, I asks her? Well, she says, she knows since I ain't got no woman of my own fixin' for me, I must be powerful hungry."

George laughed, a booming sound that carried over the meadow. "Was the cake any good?"

"Hell yes, it was good! You think a woman that size don't know how to cook?"

Hollis chuckled softly in sympathy. "Awright, Deacon. You got you some female problems, I reckon. But at least you ain't got one livin' with you! Why, my woman's been after me about this dance for days! Says I got to wear a tie. Now why the hell would I want to wear a tie for? Hell, I ain't dead. Ain't nobody gonna bury me!"

"This is all Emma's doin', y'know," Deacon whined.

J.T. sighed and shook his head. Before he could speak, though, George added his two cents' worth.

"Huh! You think that's bad? I can't even walk in my house without Myrt a-grabbin' hold of my arm and swingin' me into a two-step! She's practicin' her square dance day and night. It's gettin' so I don't dare walk across the floor!"

"Hell," Deacon spat into the dirt, "didn't nobody tell her there ain't gonna be no square dancin' this year?"

"What?"

"Now, Deacon . . ." J.T. said warningly. "I told you we'd do a couple of rounds." He glanced quickly at the other men. In the two days since he'd first spoken to Deacon, he'd been able to keep the man quiet about Emma's plans. J.T. told himself he should have known that it couldn't last.

"A couple?" George asked, throwing his hammer down. "If we're only dancin' a couple of squares, why the hell are we buildin' this here floor?"

"Miss Emma is fixin' to teach us all some fancy new steps," Deacon told him.

"Not me, she ain't," Hollis answered quickly. There was a murmur of agreement from the other men. "It's bad enough we got to dance once a year anyhow. I ain't takin' no lessons like no durned schoolboy!''

J.T. threw his hat down. He was beginning to see Emma's point. Maybe a change now and again was the right way to do things. ''You bunch beat all, you know that? One day a year the women want a little party and some dancin' and all you can do is complain about it!''

''I don't see you with no woman a-draggin' you off to dance, J.T.,'' Hollis whined.

Deacon snorted. ''He probably won't even show up.''

''Oh, yes he will,'' George added slyly. ''Myrt tells me that he's been comin' around regular for the last few days to 'help' Emma.''

J.T. frowned at the big, barrel-chested blacksmith. George talked too much.

''You mean all that time Emma spent follerin' him around finally sunk in?'' Deacon asked on a laugh.

''Pears so,'' George confirmed. ''Leastways, that's what my woman says.''

J.T. flushed slightly as the men's chuckling grew. ''We gonna build this floor or are you men gonna talk the day away?''

''All right, J.T., we're fixin' to do it.'' Hollis bent over and picked up a plank. ''Where the hell you want this blasted thing, anyway?''

J.T. snatched his hat off the ground. Jamming it onto his head, he stalked off, mumbling, ''Right where you're standin', knot head!'' He kept walking, heading toward the jailhouse. Might as well check in on Danny. See how things were doing in his absence. Besides, while he was gone, the men might get the rest of their gossiping out of their systems.

His patience shot, J.T. began to have an idea of the

problems Emma had been having since she'd started her campaign for an elegant valentine party. He'd never known his friends to be so blasted hardheaded. Or had they always been like that, and he'd just never noticed?

What was the matter with them anyway? Was the thought of a little romance that frightening? He knew darned well that those men loved their wives. But they'd rather be dragged behind a crazy mule than admit it.

J.T. stuck his hands in his pockets and told himself that he wasn't much better. Oh, he'd loved Emma for years. Obviously, according to George, the whole town except for Emma knew it. But he'd never told her. He'd never even hinted at it. He'd been so busy trying to keep her at arm's length when she was too young that he'd lost most of his chances. And now she'd hardly stand still long enough for him to talk to her.

J.T. snorted, stopped in the middle of the road, and turned away from town. He needed to think. Deliberately he stomped past the buildings at the edge of Buckshot and kept right on going. Valentine's Day. Emma gone for two long years and she comes home just in time for Valentine's Day.

J.T. walked to a lightning-struck oak tree and plopped down on the stump. He recalled clearly the last time he'd seen Emma before she'd left Buckshot. In fact, he'd do just about anything to forget it.

It was Valentine's Day then, too. And she was almost eighteen, the prettiest thing he'd ever seen. J.T. had made up his mind to ask her pa for her hand on her eighteenth birthday. But he'd never gotten the chance.

He closed his eyes against the afternoon sun and let the memory come.

J.T. had been in his home, right beside the jailhouse, that day. It was early still, he'd just finished breakfast. When he answered the knock at his door, he'd no idea that he was shattering all of his carefully laid plans.

Dixie Murdoch was standing on the porch. And Dixie, all done up in her finest dress, was quite a sight. She'd stepped right into his small parlor, carrying a plate of heart-shaped cookies she said she'd made just for him. There hadn't seemed a polite way of getting her to leave, so J.T. had let her talk. And she did. The woman rambled on for what seemed hours before she finally rose to go home.

In his eagerness to see her out J.T. leaped up and made for the door. Somehow he lost his footing and tumbled into Dixie. Being a tall, well-built girl, she kept her balance and wrapped her arms around J.T. to steady him. Before he knew it, she was kissing him. And he stood there, his arms still wrapped around Dixie, and let her.

He barely heard the front door swing open. But Dixie did, he was sure of it. Because her ardor increased and she flattened herself against him like hair on a dog. When he finally came to his senses and peeled Dixie off, he was in time to see Emma, running from his house like she was on fire.

Dixie was laughing, making some nasty remarks about Emma being a foolish child for chasin' after a man who didn't want her. J.T. was sure that Emma heard her, because she really started moving then, her running feet barely touching the ground.

And at that moment, J.T. came as close as he ever had in his life to striking a woman. Quickly he nearly shoved Dixie out the door and started after Emma. But she didn't want to be caught. She was halfway home by the time J.T. reached the street.

On his way back he saw it. Crumpled into a ball and

tossed into the mud just outside his front door was a lace-trimmed red paper heart.

He picked it up and gently smoothed it out with his fingertips until he could read it.

The message was simple. *J.T. I love you, Emma.*

J.T. opened his eyes and stared blankly at the scenery around him. Maybe if he hadn't given her an extra day to cool off before going to see her, things would have been different. As it was, when he went to her house, she was already gone. To that fancy academy. To be gone two long years.

And her not knowing that he loved her, too.

Chapter Five

Emma'd been trying to explain the dance floor and why she'd wanted to try something different.

"Ah, hush," Maybelle shouted at Myrtis. "You just want to keep doin' the same old thing 'cause you know you're the best square dancer in town and you like to hear everybody else say so!"

"Maybelle Hawken, you're a spiteful old woman!" Myrtis countered quickly.

"Yeah, but I'm right." Maybelle turned her back on Myrtis then and spoke directly to Emma. Her loud voice drowned out any other arguments and the women quieted to listen. "All right, Emma. Now just mayhap you're right about all this. Could be the men in this town need to learn that every female likes a little romance now and again. Keeps the juices flowin'."

Emma blushed and the other ladies, except for Priscilla Jeffries, laughed out loud.

"*But,*" Maybelle shouted, "if we're gonna be dancin' this waltz . . . don't you think you'd best show us how?"

"Oh, but, Maybelle"—Emma looked around her helplessly—"I don't have a partner right now."

"Don't matter none," Maybelle decreed. "You just do your share. Reckon that's all we'll need to know anyhow."

Myrtis nodded her agreement. The other ladies mumbled

sympathetically and Nell watched Emma with a disconcertingly secretive smile.

Emma tore her gaze away from the woman and faced Maybelle again. "All right then. I'll show you. But I'll have to hum my own music and it won't look nearly as elegant as it does with a partner."

"We'll keep that in mind," Maybelle said. "Now. Let's see it, girl."

Emma moved away from the group and walked to the back of the tiny church. There would have been more room up front, but she refused to perform a solitary waltz at the altar. Deliberately Emma shut them out of her thoughts. She closed her ears and her mind. Instead she pulled up the memory of the valentine's ball she'd attended in Boston the year before. Slowly she closed her eyes and took a deep breath. In her mind's eye she was again at the elegant ballroom in Boston. Crystal chandeliers hanging from an ornately painted ceiling shone brightly in the light of thousands of flickering candles. The scent of varied perfumes filled the air and a haunting, delicate melody played by the three violinists in evening attire drifted through the crowded room. In her dream creation a tall man in an exquisitely cut coat stepped up to Emma and held out his arms to her.

No one had to know that her imaginary partner was J. T. Phillips.

J.T. opened the church door slowly. It was awfully quiet in there, he told himself. Maybe he'd already missed the meeting. He stuck his head in and stopped. Humming? His gaze swept the front of the church first. Nell, Myrtis, Maybelle, and Priscilla were all staring at the back of the church, off to his left. He started to speak, but Myrtis held her index finger up to her smiling lips for silence, then pointed.

He had a notion of just who it was he'd see, but his first sight of Emma surprised him anyway.

Dressed in a mint-green gown made of some real soft-looking material, Emma was waltzing all by herself. Eyes closed, head tilted back with a slight smile on her face, she held her full skirt out to the side in her left hand, and her right she held up as if clutching an invisible partner.

J.T. moved quietly, his gaze never leaving Emma as she dipped and swayed gracefully in the soft, colored light from the church window. He didn't hear the ladies behind him begin to whisper. He didn't see the exchange of knowing looks and pleased smiles. If he had, it wouldn't have stopped him. Nothing could.

He stepped up beside Emma and immediately began moving in time with her steps. Gingerly J.T. took her right hand in his left, then slipped his right arm around her narrow waist. Her eyes flew open and her humming stopped. Her feet kept moving though, guided expertly by J. T. Phillips. His deep voice picked up the tune she'd dropped and they whirled in time to the melody.

Speaking didn't seem necessary. Emma stared up into his black eyes and, for a moment, lost herself to everything but the magic of the dance. His palm lay flat against the small of her back and she felt the warmth of his touch down to her bones. His left hand held her fingers in a gentle grip, as though he would never let go. He smelled of bay rum and tobacco. His strong jaw was freshly shaven and his full lips were curved into a smile. One lock of his dark hair curled over his forehead.

He smiled at her. Emma sighed and closed her eyes again.

He pulled her closer and her breath caught when his thighs brushed against hers. Desire shot through her as suddenly as a summer thunderstorm. Finally, she thought, his arms were around her, holding her, and she wanted this moment to never end. She'd always known it would be like this. They moved so well together. The top of her head reached to just below his chin. If she got even closer and laid her head on his chest, she would feel his heart beating.

All those years of dreaming about him and now the moment she'd longed for was here. He held her just the way she'd always imagined he would. He smiled at her as he'd done in her dreams. His touch was as warm as she'd known it would be.

"Emma?" he whispered.

She opened her eyes to find his face just a short breath away from her own.

"Emma," he said again as he guided her in a turn, "I . . ."

The church door flew open, sending a bright shaft of afternoon sunlight down the center aisle, illuminating the fascinated faces of the town ladies.

"Hellfire, boy," Maybelle called out, "close that durned door!"

Emma and J.T. broke apart, the dance's spell shattered.

"J.T. in here?" Tommy Adams called out as he closed the door behind him. Then he spotted the sheriff and grinned. "We're waitin' on you, J.T." The ten-year-old's eyes flicked to Emma then back to J.T. "You still gonna play?"

J.T. seemed to hesitate, glancing from Emma to Tommy and back again.

"It's all right, J.T.," Emma said softly. She noticed that Tommy was holding a raggedy baseball. "I think the ladies have the idea now anyway. Besides, you don't want to keep the children waiting." She turned away from him and started walking unsteadily toward the front of the church. "Now, if you'll excuse us, the ladies and I still have a lot to do."

J.T. started forward, then stopped. He looked as though he wanted to say *something,* but wasn't quite sure just what. Finally he turned and left the church.

In the silence Maybelle spoke up. "Well, Emma, honey. You just may be right about this here dance."

Emma looked over at the older woman.

Maybelle crossed her arms over her ample bosom and nodded. "Yessir, it looked real pretty. Don't think it'll do the menfolk around here any harm to learn it. What d'you think, Myrt?"

Myrtis leaned back against the pew, a smile on her face. "I think you're right, Maybelle. A little fancy dancing might not be such a bad idea after all."

It didn't seem possible, but just two days later the Valentine's Day party was beginning to take shape. The men would have the floor finished in another day or two, then they would string up the ropes for the hanging lanterns. This year they would be able to dance long after dark.

"Just set the tables up right over there." Emma pointed to the far side of the almost finished dance floor. As Danny Hanks and Deacon Barnes moved off, carrying the first of the food tables, Emma took a moment to inspect everything.

Idly she wondered if she shouldn't have hired more than one violinist for the dance. But surely one would be enough. Usually Hollis Hawken played all day long all by himself.

She glanced over at the older man as he pounded another nail into the dance floor. Emma'd heard that Hollis had been sorely disappointed at not being asked to play this year. But according to Maybelle, he'd get over it. And J.T. was probably right about having a couple of square dances in between the waltzes. Truth to tell, Emma loved the friendly, high-spirited dance as much as everyone else.

J.T. again. She sighed heavily. No matter how busy she was, her thoughts somehow found a way to get back to J.T. It probably hadn't been a good idea to have him working so closely with her on this dance. It was getting harder to keep from spending time with him. And worse yet she didn't really *want* to avoid him.

Hollis dropped his hammer and looked around in disgust. Emma's reverie shattered by his cursing, she followed his gaze and saw Maybelle standing at the edge of the meadow, holding up a brand-new, black frock coat.

"Hollis Hawken!" Maybelle shouted again. "You get on over here right this minute and try this on!"

"I'm busy, woman!" Hollis reached for his fallen hammer.

"You think I got nothin' better to do than stand around waitin' on you, old man?" Maybelle tossed the coat over one shoulder and set both hands on her broad hips. "Now, c'mon. Won't take but a minute!"

Emma bit the inside of her cheek to stifle a smile as Hollis threw his hammer down again and stood up.

"I do believe you'll look right dandy in that there coat, Hollis." Deacon Barnes didn't bother to hide the chuckle in his voice.

Hollis tossed him an angry glare as he started toward his wife. "Yeah, well, *I* hear that Dove Charles has got herself all sorts of plans for you, Deacon."

Deacon's brow furrowed and his smile disappeared.

Emma turned away from the snickering men. Her lips

curved in a grin as she walked back toward town. Everything was starting to come together beautifully. The women of Buckshot were now solidly behind her plans and the men weren't left much choice in the matter.

Since their last committee meeting, the ladies had decided that maybe some romance was just what they all needed.

"Emma!"

Deacon Barnes shouted at her again. "Emma!"

Her mind snapped out of her dreamy recollections and returned to the matter at hand. As she crossed the almost completed dance floor, she told herself to stop behaving so ridiculously. After all, she and J.T. had shared no more than a simple dance.

Hadn't they?

Chapter Six

Emma pulled the ribbon tight then tied a lopsided bow. She tossed her braid over her shoulder to hang straight down to the center of her back. Pushing a stray curl off her forehead, she glanced down at her feet and smiled. First time she'd been comfortable since she got back home.

She wiggled her toes and grinned at the pleasure it brought her. Her well-worn, stained moccasins might not be much to look at, but after two years of feet-pinching shoes they felt wonderful. Before she'd left for that academy, she'd worn her moccasins almost daily. A slight frown creased her brow as she remembered that it was J.T. who'd made them for her.

The summer she was sixteen she'd spent most of her days barefoot and had finally picked up a thorn in her heel. It wasn't too long after that that J.T. had presented her with the moccasins.

Emma shook her head resolutely. Times change. People change. She wasn't the same love-struck little girl any longer. She wasn't wearing the moccasins now as a remembrance of J.T., but because they were far more comfortable than her "fashionable" shoes.

She glanced back at the little hotel behind her. Her father would be up soon and she wanted to be well gone before then. She simply needed a little time to herself. Deter-

minedly Emma straightened her shoulders, lifted the hem
her plain blue calico dress, and started walking toward
woods outside of town.

Emma stopped halfway up the hill and frowned at
trees on the crest. For some reason she didn't remembe
ever taking her this long to get to the top. She star
climbing again and tried to forget how she'd wasted
entire day before, searching out Dutch Ingersoll's still. A
the day had been made even longer by J.T.'s insisting
going along.

She shook her head in disgust. It had all been for noth
anyway. When they'd finally located Dutch, the older n
had flatly refused their request that he not bring
moonshine to the dance. In fact, he'd been furious at
suggestion. He'd mumbled repeatedly how it was the o
real bit of cash money he made all year and he wasn't ab
to lose it.

Emma cursed under her breath and moved even faster
seemed every man she knew had a head like a rock.

J.T. squinted at the hill. Emma. It had to be. Who the h
else would be climbing that blasted hill this early in
morning?

Suddenly he turned and hurried back inside to
dressed. After the miserable day they'd spent toget
yesterday, he thought, he wanted to talk to her. And
couldn't very well do it in his long johns.

Emma tripped and fell flat on her face. Pushing herself
to a sitting position, she reached for her right foot a
rubbed her bruised toes. She hadn't even seen the blas
tree root she'd caught her foot in. Something crawled acr

her cheek and she jumped, brushing at her face with both hands.

A chuckle sounded from close by. Emma turned and saw J.T. grinning like an idiot. Wouldn't you know it?

"What's so blasted funny?" she demanded.

"You," he answered as he stepped over a fallen tree trunk, then dropped beside her on the ground. "The way you were beatin' at your face like that." J.T. was breathing heavily. He looked like he'd run all the way up that damned hill.

She dusted her hands together. "There was a bug or something on me."

"Nope. Just a leaf," he said, and pulled a dried, crackling leaf from her hair, "like this one."

"Oh." Emma reached up and ran her fingers over the back of her head. "Are there any more?"

"A few," he said softly. "They look nice."

Emma rolled her eyes at him. "Get them out, will you, J.T.?"

He stretched out his hand and gingerly pulled the leaves free. "I remember a time when you didn't care at all if you had half the forest stickin' up out of your hair."

She glanced over her shoulder at him. "That was a long time ago."

"Not so long," he said, leaning back against the tree trunk. His long fingers toyed with one of the leaves he'd taken from her. "I notice those moccasins still fit."

Emma curled her feet up under her and tried to look nonchalant. "Yes, well. I found them this morning in a bag of rags," she lied. He didn't need to know that they'd been stored in a box high on a shelf in her bedroom.

"Uh-huh," he said quietly. "Well, I'm glad they still fit anyway . . . that's a pretty dress, Emma."

She cocked her head and simply stared at him. Since
she'd returned from the east, she'd worn a new dress nearly
every day. From muslin to silk each dress was a different
color and each had a matching parasol, bag, and shoes.
When she was dressed in the height of fashion, he didn't say
a word. But, she thought irritably, let her be wearing a
threadbare blue calico, covered with leaves and dirt, worn-
out moccasins on her feet, and he thinks she looks pretty!

Shaking her head, Emma turned away and looked down
at the town below. "Well," she said firmly, "it's been nice
talkin' to you, J.T."

"Uh-huh." He didn't stir.

"What do you want?" She sighed heavily.

"Nothin' much. Just to talk awhile."

"I'd rather not," she said, tilting her head back to stare at
the cloudless sky. "I came up here to be alone."

"Me too," J.T. lied. "But we're both here now."

"J.T." Emma looked away from his eyes and took a deep
breath, hoping to calm herself. Why couldn't he just leave
her alone? "J.T., please go back to town."

"No, Em." He took her chin in his hand and forced her
to meet his gaze. "I ain't goin' anywhere."

Why were his eyes so black? Why did his hair always
have to tumble down onto his forehead? Why did his touch
have to shoot through her body like lightning? And *why*, for
goodness' sake, did he have to smell so good? Despite her
best intentions Emma felt herself leaning toward him,
drawn to him just as she always had been. Then he smiled.

Abruptly Emma straightened up and pulled away from
him. There wouldn't be any more smiling over Emma
Taylor's infatuation with the sheriff if *she* could help it! She
forced herself to recall the sound of Dixie Murdoch's
laughter. Emma remembered, too, crushing the valentine

she'd made for J.T. and throwing it into the mud. She remembered the lonely nights in Boston when she was so far from home and she remembered the vow she'd made on her return. Not to make the same mistakes all over again.

If folks in Buckshot wanted someone to chuckle over, they'd have to find someone besides Emma Taylor. Although the longer she was home, the harder it was to ignore the persistent longing to be with him.

"Emma." J.T. spoke, startling her.

She turned to face him, and when she did, he bent closer suddenly and kissed her. A soft, gentle kiss that seemed to steal her ability to breathe. Helplessly Emma sagged against him and J.T.'s arms closed around her. His fingers pulled the ribbon from her hair and he tangled his hands in the mass of curls. Gentleness gave way to desire and his kiss deepened. Her lips parted, and when his tongue slipped inside, Emma moaned softly and slid her hands up his arms until she could lace her fingers behind his neck.

His hands moved over her body and Emma wriggled closer against him. She heard him groan as though he were in pain. Suddenly J.T. tore his mouth free, held her tightly, and rested his chin on the top of her head. Emma struggled for air and listened to J.T.'s ragged breathing. She'd never experienced anything like that before. And for the life of her she couldn't understand why J.T. had stopped.

"Emma," he said, his voice hoarse, "we shouldn't be doin' that." His broad chest heaved with his efforts to calm himself.

Emma pulled back enough so that she could see his face. It was true. Regret was in his eyes. She pushed away from him and staggered to her feet. How in the *hell* had she allowed this to happen? She'd done it again. Made a fool of herself over J. T. Phillips.

And it hadn't taken him long to decide that it was all a mistake, either. She stared at him blankly for a long moment then abruptly turned and began to run down the hill toward home. Safety.

Nightfall and J.T. still hadn't found any peace. Alone in his house, he carried a cup of coffee into the front parlor. He crossed the small room to the bay window and pulled the maroon draperies back. In the lamplight his own reflection stared back at him from the shining glass. He looked like hell.

J.T. grumbled under his breath, bent over, and blew out the light beside him. If there was one thing he *didn't* need it was to look at himself. He took a long gulp of the hot coffee and swore when he burned his mouth. Irritated, he banged the cup down and sloshed liquid over the polished surface of the table.

How could he have been so damned stupid! All afternoon and into the night, he'd asked himself the same question and received the same answer. He just didn't know.

After all the years of patience, after putting up with Emma's notions the last few weeks, after *everything*, he'd shot it all to hell anyway. But Lordy, didn't she understand what she put him through every time he was near her? No, she didn't. How could she? She wouldn't stand still long enough for him to tell her.

And when he'd followed after her, racing to her house, she'd bolted the door on him. Even then, though, he'd almost been pleased. At least he *recognized* the temper. Damn it, he'd been hoping to see more signs of it. He'd been so sure that if she would just let go, let her temper and hardheadedness take full rein, she would come back to herself and stop actin' the grand lady.

'Course, he hadn't counted on this afternoon.

J.T. walked slowly over to the bookshelves on the far wall. His hand reached out for the Phillips family Bible. He carried the big, heavy book to the nearest chair and sat down.

With the Bible on his lap, his fingers flipped through the thin, well-read pages until he came to the middle of the book. Then he stopped. A soft smile on his face, he lifted the battered, wrinkled red paper from its hiding place. In the last two years he'd read it often, as if to reassure himself that it was real. That the sentiment expressed on it was real.

Gingerly he ran the tips of his fingers over the slightly torn lace and frowned thoughtfully at Emma's now faded handwriting. *J.T. I love you, Emma.*

Carefully he set the valentine back down and gently closed the Bible over it. He stared blankly at the cold hearth in front of him and hoped fervently that Emma would forgive him for what he was going to do. But by heaven he had to prove to her that she *belonged* in Buckshot . . . and that they belonged together.

Chapter Seven

Emma walked a wide circle around Main Street. She wanted to go by the church to check over the last few details for the dance . . . but she didn't want to chance running into J.T. All she had to do was stay clear of the jailhouse *and* the dance floor, where most of the men were still working. With any luck she could finish her task with Mrs. Jeffries and be back home before anyone else even saw her.

She just couldn't bear to face J.T. Not after the way she'd behaved on that hilltop. Why, it was as though she'd forgotten every lesson she'd learned in that academy. For heaven's sake, *everybody* knew that *ladies* didn't kiss men like that! Especially in broad daylight!

But all the same, Emma knew she'd never forget it, either.

"Hey, Emma!"

She stopped and turned toward the high-pitched voice.

Tommy Adams stood in the middle of a slapdash playing field, tossing a baseball in the air and catching it. Quickly her gaze moved over the rest of the town children, of various ages, spread out in their game positions.

Then she spotted J.T., hunkered down about five feet behind home plate. He grinned at her. Emma looked back at Tommy and tried to hide her disgruntlement. Wouldn't you know, she told herself, with all her sneaky maneuvers, she saw him anyway.

"What is it, Tommy?"

The boy caught his baseball again and rubbed it between is hands. "Want to take a swing, Em?" He jerked his head t the children standing in line to bat. "None of that bunch an hit a durn thing!"

Emma gave him a half smile and waved at her dainty ellow gown with the pale ivory lace. "Sorry, Tommy. But 'm a little too old to be playing baseball."

Tommy snorted his disgust. "J.T.'s older'n you . . . *he's* layin'."

"So I see." She flicked a glance at the still-grinning man. "Maybe another time," she added, and started to walk.

"What's the matter, Emma?" J.T. called out. "Scared?"

She stopped and glared at him. "Of what?"

He shrugged.

"Aw come on, Emma." Tommy's voice turned whiny. "You used to hit harder'n anybody around here. Let's see ou do it again."

"Forget it, Tommy," J.T. said loudly. "*Ladies* can't hit vorth a damn!"

Emma's eyes narrowed. She knew a challenge when she eard one. And the way he said *ladies*. Like an insult. Her rain quickly totaled up the fors and againsts for taking up he challenge and she came to a fast decision. If J.T. thought o insult or belittle her by insinuating that a lady couldn't do nything, then it was her duty to prove him wrong.

She gave J.T. a long, thoughtful look, then walked to the losest child and took the bat from her. "Sorry, Nancy," he said softly. "You can be up next, all right?"

The little girl smiled and backed up.

Emma stood at the plate, trying to find a comfortable tance. It wasn't easy in the blasted shoes she was wearing.

Tommy reared back and threw his first pitch. She swung and missed.

Billy Jenkins, stranded on second base, groaned.

"Strike!" J.T. yelled, laughter in his voice. "Mighty poor showin', Emma."

She frowned at him, tapped the plate with the bat, then lifted it high behind her head.

The next pitch came and Emma's dainty heel turned under her.

"Strike two!" J.T. chuckled softly and tossed the ball back to Tommy.

Disgusted, Emma backed away from the plate and set the bat down.

"Had enough?" J.T. asked.

"Humph!" Emma snorted and bent down. Quickly she undid the laces of her pale yellow shoes and slipped them off. Her stocking-clad toes wiggled in the soft dirt as she walked back to the plate. Comfortable now, Emma set herself and waited.

The pitch came, Emma swung and smacked that ball so hard it sounded like a gunshot. The child in left field took off at a dead run, his eyes on the high-flying ball. Emma dropped the bat, picked up her hem and headed for first base. She hardly heard the shouts filling the air. She'd forgotten everything except the sheer joy of playing the game. In front of her she saw Billy Jenkins running the bases with a broad smile on his face. Then she was rounding third base, her gown clutched in her hands, headed for home plate. She saw J.T. standing across the plate, looking toward the field. Emma knew the ball was on its way in and she also knew that she wanted to beat J.T.

Five feet from the plate, Emma put her head down, leaped through the air, and landed on her stomach with a hard thump. Stretching out her hand, she managed to touch the corner of the plate before J.T. could touch her with the ball.

The children screeched and hollered excitedly and began to jump up and down around the two adults.

Emma looked up at a grinning J.T. She could feel the dirt sifting down the bosom of her gown. Her neatly coiffed hair now lay in long, straggly tendrils, and she knew she'd torn a sleeve at the shoulder. And she didn't care.

As he helped her to her feet J.T. whispered, "Welcome home, Emma."

"Must've been quite a game," Frank Taylor said softly when his daughter passed through the parlor.

Emma smiled and shook her head. "I don't know what came over me, acting like that."

"Way I heard it"—Frank stood and closed the book he'd been reading—"the children are all fightin' now to see who gets you on their team permanent."

She laughed and picked up her shawl. "Wouldn't the head mistress at the academy love to hear that!"

Frank crossed the room and put his arms around his only child. "Emma, you know I only sent you to that place 'cause I promised your ma." She nodded and he went on: "But between you and me, I like you just fine the way you always been. Ain't nothin' wrong with bein' yourself, Em."

She hugged him tightly for a moment then broke away. "I'm gonna take a little walk, Pa. I'll be back directly."

"You go on ahead. I'm goin' up to bed." He stopped halfway up the stairs. "Emma?" he asked quietly. "Next time you tell me when you're gonna play. I'd surely like to see a hit like the one you got today."

Emma chuckled, shook her head, and stepped outside.

She stopped on the wide front porch, bent down, and took

off her shoes. If she could play baseball just off Main Street, she could surely walk barefoot in the middle of February. Smiling, Emma remembered J.T.'s words that afternoon. He'd said, "Welcome home." And he was right. She'd finally come home. Oh, not just to the town. But to herself. To the person she'd always been.

She stepped into the slightly damp grass and sighed. It felt good to let go and just be Emma again.

Walking slowly, to enjoy the night air, she moved down the slope of the yard away from the house. Moonlight skittering from between the clouds dappled the familiar sights with patches of light and shadow. Crickets cut their song short as she passed, only to start up again moments later.

In the distance she could see lamplight in the houses lining the main street of Buckshot and Emma knew she should turn and go back inside. But she needed time to think.

She glanced over her shoulder. Her father must have gone to bed. He'd left one lamp burning downstairs and its meager light shone in the night from behind the lace curtains in the front parlor.

Emma breathed deeply and exhaled on a rush. Even though she was tired, she wasn't quite ready to go inside. Instead she turned her back on the silent house and continued her walk to the ancient maple tree at the edge of the Taylor property. She dropped to the ground, leaned back against the craggy trunk, and stared out at the night. It was so good to be home.

"Hello, Emma," J.T. said quietly as he stepped out of the surrounding brush.

She turned to look at him.

"I've been waiting for you." He moved closer and sank

to the ground beside her. When he leaned back against the tree trunk, his shoulder pressed against hers. She didn't move away.

"How did you know I'd be out here?" she whispered.

He smiled. "You always did favor a walk in the night."

She said nothing and J.T. went on: "You were really something today, Emma."

"You mean you're willing to admit that ladies *can* hit a baseball?" she asked on a soft laugh.

J.T. reached for her hand. Running his thumb across her knuckles, he said, "If the lady is *you,* I reckon she can do just about anything."

She stared up at him. Moonlight filtered through the old tree's branches, dappling his familiar face with moving shadows. Somehow she knew that *he* was the reason she hadn't been willing to go inside. Somewhere deep inside her, Emma'd been expecting J. T. to show up.

Everything was finally clear to her. Emma was now ready to admit what her heart had been telling her all along. She still loved J. T. Phillips. Always would. Whether he loved her back or not, simply didn't matter.

When his hand cupped her cheek, Emma leaned into it, moving her face across his flesh. She'd yearned for this for so many years, she wouldn't deny herself now.

"Oh Emma . . ."

She laid her fingertips across his mouth, then bent toward him and pressed her lips there instead. J.T.'s arms closed around her, pulling her tightly against him. Emma heard him groan softly and she echoed his call when one of his hands snaked around and caressed her breast. His long fingers teased her hardened nipple and Emma gasped with surprise at the depth of the feelings he created.

As his mouth moved down the length of her neck and his

tongue traced warm patterns on her skin, Emma arched herself against him, flattening her palms on his chest. Head back and eyes wide, she stared up through the tangle of branches overhead to the clear night sky. Her body seemed to come alive under his touch. She licked dry lips and sighed on a smile. Emma'd wished and hoped for this night for so long, she wanted to capture every sensation, so that years from now, she could reach into her heart, pull out the memory and relive it.

She lifted her head and looked into J. T.'s eyes. Their gazes locked, Emma's fingers seemed to move of their own accord. Deftly, she undid the buttons of his shirt. As each one slid free, Emma watched a flash of restrained passion in J. T.'s eyes brighten and grow. When his shirt lay open, her hands smoothed over his flesh. Her breathing staggered, her heartbeat frantic, the warm strength of him filled her. Beneath her palms, J. T.'s heart pounded out a rhythm she knew matched her own.

He dipped his head and brushed her lips with his. Emma gasped at the lightning-quick shiver that raced up her spine and she tried to pull him back when he drew away briefly.

So shaken by the tingling sensations coursing through her body, Emma barely noticed when he slid her dress down her shoulders. But as J. T. pressed their naked chests together, Emma's breath stopped. Curls of desire spread through her body like a brush fire, threatening to consume her entirely. The coarse, dark hair covering his muscled chest brushed against her too sensitive nipples and Emma groaned softly at the exquisite torture of being close to him and yet not close enough.

He moved to kiss her and Emma's mouth parted under his. As their tongues met and danced in silent promise, their hands and fingers moved frantically over each other's body.

In seconds, their clothes were discarded in a pile beneath the old tree. The soft chill of the February night descended on them, though neither of them noticed. Emma looked up into J. T.'s eyes and saw his hesitation. She knew instinctively that he would stop now and leave her if that was what she wanted from him. A swell of love for him washed over her, closing her throat with the force of it. She reached up and tenderly cupped his cheek. He smiled at her touch and Emma whispered, "Be mine, J. T. If only for tonight, be mine."

He placed a kiss on her palm and wordlessly moved to cover her body with his own. Gently, quietly, J. T. entered Emma's soul and they paused for a heartbeat as if to savor the joining. Then she pulled his face down toward hers for a kiss and lifted her hips slightly to urge him on with the dance.

As J. T. moved inside her, his fingers slipped down between their bodies and caressed the core of her. Emma's head twisted from side to side, as she struggled to find what he was offering. Her fingers tight over his shoulders, she fought for breath as her body went higher and higher until she burst and floated back to the soft, damp grass. Seconds later, J. T. arched against her and she heard him call her name softly.

Emma lay quietly beneath him, running her hands over his back as she tried to steady her breathing. J. T. raised up, twisted slightly and bent to her breast. Tenderly, he took her nipple into his mouth and rolled his tongue around the sensitive bud. He smiled when her hand tightened in his hair and held him fast. After another moment though, he straightened, propped himself on one elbow and looked down into her face. Gently, he stroked the matted hair from her forehead, then ran his hand down the length of her nude body. Emma shivered.

"Cold?"

"No," she whispered through dry lips. "I've never been so warm."

Reluctantly, he rolled to the side and pulled her into his arms. He could hardly believe what they'd just done. J. T. hadn't *meant* to seduce her. He'd meant only to *talk* to her. Make her listen to him. With her head pressed against his chest, he said softly, "I didn't mean for this to happen, Emma."

"I know, J. T." The regrets she'd expected him to feel had already started. But no matter his feelings, she would always cherish the memory of this night. Her fingers moved over his flat nipple and his flesh quivered under her touch. "I think it *had* to happen." She tilted her head back to look at him, determined to etch every moment of this time with him into her brain. And just as determined to keep him from feeling any guilt over what they'd done. What had happened between them wasn't really his fault. At least not his alone. She could have stopped him. If she'd wanted to. "I think we were owed at least *one* time of being together."

"One time?" He stiffened.

She nodded, sat up and reached for her clothes. It would be much easier to bear, she knew, if she left quickly. This moment of tenderness had changed nothing. She loved him, but one-sided love wasn't enough for her anymore.

"What do you mean?"

Emma's practiced fingers quickly did up the buttons running down the front of her dress. "Oh, J. T.," she said softly, "I chased you for so long." She glanced at him for a moment and smiled half-heartedly. "This was *bound* to happen. I'd wanted it most of my life and you . . ."

"Yeah?" he said harshly, "what about me?" He pulled on his pants, his eyes never leaving her bent head.

"Well, J. T., you're a kind man . . ."

"*Kind*?" He stood suddenly and leaned against the tree to pull on his boots.

"Well, *yes*." Emma rose slowly, her body unaccustomedly stiff. She still didn't look at him, but kept her head down. "I know that I was a pest . . . interfering with your time with other women . . ."

"Other women?" Disbelief colored his voice.

"Yes. Like Dixie for instance." Emma managed to say the woman's name without releasing the tears clogging her throat.

"Emma . . ." He threw his arms up in the air. "Of all the . . ."

"Please, J. T.," she interrupted in a rush. She didn't want to hear any stammered apologies. She didn't want to listen to him list his regrets. "Let it end here. I'll always keep the memory of this night." She started walking, and just before she broke into a run, she added, "And I'll always love you for it."

"Emma!" J. T. stared after her and could hardly believe it when she went straight into her house and closed the door. For a minute he considered breaking the damn door down and *forcing* her to listen, then he discarded the notion.

Talking wouldn't be enough. She'd never believe that he'd loved her probably longer than she had him. No, he told himself, it would take more than talk to convince her. Then he smiled. And he knew just what would do it, too.

Chapter Eight

The valentine's dance was a huge success. Red paper hearts with trailing pink and white ribbons were strung along the length of the ropes holding the lanterns that would be lit later that evening. The food tables set up along one side of the dance floor groaned with the weight of full platters and bowls containing everything from fried chicken and turnip greens to chocolate cake.

An explosion of children streaked past Emma, their laughter and good-natured shrieks an accompaniment to the adults' loud chatter. Bright sunshine spilled over the gathered crowd while friends greeted each other as if they'd been separated for a lifetime. Emma turned toward the dance floor and watched the dozen or more smiling couples move through the intricate steps of yet another square dance.

She quirked her lips slightly and glanced toward the far corner of the floor.

Monsieur Henri Blanc, the French violinist, had turned out to be Hank White from Silver City, New Mexico. Of course, no one knew that until the man had spent a couple of hours with Dutch Ingersoll, sampling the "finest moonshine in California."

Emma shook her head and sighed. Even now Dutch and Hank, fast friends already, were bending their elbows, tipping two of the ceramic jugs Dutch had brought with him. She turned her gaze on the opposite corner then and smiled to see Hollis Hawken, proudly playing his fiddle for all he was worth. Maybelle sat by his side, smiling at the whirling couples as they passed in front of her.

Deacon seemed to be in fine voice, Emma told herself. In fact, his calls only faltered whenever he chanced to look in Dove Charles' direction. The big woman stood only a few feet away from her adored one, sending him coy smiles and hungry stares.

George and Myrtis Hartsfield sailed past just then and Emma would have sworn she could hear Myrtis's stiff petticoats rustle and snap with her movements. Everyone was right. The older woman really *was* the best square dancer in town.

Emma's gaze moved over the crowd, absently noting familiar faces. Her father stood talking with Preacher Jeffries and his wife, and from the corner of her eye Emma noticed Nell carrying a cloth-covered canvas toward the easel she'd set up earlier.

People had come from miles around. From every farm and ranch. Everyone was there. Everyone but J.T.

She hadn't even seen him since *that night*. A flush of heat stained her cheeks every time she thought of it. In fact, that was the main reason she'd hardly left her house in the last two days. She couldn't bear the thought of blushing and stammering like an idiot in front of J.T. But Lord, how she missed him. The fire J.T. had started still burned in her veins. It probably always would.

"Pretty dress, Emma."

She looked up to see Nell, dressed in a bright red shirt and her favorite beige pants.

"Thank you," Emma mumbled, and smoothed her skirt

unnecessarily. The white silk dress adorned with tiny red dots, its scooped neck and long sleeves edged in stiff scarlet lace, had been ordered especially for this dance. Now Emma knew that she could be wearing an old buffalo hide and not care at all.

J.T. wasn't coming.

"Folks seem to be havin' quite a time," Nell said with a glance at the dance floor.

"Uh-huh," Emma answered halfheartedly.

"Something wrong, girl?"

Emma took a deep breath and forced a smile. "No, Nell. Nothing."

The older woman nodded doubtfully.

"'Scuse me ladies." Frank Taylor stepped up. "Nell, would you mind if I borrowed my girl here for a dance or two?"

"Not at all, Frank," Nell answered, and turned to walk away. After only a couple of steps, though, she said over her shoulder, "I brought your portrait with me, Emma. I want to show it to you today."

Frank's gray brows arched. "A portrait? Of you?"

Emma nodded and watched Nell's back for a long moment, a sense of misgiving creeping up her spine. Then she wrenched her gaze away and faced her father. "Never mind that, Pa. About that dance . . . if it's all right with you, I think I'd rather just go home now."

"Well, it ain't all right with me," her father said, and tucked her arm through his. "I want a chance to dance with the prettiest girl here before some young fella steals her clean away."

Small chance of that, she thought. Sighing softly, Emma agreed and stepped up onto the floor with her father. As if at an unseen signal, Hollis began to play "Greensleeves" and the Taylors moved easily into the waltz that Emma had taught her father.

"You did a fine job on this dance, Emma," Frank said, trying to coax a smile from his child. "Why, even Deacon's waltzing!" He inclined his head at a passing couple.

Emma looked and fought down a smile at the sight of skinny Deacon Barnes being half carried around the dance floor by Dove Charles. Emma's gaze touched on everyone and she was pleased to see that the people of Buckshot seemed to enjoy the waltz as much as a square dance. Maybelle Hawken danced by on the arm of Preacher Jeffries. And big George Hartsfield led a smiling Myrtis around in a surprisingly light-footed turn, her new red dress flaring out behind her.

Surrounded by happy, laughing people, Emma felt a sudden, overwhelming desire to sit down and cry. Everyone was having a good time at the dance she'd planned so carefully. Everyone but her.

"What is it, honey?" Frank whispered, concerned.

She shook her head then leaned into the warmth of her father's embrace.

"Can I cut in, Frank?"

Emma's eyes squeezed shut at the sound of J.T.'s voice.

"Well." Frank leaned back and studied his daughter's face for a moment before saying, "All right, J.T." Then he added as he handed Emma over to the tall man, "But you best take good care of her. . . ."

J.T. nodded briefly then whirled Emma into the center of the dancing couples. "Your pa all right? That sounded almost like a warning."

Emma looked up briefly. "He's fine."

"You sure do look pretty, Emma." J.T.'s voice came soft

as his breath against her ear. "But not near as pretty as the other night . . ."

Emma stiffened and pulled free. She didn't want to talk about that night. Not to him. Not to anyone. Quickly she threaded her way through the dancing couples and stepped off the edge of the floor. J.T. caught up to her in seconds.

"Wait a minute, Emma. Where you goin'?"

"Home." She started walking again.

He grabbed her arm. "Look, I'm sorry I'm late but—"

"You don't owe me an apology." She pulled away.

"Will you just stand still for a dirty minute?" J.T. snatched his black hat off and dusted it angrily against his thigh. "Hell, I haven't even *seen* you in two days!" He took a deep breath as if to calm himself before saying, "I . . . brought you something, Emma. Will you come look?"

His eyes held her. But Emma knew she had to find a way to refuse. She had *some* pride left.

"If you don't like it . . . well, then you can leave and I won't try to stop you."

Emma stared up into his fathomless black eyes and heard herself agree.

J.T. took her hand and folded his long fingers over hers. Gently he led her away from the crowd to the foot of an ancient elm tree. There in the shade lay a small package, wrapped in bright red paper and tied with a clumsy white bow. He bent down, scooped his gift off the ground, and handed it to Emma.

He smiled at her and Emma's heart thudded in response. Slowly she pulled at the ribbon then slipped the paper off. She could feel J.T.'s eyes on her, but couldn't quite manage to look up at him. Instead she concentrated on the small box.

Lifting the lid, Emma smiled softly. Inside was a brand-new pair of soft, white moccasins. Her eyes blurred slightly as she ran one finger over the tiny stitches.

"Do you like 'em?" J.T. whispered.

She nodded. "They're perfect."

"See, that's why I was late. I wanted to finish 'em so I could give 'em to you today . . . but it took me longer than I thought it would."

"They're beautiful, J.T.," she said, and forced herself to meet his gaze. It must have taken him days to make such a fine gift. His care and thoughtfulness showed in every stitch. "Thank you."

"There's a card, too," he said softly, and pulled an envelope from his breast pocket.

Emma handed him the package and accepted the envelope. His features betrayed his nervousness and Emma felt her heart skip unevenly. Her hands shaking, she opened the envelope. She only needed a glimpse at its contents to recognize the card she'd brought to him two years before.

Slowly she drew out the wrinkled, stained valentine and stared at it through her tears. The lace bedraggled, the paper creased and worn, she read her own faint handwriting and just below it the message J.T. had added.

I love you, Emma. Marry me.

She bit at her lip and took a slow, shuddering breath. He'd kept it. He'd rescued her token of love from the mud and kept it safe. And now he was offering her his own token. Emma's fingers played over the surface of the valentine as she concentrated on J.T.'s voice.

"I *do* love you, Emma. Always have. I want you to be my wife." He stepped closer and tipped her chin up with his fingertips. "I want to spend the next forty or fifty years showing you how much I love you. Will you let me?"

Everything she'd ever dreamed of was shining in his eyes. Emma held the old valentine close to her heart and felt her fears and doubts melting away. This was what she wanted. What she'd always wanted. J.T.

"Yes, J.T. Yes," she whispered.

He grinned suddenly and bent down to kiss her. His lips moved against her mouth in a slow, leisurely caress that promised a lifetime of attention. When he finally broke away, he said, "Let's go see your pa."

"All right." Emma laughed delightedly. "But first . . ." She plopped down on the grass and quickly undid the laces on her beautiful but painful shoes, then tossed the offending objects over her shoulder. J.T. chuckled, lowered himself to one knee, and slipped her new moccasins on. Emma wiggled her toes and sighed her pleasure.

It was all so simple. Her beautiful gown and moccasins. Square dances mixed with waltzes. Love and laughter. Good friends and family. And above all, J.T. The one person who knew her well enough to know that *moccasins* were the perfect valentine's gift!

J.T.'s eyebrows rose slightly and he smiled as he said, "Comfortable, but not very elegant, Emma." He stood up and drew her to her feet.

She leaned into him and hugged him tightly. "J.T., sometimes a compromise is enough of a change. And 'elegant' isn't everything."

Their arms linked, they walked together toward the small knot of people gathered around Nell's latest painting. Emma could see her father at the forefront of the group, and even from a distance she could see his grin.

Emma quickly looked around for Nell and finally spotted

the woman sitting in the shade with George and Myrtis. As one, the three old friends raised their glasses of Dutch's moonshine in a toast, then drank.

Hurriedly J.T. and Emma moved to the portrait. At their arrival the people parted and allowed the couple to get closer.

Dumbfounded, the two stared at the exquisitely done painting. Nell had captured the valentine's dance perfectly. And in the center of the canvas was a remarkably rendered likeness of J.T. and Emma, dressed in their valentine finery, waltzing. In the shadowed background was a smaller scene. In it Emma and J.T. in wedding clothes stood on the dance floor surrounded by the people of Buckshot as Preacher Jeffries married them.

J.T. leaned toward the painting, studying the background scene and shaking his head in wonder. A few chuckles from the waiting crowd drifted toward him.

"Well, he's good and caught now," someone said.

"Yep," another voice agreed. "If Nell paints it . . . it's bound to happen."

J.T. stood up and looked down at Emma, his grin fading as he studied her thoughtful frown. "What's wrong, darlin'?"

"It's the painting, J.T." Emma chewed at her lip and ignored their audience.

"What about it, Em?" J.T. shrugged. "Hell, anybody in town could have guessed that we'd get married!"

"Yes, but . . ."

"But what?" J.T. followed her gaze to stare at Nell, George, and Myrtis, laughing together over some shared joke.

"My dress, J.T.," Emma mumbled. "My valentine's

dress. I never showed it to anybody.'' She looked up at the man beside her. ''How did she know?''

J.T. looked at the canvas again and saw that Nell had indeed captured Emma's dress exactly. After a long moment he turned back to the woman he loved, pulled her into his arms, and whispered, ''Who cares?''

Then he kissed her.

PENGUIN PUTNAM INC.
Online

Your Internet gateway to a virtual environment with
hundreds of entertaining and enlightening books
from Penguin Putnam Inc.

***While you're there, get the latest buzz on
the best authors and books around—***

Tom Clancy, Patricia Cornwell, W.E.B. Griffin,
Nora Roberts, William Gibson, Robin Cook,
Brian Jacques, Catherine Coulter, Stephen King,
Jacquelyn Mitchard, and many more!

**Penguin Putnam Online is located at
http://www.penguinputnam.com**

PENGUIN PUTNAM NEWS

Every month you'll get an inside look at our upcom-
ing books and new features on our site. This is an
ongoing effort to provide you with the most
up-to-date information about
our books and authors.

**Subscribe to Penguin Putnam News at
http://www.penguinputnam.com/ClubPPI**